Apr 2016

Three Rivers

Three Rivers

Tiffany Quay Tyson

THOMAS DUNNE BOOKS
ST. MARTIN'S PRESS
NEW YORK

THOMAS DUNNE BOOKS.
An imprint of St. Martin's Press.

THREE RIVERS. Copyright © 2015 by Tiffany Quay Tyson. All rights reserved. Printed
in the United States of America. For information, address St. Martin's Press, 175 Fifth
Avenue, New York, N.Y. 10010.

www.thomasdunnebooks.com
www.stmartins.com

Designed by Jonathan Bennett

The Library of Congress Cataloging-in-Publication Data is available upon request.

ISBN 978-1-250-06326-7 (hardcover)
ISBN 978-1-4668-6836-6 (e-book)

St. Martin's Press books may be purchased for educational, business, or promotional use. For
information on bulk purchases, please contact the Macmillan Corporate and Premium Sales
Department at 1-800-221-7945, extension 5442, or write to
specialmarkets@macmillan.com.

First Edition: July 2015

10 9 8 7 6 5 4 3 2 1

For Judy and Jerry Tyson, who raised
me in a home filled with books

Acknowledgments

Thanks to Andrea Dupree, Michael Henry, and everyone at Lighthouse Writers Workshop. I owe so much to William Haywood Henderson, an extraordinary reader, teacher, and friend. Thanks also to Nick Arvin, Catherine Hope, Jennifer Itell, Greg Jalbert, Shana Kelly, Amanda Rea, Scott Sawyer, Gary Schanbacher, Emily Sinclair, and other careful readers who gave me more of their time and wisdom than I deserve. Thanks to Corinna Robbins for allowing me to use her mountain home as a writing sanctuary. And thanks to the members of Denver Salon for all the support, laughter, friendship, and wine.

I am so grateful to Sandra Bond for her unflagging support of this book and this author. Thanks to Toni Kirkpatrick for believing in this book, and for providing the feedback that made it better. And thanks to Jennifer Letwack, Eliani Torres, and everyone at Thomas Dunne Books.

Finally, to John, who knew I was a writer and married me anyway, I love you.

1990

Chapter One

SATURDAY

The preacher's wife delivered the crumpled note early that morning. *Come home. I must leave. Your father is dying. Your brother is not able.* The woman, who was balancing a grimy toddler on one jutted hip, asked Melody if there was anything she could do to help. Melody asked about a phone. The woman used her hand to wipe a streak of snot from the toddler's upper lip and told Melody the church office would be unlocked at eight. By quarter after, Melody perched on the corner of a polished wooden desk and dialed her childhood home.

Except for a row of yarn-woven God's eyes and a stack of Jesus pamphlets, there was not much about the office that marked it as religious. The fire-and-brimstone, hand-to-God preachers of Melody's youth had retired. Nowadays, churches were led by slick men in designer suits, who preached more often about prosperity than about eternal damnation.

Against her ear, the phone rang and rang. No one hurried to pick up a phone in her house. Mama could very well be sitting right next to the phone, painting her fingernails

3

bright red, and saying, as she always did: *A ringing phone does not demand urgency on my part.* Daddy would still be sleeping. Bobby could be anywhere.

Years earlier, Melody had bought her parents an answering machine, thinking it would be the perfect gift. "Now you can just let it go to the machine and call people back whenever you feel like it," Melody told them. "Oh, my," her mother said. "I hope you kept the receipt. I can't have people calling and getting a machine. It's just so tacky." What Melody wouldn't give for a bit of tacky right now.

"Well, hell's bells." She wanted to say something stronger, but manners or superstition prevented her from swearing in a church, even though she was alone and it was just the office, and even though she'd stopped believing in God. Oh, she still believed it was possible God existed, but she didn't believe he cared. She didn't believe anyone was going to answer her phone call, either. She pulled the phone from her ear and nearly had it back in its cradle when she heard her brother's voice. Bobby shouted, "Hello? Hello!"

"Hey there." Melody tried to remember the last time she'd actually spoken to Bobby. "What's going on? Mama called."

"When are you coming home?"

She coiled the phone cord around her finger. "I'm not sure. Can you tell me what's going on with Daddy?" The cord was sticky, the victim of an exploding soda or some kid with jam-coated hands. She wiped her finger on the hem of her T-shirt. "Is Daddy around? Maybe I could just talk to him directly."

Bobby barked a harsh laugh into Melody's ear. "Oh, he's around, all right. He's around." Melody was supposed to be patient with Bobby. Since the baptism, he'd been a little off. It was like his brain got switched to a channel that didn't come in clear for anyone else.

"Why don't you run and get him?" She kept her voice as even and pleasant as she could.

"I thought you were home coming, home coming, coming home." Ah yes, there it was, not quite a stutter, but a vocal tic that was the most visible (or audible) reminder of Bobby's baptism.

"I will," she said. "I just want to talk to Daddy for a minute. Can you fetch him for me?"

Bobby huffed. "Well, he can't talk. He's hooked up to tubes. Phone won't far, far, far reach. Reach that far."

"Tubes? What sort of tubes?"

"Hang on."

A loud clattering echoed through the line. She heard Bobby's voice, distant but still clear enough. "I'm checking. I'm trying to find out."

"Daddy wants to know when you're coming home."

Melody sighed and made a request of last resort. "Okay, then, let me talk to Mama. Can you just put Mama on the phone?"

Bobby said Mama had disappeared, gone that very morning. Melody was annoyed but not surprised. Mama had a long history of leaving for days or weeks at a time.

"I don't suppose she said where she was headed this time, did she?"

"She doesn't ever," Bobby said. "You know that, Sissy."

He hadn't called her Sissy since they were very young. Melody softened. He was still her little brother.

"I'll be there tomorrow," she promised. "I'll get there as early as I can." She hung up the sticky phone and headed out into the rising heat.

A Christian music festival is no different from any other music festival except there are more young children, fewer tattoos and halter tops on display, and no alcohol for sale. At nine in the morning, however, there was nothing about the festival grounds, a scrubby field behind the Holy Redeemer Baptist Church just outside Memphis, that set it apart from any of the dozens of weekend music festivals being held in cities across America. Melody meandered a bit, not ready to break the news to her bandmates that she wouldn't be traveling on with them to Orlando. The girls would be furious. There was no way they would find another keyboardist who could harmonize on such short notice. They'd have to cancel the gig. They were scheduled to perform tonight and Melody decided that would be her final performance with Shout with Joy.

She strolled past the shuttered booths that flanked the grounds. Later, these booths would offer up greasy corn dogs, fried Twinkies, chicken on a stick, cherry lemonade. Even now, the scent of fried dough and sugar hung in the air along with citronella and diesel fumes. Melody was hungry. She was always hungry. Food was the last temptation of the Christian musician, and Melody was weak. It would be a relief to leave this behind. She didn't know how she'd stayed for so long. She'd started playing with Joy and Shannon in college. It was a way to earn a little money on the weekends. Before she knew it, Joy had slapped her name on the band and found a manager. Melody thought she'd play with them until something better came along, but nothing better ever had.

It was early evening when they took the stage. Melody's polyester pants strained against her stomach and thighs. A day of arguing with Joy and the girls had sent her off to the food trucks, where she'd scarfed down a bratwurst and funnel cake in the heat of the afternoon. Now she felt bloated and angry. Mosquitoes buzzed around her head, drawn by the massive amount of hair spray she used to keep the teased and curled strands in place. Thank goodness it was a short set, just five songs unless the crowd demanded an encore. Unlikely.

Melody leaned in and struck the chord for the last number, a dreadful song she'd never have to play again, but something was wrong. Her mic was dead. None of the other girls were playing. Melody leaned back, raised an eyebrow at Shannon, who looked away.

Joy addressed the audience. Her mic was working fine. "I wanted to take a moment and let our fans know that one of our group is leaving the flock. Our keyboardist and backup singer, Melody, has decided to abandon the path. I know you'll all join me in praying for her, praying that she'll see the light and seek truth in the love of Jesus Christ."

Melody seethed. How dare she call her a backup singer. Melody's voice carried the band, and Joy knew it. Joy's voice was just good enough for bad karaoke. Her face went hot.

Sweat trickled beneath her bra, soaking the cheap blouse to her skin. Her chest burned, both from anger and the bratwurst.

"And now," Joy said. "Our final number, 'Heart Happy Heaven.' Join in if you know it."

Melody struck the keyboard, her muscle memory ingrained with the instinct to perform. She harmonized. Her mic was live now. Of course it was. They needed her voice. Shannon's voice was flat and tended toward nasal. Joy's was predictable, bland. Worse, she insisted on writing songs like this one, full of sappy lyrics and lazy rhymes. "Heaven" paired with "seven," of course, and "rise" with "lies," but the kicker was the last line of the chorus: *And the angels appease us / when first we see Jesus.*

Melody had argued with Joy over that line. "Why would the angels need to appease us? Is Jesus a disappointment?" There was no reasoning with Joy. She was convinced the song would be a hit. It wasn't.

She sang the horrid line and then, as the music ended and before the applause, she said the following: "Joy, you're an enormous cunt."

The nasty word echoed across the stunned crowd. A baby cried. A woman coughed. Otherwise, silence. If Melody accomplished nothing else, at least she'd squelched the polite applause that usually followed Joy's dreadful song. And Joy, oh Joy, stumbled backwards like she might faint. Melody turned her back on the audience and stomped off the stage. She tried to muster some dignity, but as she stepped off the back stairs, the too-tight polyester fabric of her pants ripped right along the seam of her ass.

Chapter Two

Obi snuck out into the predawn mist while Liam slept. When they first took to the land, he had worried about leaving his young son alone, even for short stretches. It wasn't that he worried anything would happen to the boy—there was more danger in the city—it was that he thought Liam would be afraid. Now, though, Liam was at home by the river and Obi didn't fret about whether he might wake up and believe Obi had abandoned him as his mother had. They were a team. Together they had become so used to the constant rush of the river flowing past that the noise of the water was the same as silence. Together they made the land their home.

Obi picked his way through the pine trees, placing his feet by instinct to avoid cracking branches hidden beneath the needle-covered ground. He crouched down in the midst of a circle of trees, a place where he could hear the bubbling water of an underground spring, and he waited.

He'd chosen this spot the day before, when he noticed the smooth areas rubbed onto the bark of the trees and the piles of shiny brownish-green pellets scattered on the ground. It was close to their campsite, but not too close. Obi peered in the direction of the spring and listened for the telltale rustle among the trees. He heard the buck before he saw it and he shouldered his rifle in anticipation. The buck stepped out into a small clearing, sniffing the morning air and stretching out its neck toward the sunrise. It was a beautiful deer, reddish brown with a soft streak of white across its throat. Its antlers were symmetrical, with three points on each rack. The deer was just beginning to shed the velvet coat of spring.

Obi squeezed the trigger. The buck crumpled to its knees, head and chest falling first, back end timbering down behind. A doe and a young, spotted fawn leapt across the clearing and crashed into the woods.

Obi stayed put, watched the downed buck just long enough to be sure the animal was no longer breathing. He approached his kill and pulled his bowie knife from a sheath strapped onto the belt loops of his jeans. He figured the buck weighed about 150 pounds, small enough to handle but large enough to yield a generous amount of meat. He sliced the animal open from breastbone to penis, removed the buck's testicles and also its bladder, which was thankfully empty. Entrails spilled out onto the pine needle nest of the forest floor when he rolled the carcass. Obi's hands and shirt were covered with blood and the warm salty smell of the animal clung to his nose. He separated the tough muscle of the diaphragm from the chest cavity with a few sure strokes, severed the esophagus and the windpipe, and pulled out the heavy heart and slippery liver. Obi dragged the animal back to his campsite, where he strung it from a tree to allow the blood to drain. As he reached above his head to cut the rope, he dropped his knife. It came down, blade first, on his cheek, missing his left eye by less than an inch. Obi put his hand to his face and felt warm blood pulsing from the wound. His knife was sharp and the incision was clean, so it didn't hurt much. His heart pounded with the knowledge that he could have lost his eye.

"Ow, Daddy!" Liam pointed at his father.

"I'm all right," Obi said. "How about a trip into town?" Liam rubbed his eyes, yawned and stretched like a satisfied cat.

Sunlight was just beginning to filter through the trees. He'd strung the carcass up on a high branch to discourage predators, but he didn't have much time to dress and butcher the deer. The heat rose quickly at this time of year.

He drove to a truck stop that was also a small grocery on the side of the highway. It was open twenty-four hours a day, and Obi knew it would have what he needed. "Stay in the truck," he told his son. Liam was stretched out with his back against the seat and his feet propped up on the dashboard. His eyes were closed, but Obi knew he was awake. He wore nothing but a pair of faded red shorts. A cluster of mosquito bites decorated Liam's calf. His chest and arms were smooth and flawless. His hair was long and curly and the color of soft brick, and it framed his freckled face like a halo. Obi reached out and gave Liam's tummy a tap. "Hear me?" Liam nodded without opening his eyes. He looked like a starfish splayed on a bit of dry sand.

The store was empty but for the clerk reading a magazine behind the counter. She didn't glance up when Obi entered. Air-conditioning blared, though the morning was cool. He picked up a container of kosher salt, a sack of red potatoes, and a bunch of carrots. He'd rather take the vegetables from a backyard garden and save his money, but the season was wrong and the carrots grown in Mississippi were puny anyhow. He grabbed a cheap tube of antiseptic cream and a box of large bandages. On impulse, he grabbed a handful of chocolate bars that were on sale beside the register. The woman working behind the counter put her magazine aside and rang up his purchases. She looked at him and recoiled. "You okay, mister?"

Obi knew he should have changed his shirt and cleaned his hands before coming here. It was not deer season, and there were heavy fines associated with hunting out of season, besides which, he did not have a hunting license. He knew he looked terrible, probably smelled worse. It was never a good idea to attract attention. He smiled at the woman and felt the gash under his eye open up; a warm trickle of blood ran down his cheek. "Little accident." He wiped the blood with his palm. "Looks worse than it is."

She pushed his change across the counter, not touching his hands. Obi gathered his purchases and returned to his truck. Liam was on his stomach now, his head facing the seat back, his knees bent against the passenger door and his feet dangling out the window, soles toward heaven.

When they got back to camp, the deer had dripped the last of its blood onto the ground. Obi cut the buck down and then hung it again, this time with the head up. He sliced around the animal's throat to free the hide and pulled the skin off using his knife where he needed to release the muscles. He sliced off one of the buck's ears, washed it in a bit of cold river water and set it aside to dry as a gift for Liam. While he worked, Liam ran back and forth, dipping his feet into the icy cold river water. Obi was proud of how the boy moved, swift and silent and graceful. He belonged to this place, and Obi had no regrets about taking him from that other life. That woman from Social Services might even be impressed by how much Liam had grown.

Obi sliced through the joints of the deer's back legs and cut away the rump steaks. Most of the meat he cut into bite-sized pieces for stew, peeling away the tendons and connective tissue. He sliced the hams into strips and buried them in a pile of kosher salt. He filled his largest stew pot half full with water from the fresh stream and built two fires: one from coal and soft woods that sent up licks of flame and boiled the water in the pot, the other smoky and dry, a bed of coals topped with oak chips. Over the dry fire, Obi set up a crisscrossing frame of branches and stretched salted strips of meat across the wood. The smell of the smoke mingled with the fresh game and wafted out along the banks of the river.

Obi used the side mirror on his truck to examine the cut beneath his eye. The gash was deep and swollen. Obi dipped a cloth in a bit of river water and ran it along the wound. He scraped out the dried blood and the dirt and pressed to staunch the flow of fresh blood. It stung. Liam stood beside him, took the bloody cloth from him, and handed him a fresh one. When the blood coagulated, Obi smeared the antiseptic cream into the wound and covered it with a bandage. It needed stitches, but he didn't have the guts to stick a needle so close to his eye.

"I'm hungry," Liam said.

Obi touched the boy's hair. "Let's make some breakfast."

"Can we eat the deer?"

"Not yet," Obi said. "Tonight we'll have a feast." He rummaged around in the back of the truck, searching through their supplies. "How about pancakes? We still have some of those blueberries we picked."

Liam pulled out the skillet and held it up like an offering. "Pancakes it is."

Chapter Three

Geneva lay still and let the heat and shifting colors of the sauna wash over and through her. Guilt and obligation seeped from her pores, the flop sweat of family dysfunction. She itched to wipe her eyes and shake out her hair, but she resisted. The sweat, the poison, would evaporate at its own pace.

Some of the other women in the room moaned or cried out. One seemed to be performing a solo drum concert on her thighs. The slapping sound wasn't quite loud enough to drown out the nagging voice of Geneva's own weak conscience. Oh, shut the hell up, she told the voice. She knew damn well what people thought of her. No need to condemn herself.

These were the judgments against her: mad as a loon, unbelievably selfish, a bad mother, and a terrible wife. Fact is, Geneva's life was one long string of tragedy and yet she went right on living, getting stronger and more powerful in spite of it. People with ordinary problems believed they knew suffering. They thought they had a right to judge her. They had no right.

The moist cedar scent of the room mixed with the body odor from so many women sweating together. The air was thick and blood rich. She'd been away too long, allowed the anemia of her daily life to drag her down. Between deep breaths, her naked body filled with color. She forgot everything she ever knew. She remembered things she'd never known before. Her soul went blue, a deep cool blue like the color of the sky in springtime, her favorite turquoise bracelet, her grandmother's Spode china. Just when she was good and settled into the blue, it deepened. Purple gathered in her belly and spread out in a sensual, pulsing rhythm. She shuddered with pleasure. When she was wrung out and weak, red took over. It rushed through her like a wildfire, burned her skin and brain, then seemed to double back and tighten into a small, hot fist. Red gathered up all her anger into a tight mass at the base of her spine. It grew hotter until she feared she'd burst into flames. When it was as hot as she could bear, it faded to an ember, then snuffed out to blackness. Black as a shroud of protection, black as a mask of death, black as the Delta soil. She huffed out a burst of air like someone punched in the gut. That was better. Light. Clear, pure white light remained.

A soft hand stroked her arm. She was in a cool room now, a cave. Candlelight flickered on the mud-scraped walls. The dirt floor was raked into concentric circles. She sat in a circle of women, all of them woozy and disoriented from the heat of the sauna. Plus there was the tea they were served before entering the sauna, some mixture of ginger and funny mushrooms that helped the enlightenment along.

Geneva bent at the waist and let her tongue flop out, dog-like, onto the cool ground. Saliva poured from her mouth and turned the soil to pudding. A pair of hairy arms pulled her back. "Careful, love," said a woman's silky voice against her ear.

Geneva smiled. Careful had never really been her style.

Chapter Four

Melody picked her way across the gravel parking lot. Her pants ripped a bit wider with each step. Big deal. She would never wear them again, and there was no one she hoped to impress between here and White Forest, Mississippi. Then she heard her name called and realized she was being followed. It was Chris. She ran faster. Chris had been trying to catch her for months. She wasn't about to slow down for him now.

Six months ago, Melody had walked off the stage after a performance in Oklahoma City and slammed into Chris Perkins, radio host, producer, up-and-coming tastemaker in the Christian music scene, almost as important as he believed himself to be. Chris was the voice of the Christian Radio Network, a syndicated service that aired wherever people listened to gospel music, which was most places in America.

Melody had not been paying attention and she walked into Chris, who was hanging out backstage. "Whoa!" He grabbed her shoulders and grinned like the Cheshire cat. Melody, as she always did under such circumstances, flushed purple and babbled out an apology. "Did I step on your foot?"

Chris laughed. "You're still standing on my foot."

"Oh." She stepped back.

"Yes, but it's fine. My foot is fine." Chris jogged or danced or something, as if to prove his foot was in good working order. He looked like a puppet on a string.

"I'm glad." She'd tried to walk around him, to catch up to the other girls. Joy liked to have a post-performance prayer and then tell everyone what they'd done wrong. She'd be furious if Melody was late, but Melody was going to be late. Chris took her hand and dragged her toward a heavy door. It led out into the alley and blessedly cool air.

"I couldn't hear myself think in there," Chris said. "You were great."

Melody shrugged. "It's Joy's group."

"That's the problem," Chris said. "Your voice should be front and center. Joy sings about as well as a canned ham."

Melody laughed. "I don't even know what that means."

"Me neither." Chris was sweating, his upper lip glistening, and he stood so close Melody could feel the heat coming from his body. "These outfits are ridiculous. You look great, but no one should wear this blouse. It makes you all look like Captain Cook or something."

"Mine doesn't fit so great. I've gained a few pounds since we ordered them."

"It's not you. It's the clothing. You're beautiful. You're beautiful in spite of the clothes. You are doing these clothes a huge favor."

Compliments like these were so outside the realm of

Melody's experience that she did the only thing she could think of to shut him up. She kissed him.

He kissed back, pressing against her and putting his hands on either side of her face. His fingers tangled in her hair and she wished her hair were soft and flowing instead of brittle and sticky from all the hair spray. Not that he complained. It was good stuff, this kiss. Despite running with a crowd that encouraged virginity until marriage, Melody had managed to shed that albatross during a particularly awkward, drunken encounter with a Kappa Sig in college. So she wasn't completely without experience. Still, there was more going on during this kiss in an alley than had happened during an entire night with the frat boy at a decent hotel. Just as she was beginning to really relax and enjoy things, Shannon's shrill voice bleated out into the alley.

"I found her. I found her!"

For about half a second, Melody was prepared to tell Shannon to get lost, but Chris was not so unconcerned about being discovered. He pushed her away, wiped his mouth with the back of his hand, and sprinted from the alley without so much as a thank-you. As it turned out, Chris was engaged to some girl in Nebraska. This was common knowledge, according to Shannon and Joy. "What kind of person just makes out with someone in an alley?" Joy asked. It was not a purely hypothetical question, and the implication was clear: a cheap girl with loose morals, that's who.

She'd avoided Chris since that night, and she had no intention of talking to him now. She stepped into the road and flagged down a faded gray sedan. The setting sun turned the sky orange and obstructed her vision. She squinted but could not see inside the car. She decided a car full of rapists and ax murderers would be preferable to a confrontation with Chris. Thankfully, a woman with severe black hair poked her head out the passenger-side window and told Melody to hop in. The woman looked Pentecostal, which wasn't great, but she didn't look like a killer.

Melody slid into the backseat, her heart pounding. Sweat soaked her horrid blouse to her stomach. The driver, a man with the same dark hair as the woman, said, "Welcome, sister."

"Hey there." She plucked at the sleeves of her blouse, desperate to get some air between her skin and the god-awful fabric. "Thanks so much for stopping. I'm hoping to get to the train station."

"Ah, a journey on the rails. Where are you heading on this fine summer evening, sister?" The man's voice, deep and musical, gave Melody the creeps.

The woman turned her head and beamed. "I'm Bernice and this is my husband, George Walter."

Melody wasn't sure if the couple's last name was Walter or if the man used two names. "I'm Melody."

"Melody," George Walter said. "Melody. It's a beautiful name, sister. A musical name. Is your family musical?"

"Sort of," Melody said. "Mama used to play the piano, sing a bit." Her own musical career felt too freshly failed to mention.

"That's the saddest thing I've ever heard." George Walter

glanced at her in the rearview mirror. A milky film floated over the brown iris of his right eye, ghostly and ghoulish.

"Sad?"

"That she *used* to play. Once you find the music inside you, you have a duty to keep playing, keep singing. Music must be shared with the world, sister. Music is a gift that should never be squandered."

Melody wished she could close her eyes and ignore this odd man, but he'd offered her a ride and she felt obligated to respond. "She had more important things to do. She had to drop out of college and take care of her mother. Her mother was very sick."

"Ah," Bernice said. "Family obligations. Your mother is a godly woman?"

"I don't know about that. She did what she had to do."

"No one has to do anything in this world, sister." George Walter slowed the car as they entered city traffic. The sun had faded and Melody felt bathed in the passing headlights and bright neon of Memphis on a Saturday night. The air was cooler now. "You make your choices and you live with them," George Walter said. "Don't forget that. Everything is a choice, sister."

"Don't mind George Walter," Bernice said. "He has strong opinions."

Who doesn't? Melody thought. What she said was, "It's okay. I appreciate the ride."

"And where is your destination, sister?"

"White Forest, Mississippi. My father is sick."

"Aha!" George Walter removed both hands from the wheel and raised them in the air. "The daughter becomes the mother. The mother becomes the daughter. One and the same. All of a package. The circle of life continues. History repeats."

"No!" Melody shouted. Panic rose in her throat when George Walter compared her to her mother. "No. It isn't like that."

"What is your music, sister?"

"I don't know what you mean."

"What are you leaving behind?" George Walter asked. Bernice smiled and hummed something tuneless.

Melody reached over to roll down a window, but there was no handle on the back doors. Maybe she'd misjudged this pair. The old couple with shoe polish hair might be killers, might be part of some strange cult that practiced blood ritual and handled snakes. "I'm not leaving anything," she said. "I'm just taking a break."

"You are your mother, sister. You are your mother."

"No. No, I am not." Melody clawed at the doors. She was desperate for fresh air, afraid she might faint. "Can we please just crack a window or something?"

Bernice reached back, patted her leg with a bone-white hand, fingernails chewed to the quick. Melody got a whiff of Bernice's perfume, a sickly combination of lavender and decay. "Relax, honey. George Walter doesn't mean anything by it. He has a bit of the gift, you understand. When it comes upon him, he feels compelled to use it."

"I don't have a bit of the gift," George Walter bellowed.

"I have the gift. The whole package. I don't predict the future. I see the possibilities unfolding. I see the nature of your soul. I see the truth."

Now, Melody was used to fervent preaching, and this was not the first time she'd met someone who claimed to have the gift of prophecy. Her own mother had once taken her to see a Native American woman who claimed the gift of sight and healing. No, it wasn't the foretelling that terrified her, it was George Walter's gleeful certainty and that awful milky eye.

"Be warned," he said. "I have come into your life for a reason. No one crosses my path without purpose. You have choices to make. You must make different choices if you want to be spared the fate of your mother."

"I am nothing like my mother. I assure you of that."

George Walter chuckled, then rocked with laughter. Tears streamed down his face. The milky eye seemed to darken in the rearview mirror. Melody braced herself, waiting for the car to crash, waiting for George Walter to steer them into oncoming traffic or off the side of a bridge into the rushing river.

"Did you hear what she said?" George Walter choked with laughter.

"I heard her." Bernice laughed, too, a high-pitched giggle.

"Nothing like her mother," George Walter said.

"Nothing like her mother," Bernice said.

Their laughter filled the car until Melody felt she would drown in it. "Stop." Her voice was no louder than a whisper. "Please stop."

The car slowed to a crawl. The lights of Central Station flickered in the windows. She was safe. These people were nuts, but they did not plan to kill her and feast on her liver. She pushed the door open before the car came to a complete stop and flung herself out onto the sidewalk. She pitched forward, caught her balance, and sprinted toward the front doors of the station. Safely inside the bustling building, she looked back and saw George Walter and Bernice still laughing together under the glowing streetlights.

Chapter Five

Obi dumped a handful of chopped carrots into the simmering stew. He tasted the rich broth, added a good stream of salt and black pepper. Liam ran in circles in the clearing near the water. His naked skin was the color of polished cedar. The freckles on his face were dark and his green eyes flashed like the eyes of a wildcat. His hair, a dark red tangle, flopped over his forehead and curled around his ears and neck. The boy's penis bounced between his legs. It was as big as Obi's thumb and Obi had large, strong hands. The red hair and freckles and green eyes were a gift from the boy's mother, but that was all she gave him. That, and his name.

"Liam," Obi called. Obi had considered renaming the boy. He'd thought about naming him after one of his Chickasaw ancestors or using the boy's middle name, which was Land and at least sounded like a man's name. He'd called the boy Land for a while, but the child never responded. He smiled and toddled toward Obi only when he called for Liam. Now, at the age of five, Liam no longer toddled. He ran and jumped and skipped and walked with the long sure strides of a grown man.

For the first six months or so after Liam's mother left, Obi thought she would come back. Of course she could leave him, but how could a mother leave her son? Obi did not know how powerful the pull of alcohol was for some people, although his own family was full of men and women grown fat and lazy and perpetually drunk. His own father hadn't seen the world through clear eyes in all the years that Obi knew him, but his mother never touched the sweet brown liquor or smoked anything stronger than tobacco. She would not have abandoned him for anything on earth or beyond, and she protected him from his father's rages until Obi got old enough and big enough to protect himself.

In the months when Obi was waiting for Eileen to return, he lived in the little box they shared out at Chickasaw Mound, which some people call Memphis. He lived in the square, squat concrete box with curtains on the square windows to block out the sun and a poured concrete square out front for parking his truck. He slept underneath the square roof, which blocked out the moon and he fell asleep listening to the hum of the square appliances, which obscured the sound of the wind, the birds, the howl of the coyotes, the rustle of the trees. He went to work every day and welded sheets of iron and steel together, pounded nails into slabs of wood, measured, cut and leveled lumber to make more square boxes where people would live and work and die. As if the boxes weren't bad enough, the woman from Social Services kept harassing him. She dropped by unexpectedly and lectured Obi about the food in his cabinets, about sweeping and wiping down the counters and vacuuming the old gray carpet, as if he had loads of extra time for chores. He kept the house as neat as he could, but she found fault. She asked Liam questions, too, about whether he was ever hungry and if he was happy and if he felt safe. Liam was too young to understand that the woman might be dangerous, that the wrong answer could be devastating. The woman asked Obi about Eileen, where she'd gone and when she'd be back. Useless questions with no answer. She set up hearings at the courthouse and Obi had to take off work, fill out forms, and answer questions from the family court judge. No matter how hard he worked, it wasn't enough and the woman never let up. She said they could take Liam away, put him in a foster home. If he didn't follow their rules, he could lose his son.

One week, he took Liam camping out by Wolf River though he knew the woman would disapprove. It would be one more strike against them. For seven nights, they slept on the ground. When it rained, and it often did in the midafternoon, they took shelter in a small tent Obi pitched near a cluster of water ash trees. Obi hunted during the early morning while Liam slept, always staying within earshot of the campsite in case the boy cried out. They ate squirrel that Obi killed, skinned, and soaked in milk to tame the flavor of blood and wildness, or crappie he caught in the river, dredged in cornmeal and fried in a black skillet. With just milk and cornmeal, he stirred together hush puppies or corn cakes to serve alongside the meat or fish. For the first time in years, Obi felt free. Stars shone down on his son; the gentle trickle of the river lulled the boy to sleep.

Obi noticed how Liam ate hungrily and asked for more. At home, where the boy lived on a steady diet of crackers and cereal, he grew lethargic and had to be coaxed to eat at every meal. Obi saw then that despite the freckles and red hair and green eyes, this boy was truly his son. He was not meant to live in a box, to eat things produced in factories halfway across the world, to spend his days in a sterile day care with other children who all dressed alike and looked alike and went home to their own boxes every night until they grew up and moved into boxes of their own and had children who looked just like them and just like everyone else around them, with no idea that there could be another way.

On the eighth day, Obi returned to his box and spent a day gathering things he thought they would need. He picked up his paycheck from the construction crew. His boss, a small, quiet man, told him he would be missed and to come back if he ever needed work. He was supposed to contact Social Services, but he could just imagine what the woman would think of his plan to live in a place where the floor wasn't just dirty, it was actually dirt.

He cashed the paycheck and emptied out his bank account and found that he had plenty of money. They would be able to live for a long time if they were careful and ate food they hunted or harvested from the wild berry bushes that grew along the river and from the gardens so carefully planted in neat rows behind people's homes. Obi knew he could find work when he needed money. People always needed a fence mended or a roof repaired.

Traveling with a small boy proved fortuitous. Women

wanted to get their hands on the child, to make sure he was well fed and healthy. They wanted to hold the boy and coo at him, poke his round tummy, tickle his dancing feet, stroke his rust-colored hair, peer into his green marble eyes, kiss his freckled cheeks, and smell his wild child scent. Obi was happy to let the women hold Liam while he worked or talked with the men and figured out the best places to camp. The biggest problem he ran into were single women, who would offer Obi a bed for the night. It felt good to sleep with a woman and he could trade his freedom for one night or even a week in exchange for that pleasure. Soon, though, the women wanted him to stay. *Liam needs a mother,* they said, *a home, a schedule. What about school?* they asked. Obi wised up and turned away from the single women. He sometimes slept with other men's wives while the men were at work. The wives didn't want him to stay, and Obi, satisfied, could move on without guilt.

The money he carried with him plus the cash for odd jobs kept his truck filled with gas and allowed him to purchase the few items he couldn't capture or take. Every month he bought cornmeal, flour, powdered milk, a few canned goods, and a surprise for Liam. The surprises were small: a box of lemon cookies that made Liam's mouth pucker when he ate them, a bag of oranges, a loaf of fresh bread. Liam loved the treats. Once it was a package of bubble gum. Obi and Liam spent an entire afternoon chewing the gum and pushing their tongues through the rubbery sweetness to blow bubbles. Liam spat the first piece out onto the ground with his effort to create a bubble. His face screwed up and the corners of his mouth drooped; the gum was covered in dirt and twigs. Obi unwrapped another piece and popped it in Liam's mouth before he could cry.

Obi met other people who lived as they did, single men who traveled along the rivers in canoes and families piled into trucks and campers. The single men were outlaws or deadbeat parents. On the river, though, they were just men, strong men who lived freely and from the land. The families Obi met traveled for many reasons, but it all boiled down to this: They couldn't bear to live in a box, to raise their children in the cold, generic suburbs of America.

Sometimes luck or fate or the weather brought a group of them together in the same area and then it was a party. Tonight would be one of those nights, Obi knew. The smell of the stew and the salty smoked meat filled the air with invitation. Once the river people set up or returned to camp for the evening, back from a day of fishing or hunting or just floating along the river, they would follow the scent of Obi's stew. The sun dipped its white light into the green tips of the pine trees on the far side of the river. They would be here soon.

"Liam!" he called. "Come and put some clothes on."

Liam ran over and pulled a pair of jeans from a duffel bag in the bed of the truck. He shimmied into them and slipped a T-shirt over his head. Obi had taken the clothes from a charity donation bin outside a Goodwill store just south of Batesville. The jeans were a good fit, but the T-shirt hung on Liam's small shoulders like a nightgown. The shirt was dark blue with flaking red and white letters that read OLE MISS on the front. People were always throwing out perfectly good stuff and Obi figured they needed the clothes as much as anyone who might visit the thrift store. He figured that by taking the clothes directly from the donation bin, he was saving someone the trouble of paperwork.

This was the kind of thinking that got Obi in trouble. He and the other people along the river shared a philosophy. Some things could not be owned; some things were ripe for taking. Corn and tomatoes, sacks of pole beans, heads of lettuce, and the occasional live chicken disappeared from homes in the small towns along the Yalobusha, the Tallahatchie, and the Yazoo rivers. Obi never took more than he needed and he never took the best of anything. People blamed deer or a fox or some other wildlife for the loss. It was the price of living in a place where you could grow enough food in a backyard to feed a small army. Sometimes, though, homeowners and farmers called the sheriff and accused the river people of stealing. It was not a crime to live as Obi did, but sometimes crimes were committed.

In the same way they believed living things could not be owned, whether it be animal or vegetable, they believed some things must be shared. There was no hoarding food on the river. Money, scarce as it was, belonged to the individual. Guns and vehicles and boats were owned. Food and drink and smoke were shared. Most people provided for themselves by fishing or hunting or foraging, but when someone struck it rich, as Obi had done this morning, they were obliged to share. Obi made a point of sharing a big meal every so often, just to keep on the good side of all the river people. Most of them were solitary men who didn't want trouble and who wouldn't cause trouble. Lately, though, there had been an influx of young, brash men who looked at living off the land as an adventure rather than a life. These new men—boys, really, in Obi's opinion—did not understand how important it was to be inconspicuous. They were the children of the wealthy and they had been to college and dropped out, or they had graduated and decided work didn't suit them. They lived off their parents' money. They drank too much, drove recklessly, smoked excessive amounts of marijuana, took pills, manufactured drugs that smelled of cat piss in old trailers they set up by the river, swung from the trees in imitation of Tarzan, left trash on the riverbanks, left fires smoldering, chased women who didn't want to be caught, and generally terrified everyone in their path. These boys brought unwanted attention to the river people, and attention turned into trouble. The small-town sheriffs and their deputies were capable of violence and cruelty. It was best to avoid their attentions. People who lived in boxes and liked it didn't understand why anyone would choose to do otherwise.

Obi waved to a couple approaching the campsite. Samuel carried a bucket in one hand and it sloshed as he walked. His wife carried a cast-iron dish with a towel across the top.

"Glad you came," Obi said.

"We smelled the stew starting around lunchtime, and Margie said she knew it was you."

Margie set the dish she was carrying on the tailgate of Obi's truck. "I love a man who knows how to cook." She kissed Obi on the cheek and rubbed Liam's curls. "The boys are right behind us."

Obi watched as the two young boys wrestled their way toward the fire. They looked like puppies fighting to get the first sip of milk. The boys were older than Liam by a few years, but they included him and made him feel a part of their games.

"I caught a mess of bream today." Samuel set the bucket down on the ground. "Thought I might add to the meal for anyone who wants a bit of fish."

"Appreciate it." Obi nodded.

"Still need to clean 'em and fillet 'em." He gestured toward the bed of Obi's truck. "Do you mind?"

"Not a bit."

"John David! Sam! Cut it out." Margie watched, to be sure her sons quit doing whatever it was she didn't want them doing, and turned back to Obi. "I made a berry cobbler. We can stick it on the fire for after dinner."

"Mmmm, that's perfect." Obi had very little interest in another wife, but if he did settle down again, it would definitely be with a woman who could make a good cobbler.

Before long, there were a dozen people in Obi's camp. Many brought something to share—a bottle of whiskey or jug full of lemonade or a salad of wild, bitter greens. Obi's stew was delicious and Samuel's fish was just right. Everyone made a fuss over Margie's cobbler, and more than a few people wished for ice cream. Liam and John David and Sam carried around fish eyes like talismans, rubbing the slimy orbs across their palms and looking at them closely to uncover their secrets. One of the older men pulled out a guitar and strummed on it without evoking any sort of melody. The night grew darker and the stars came out, hanging like ornaments in the black sky. The air cooled and there was almost a breeze if you stood still enough to feel it. Mosquitoes swarmed and dispersed, biting flesh that had been bitten too many times before.

One by one, the men drifted off, back to their own campsites along the river or to sleep in the cradle of canoes. Samuel and his family stayed on longer than the rest. The boys played an elaborate game of tag.

Samuel and Margie and the boys had a camper, which practically made them of another world among most of the river people. They were traveling for one year, Samuel told Obi, one year of freedom from television and movies and from working like a dog for money to pay for the things Samuel hated.

Samuel and Obi sat side by side while Margie cleaned up her cobbler dish in the river. A loud whine and the tinny sound of music blared through an old radio, distant at first and then louder. A light bounced toward them. Obi jumped up first. The light split in two and grew bigger, revealing a vehicle careening through the woods before coming to a stop just inches from Obi's own truck.

"Good God Almighty Christ in Heaven!" Samuel rose up. Obi almost laughed at his friend's choice of words, but there was nothing funny about the young men climbing from the Jeep. Obi looked to make sure Liam and the two boys were safe. Margie had all three of them in her arms.

Three boys spilled from the Jeep, young men with wild eyes and wild hair but wearing clothes that probably cost more than Obi's truck was worth.

"Hey," one of them said. The boy was tall and looked strong if a bit soft around the middle. His hair was blond and curly and his eyes were glassy with drink or something stronger. His face was scratched, four long red gashes across his right jaw, fresher than the wound on Obi's cheek. "Got anything to drink?"

Obi shook his head. "We have clean water and a bit of orange juice. You are welcome to the water, but the juice is for my son."

"Naw, man." The boy looked at his friends and grinned.

Samuel spoke. "We don't drink alcohol and we don't have any, so move along."

"See," the boy said, as if Samuel hadn't spoken. "We just need a little shot of something and then we'll head on down the river."

"We don't have any liquor," Obi said.

"Okay." The boy sighed like Obi was dense and he was just trying to be reasonable. "Okay, then how about you run into town and buy us a bottle? We got money." The boy who had been speaking nodded at one of the others, the smallest one. The small boy lowered his head, his face shaded with a baseball cap, and reached into a pocket to pull out a wad of cash.

"You have money, buy it yourself," Samuel said.

Obi studied the smaller boy, the one with the money. Something about him was different from the others. His skin was darker and smoother, not a trace of a beard.

His denim shirt would fit someone twice his size. His blue jeans were rolled up and cinched tight at the waist. Obi wondered how old he was. He looked to be a teenager—a runaway, perhaps.

"You know," the first boy spoke. "We would. We really would. But there's been a, uh, misunderstanding. We can't be seen in town right now."

"Move on," Obi said. "Go to the next town." If there was going to be trouble, he wanted the boys far away.

"It's a pretty big misunderstanding." The boy reached up and touched the scratch on his jaw. "I'm gonna have to stay low for a while and I need a drink. I really need a drink, man."

"Looks to me like you've had plenty to drink already," Samuel said.

"Aw, man, don't give me that and don't tell me you don't got anything to drink either. See, I know you guys drink. Everyone drinks on the river."

Plenty of people drank on the river, it was true, but these boys managed to find the one camp with no liquor. There was not even a bottle left over from the party. People who brought whiskey to pass drank until the bottle was dry.

One of the other boys spoke, a boy with brown hair and a face with features so vague that he looked like an unfinished sketch. "Yeah, you're all a bunch of drunks."

"We have children here," Obi said. "Can't you see that?"

The first boy, the blond, laughed. "So what? I didn't tell you to bring your bastard kids out in the woods. You want your kids safe? Keep 'em indoors."

"Yeah," said the featureless boy. The small one didn't say

a word, just kept staring down into the fistful of cash he held.

"Daddy!" Liam yelled. Margie tried to grab him, but she was already holding on to her own sons, and Liam was quick. He raced over, wrapped his arms around Obi's legs.

Obi touched Liam's soft curls. "It's okay, son."

"Hotty toddy, kid," the blond boy said.

"Huh?" Liam pressed his face into Obi's thigh.

"Your shirt," the boy said. "Ole Miss Rebels. Hotty toddy, gosh almighty, who the hell are we?"

The featureless boy joined in. "Flimflam, bim bam, Ole Miss by damn!"

The smaller boy smiled, revealing a row of straight white teeth.

"Okay, that's enough," Samuel said. "You're scaring the kid. You can see that. You don't want to scare a kid, do you?"

The blond boy laughed. "Hey, kid, are you scared?"

Liam kept his face turned into Obi's leg.

The blond boy reached behind his back, and Obi knew what he was going for; he intuited the cold steel glint of the blade before he saw it. "I don't want to scare a kid, man," the boy said. "I just want one of you to get us something to drink. It's not such a big deal. I don't know why everything has to be such a big deal."

The whine in his voice told Obi everything he needed to know about this boy. Obi pulled Liam's chin up, looked him in the eyes. "I want you to go with Margie. When I say so, I want you to run to Margie as fast as you can, you hear me?"

"I wanna stay with you."

"It's just for a few minutes," Obi said.

"Come here, baby," Margie cooed. "Come see Aunt Margie."

"I wanna stay with Daddy."

"Daddy'll be right along," Samuel said.

"Go on," Obi gave him a push. He wished more than anything that his rifle wasn't stuck behind the seat of his truck, but Obi kept his best knife strapped to his belt. It would have to do. He let his right hand float up to the level of the knife, keeping his eyes on the boy.

"Hey!" the featureless boy yelled.

The blond boy charged at Obi, holding his knife out in front of him like a sword. It was ridiculous, but too dangerous to mock. Obi crossed his left forearm in front of his body to deflect the blade. He grasped his own knife firmly in his right hand and arced his arm around in front of him. The boy's blade glanced off Obi's arm and drew blood. Obi barely felt a thing. He yanked the boy's head back and held his knife to the boy's throat.

"Let go of me." The boy's voice squeaked.

Obi's blade rested against the boy's pale throat. Up close, Obi saw how dilated and glassy the boy's eyes were; his skin glistened and a bubble of saliva danced on his bottom lip. The boy's pulse thrummed against Obi's wrist, hard and erratic.

"Look," Obi said. "Why don't you move along and sober

up? Whatever the trouble is, it's probably not as bad as you imagine." The boy grimaced and flailed his arms.

"Look," Obi said. "Even if one of us drove into town for you, how do you know we wouldn't bring back the sheriff? How is sending one of us any safer than going yourself?"

"You wouldn't dare get the sheriff," the featureless boy said. "You're all criminals, too. Look at your face. You're telling me you got that cut doing something legal? Hell, you're probably a killer. You're a monster. You're hiding out here just like we are."

Obi was no monster, but he didn't intend to invite the law into his life. "If I'm a killer," he said. "How come I haven't killed your friend yet?"

"Oh, God." The blond boy struggled to break free.

Obi told Samuel to take the boy's knife. Disarmed, Obi figured he'd move on. The boy shook under his grip, terrified. Obi laughed, not because he was amused but because the whole situation was ridiculous. These boys were playing at being men; that was all. They were scared and in trouble. Obi knew what it was like to be scared and in trouble, but he couldn't allow anyone to threaten his son. When he laughed, the boy screamed and writhed violently. The knife Obi held at the boy's throat slipped, spilling a warm, wet gush across Obi's hand. Samuel stepped away, looked at Obi with shock or anger or fear. The boy fell to the ground. He twitched and moaned. The featureless boy screamed and ran into the woods. The smaller boy, who hadn't spoken yet, ran to the boy on the ground. "Reese?"

he said. "Are you okay? Oh, God, please be okay." The boy on the ground responded with a desperate gurgle; a low rattle escaped from his bleeding throat.

The boy removed his hat and knelt. He looked up at Obi and narrowed his eyes. "How could you? He didn't hurt you. He was just a little messed up."

The blond boy grasped at the ground with his hands as if to keep from falling, though he was already splayed flat. Blood spurted from his neck like a fountain, then slowed to a steady stream. It was so much blood. The gurgling stopped. He stared up at Obi, eyes wide.

Obi shook his head. "It was an accident. I didn't mean to."

Samuel backed away. "I can't stay here. I have a family."

Liam called to him. "Daddy."

"It was an accident," Obi said. "He came at me first." He looked at the smaller boy, saw his face for the first time, and realized he wasn't a boy at all.

"I'm sorry, miss. I'm so sorry." Obi wished he'd never shot the deer, never camped on this piece of land, never pulled the knife from his belt.

Liam was at Obi's side. Samuel disappeared with his family.

"My father is going to kill me." The girl sobbed; her nose ran. "What am I supposed to do?"

Reese was still alive, still grappling the earth. Maybe the cut wasn't deep enough to kill. Obi didn't want to be a killer, didn't want his son to think of him as a killer.

"I'm not even supposed to be here. He's going to kill me."

Obi put Liam in the truck and locked the door. "Don't move," he said. He yanked down their tent and tossed it into the bed of the truck, a heap of poles and canvas. The stew pot went on top. The campsite was a mess, bottles and scraps of food, cigarette butts and debris lay scattered around the fire. Normally, Obi left a campsite cleaner than he'd found it. He wished he could clean up now, leave no trace, but there wasn't time. Better to leave a bunch of fingerprints than to risk leaving only his own.

The boy on the ground moaned and the girl continued to cry.

"Oh, I'm in so much trouble," the girl said. "I'm not even supposed to be with these guys. My father is going to kill me."

Obi paused for just a moment as he climbed into his truck. "Maybe you shouldn't tell him about this. Maybe you shouldn't tell anyone." He hadn't meant it as a threat, but that's how it sounded. The girl's eyes got wide and she stumbled, falling back onto the ground.

Obi drove as fast as he dared. He didn't want to scare his son any more than he already had, and he couldn't risk being pulled over. He leaned forward, both hands on the wheel, his jaw clenched; sweat poured down his back collar.

"Everything's okay," he told Liam. "Everything's gonna be fine. Don't you worry. I won't let anything bad happen to you." It was a promise Obi intended to keep, no matter what.

Chapter Six

Geneva was at that point in her pilgrimage when clarity returned. Whatever magic plants the women spiked her tea with were wearing off, and her hallucinations faded into revelation. She understood one thing good and clear: It was time to tell her daughter everything. She'd been trying to protect Melody from the awful truth, but she couldn't protect anyone from the truth by keeping her mouth shut. The truth was there whether she gave voice to it or not.

Greedy as a suckling pig, she squeezed ice-cold water from a soft cloth into her mouth. It dribbled down her chin and chest, and it carried the flavor of memory. Sharp and metallic and pulled up from a deep well, it carried the taste of things most people want filtered out of their water. Geneva shivered. After the hot sauna and the cave, she was so thirsty she forgot what it meant to drink. If the woman beside her hadn't grabbed it, she'd have swallowed the cloth.

The water brought Geneva fully to her senses. Melody had to know the truth. Without the truth, she would never understand. Melody blamed her for every damned horrible thing that ever happened. Maybe she deserved it. Maybe not. Either way, Melody needed to know what she'd been spared. She needed to know how much worse things could be, and how Geneva had saved her, saved them both. Geneva wished her own mother had bared her soul at some point in her own pathetic life. Perhaps she could have saved herself. Perhaps she could have spared Geneva.

"Let's get started," the woman at her side said. "It's time."

Geneva followed her out into the settling heat of the early evening. The horizon shimmered in the distance, and for all she could see, there was nothing but grass and trees and the dark rich dirt of the land stretching out to eternity. Like Lot's wife, she turned to glance at the small gray house with the sauna and the few cool rooms where women waited to begin their journey. The haint blue windows and doors seemed to wink at her. The color, crayon bright and deceptively cheerful, was rumored to ward off ghosts and repel evil. The front door was flanked by an impressive pair of bottle trees, the largest Geneva had ever seen. Sometimes when the sun was high and bright enough, the bottles would glint and glimmer until people claimed the light could be seen shining clear to Memphis. People claimed all sorts of things.

She turned her eyes back to the vast landscape and walked. The woman led her in the direction of the waning sun. The soft dress swirled around her legs like a purring cat. Her bare feet sank into the cool black soil. Staring ahead made Geneva's eyes swim with dark spots, ghosts, and ghoulies from her past. She swatted at them, shielded her eyes from the sun's glare with a cupped hand. Her head throbbed as the sun slid slowly down the sky. Finally, the old beast melted into the far horizon. The air cooled just enough as the sky went orange, then pink, then gray. Fireflies filled the darkness. Glow and fade, glow and fade, like fairies lighting the way. Geneva smiled, remembered rare summer evenings as a girl when she was free to run outside and dance with the fireflies.

The sharp, sour scent of fertilizer filled her nose. Memories of dancing gave way to memories of her father working the land. That land had been something of value once, not because anyone would give them a heap of cash for it, but because it produced cotton and good food and honest work. Now it was just one more burden she had to tote.

They walked on through farmland that was still being farmed. The scrubby stalks and tender shoots that would soon turn into something worth wearing or eating or pressing into oil lay all around them like a great promise. She knew farmers and their wives all over the Delta were home now, praying for the weather. Dear God, send us rain, but not too much. Bring us heat, but not too high. Bring us breezes, but not wind. Worthless conversations, because God never listened. Or if he listened, he didn't give a hoot. That was probably more like it. God just didn't give a hoot about a bunch of poor farmers in the Mississippi Delta. Well, they could keep their god, Geneva thought. She had Pisa.

By they time they stopped walking, Geneva was so tired, she could spit. The woman spread an old wool blanket on the ground, and Geneva collapsed onto her back. The ground beneath her was unforgiving, but she didn't care. She closed her eyes to the fisherman's moon. Crickets chirped and a lone bullfrog croaked. Geneva slept like a corpse.

Chapter Seven

Melody's train pulled into the station at just after nine in the morning. It had not been a restful night, but that was nothing new. Three years of sleeping on the cramped tour bus or in cheap hotels had left her feeling perpetually hungover. She squinted into the morning sun and raised her hands above her head, bending backward and forward to loosen out the kinks in her body. In some parts of the country, people would pay good money to be ordered into these positions, but yoga had not yet brought its sun salutations to White Forest. Melody sighed and set out walking.

After George Walter and Bernice had dropped her off at the Memphis station, and after she'd checked the schedule and purchased a ticket for the 6:50 A.M. train, she'd wandered into the gift shop and bought a T-shirt featuring the BeDazzled face of a young, thin Elvis. The extra-large T-shirt hung on her like a dress or a nightgown, but it covered the rip in her pants.

She'd tried to sleep on the hard wooden benches at the train station, but they reminded her of church pews and sent her dreaming about Bobby's botched baptism. She

47

dreamed about it plenty, no matter where she slept. In the early morning, she startled herself awake shouting, "Mama, no!" When she opened her eyes, still half in her dream, an old whore wearing a hot-pink halter top stood over her, breasts sagging dangerously. "Mama's here," the old whore rasped and Melody saw that the woman had no teeth. After that, she'd given up on sleep.

Melody awakened to a truth most people discover at some point: The more you try to forget something, the larger the memory looms. Melody had been trying to forget about Bobby's baptism since she witnessed it at the age of fourteen. As a result, she thought about it all the time. It came to her in flashes throughout the day, stalking her and pouncing when she was most vulnerable. She didn't understand why it should haunt her so relentlessly. Bobby didn't seem to dwell on it. Her mother did not speak of it. Her father handled it as he handled everything, with a mix of resignation and rage.

This was what she tried to forget.

Bobby was eleven when he answered the call of the Lord. It was summertime and hot then, as it was now. They worshipped in a small, old church while a new sanctuary was built. The congregation looked to that new sanctuary with as much reverence as they looked toward God. When Pastor Tuttle announced they would worship in the new church the very next week, Bobby sprinted up the aisle to dedicate his soul, determined to be the first body dunked in the new baptismal pool.

For the past year, the church had contracted with a

nearby hotel to use its pool once a month for baptisms. It was awkward when guests in town for reunions or weddings came down on Sunday mornings to swim off their Saturday night hangovers. Before that, they'd done all their baptisms in the Tallahatchie River. That's where Melody was dunked, where she felt the cool squish of mud between her toes, where she ate sour cream cake and fried chicken while the sun and a warm breeze dried her hair. It was perfect until little Johnny McPherson was bit by a water moccasin at his baptism. Plenty of folks said Johnny was an evil child and the devil had come back in that old familiar form to claim his soul. That Johnny survived and went on to brag about his brush with death just reinforced the gossip. Most people, though, knew you could enter snake-infested waters only so many times without getting bit. Those people began raising money for a new sanctuary, snake-free baptismal pool included.

Bobby didn't care a bit about being baptized, but he cared quite a lot about being first. He was beautiful, with eyelashes that cast shadows on his porcelain cheeks and thick black hair that he wore just a little too long. He was vain and dramatic and stubborn. Melody reminded him his mortal soul was on the line, but she didn't mean it. She wanted to see her brother dunked in that magnificent, elevated, tile-lined pool as much as he wanted to be seen.

On the morning of the baptism, every seat was filled. People who showed up for church only at Christmas and Easter were there, wearing their finest clothes. The new sanctuary was spectacular with gleaming polished oak pews. The choir wore new rich purple robes with gold embroidery around the neck and arms. Melody, Bobby, and Mama sat in the third row. Melody's father could not be lured to church for any reason. When the choir rose to sing "Just a Closer Walk with Thee," Bobby slipped through a side door behind the choir loft. Pastor Tuttle followed. The choir sang on and on. When they finished, Pastor Tuttle emerged clad in dark robes. He stepped down into the pool. A soft light emanated from the water and shone on his face. A microphone was attached to one side of the pool, and Pastor Tuttle took it in his hands. "Friends and family in the Lord." His voice boomed, magnified by the microphone and tiles. When Bobby appeared behind the pastor, poised to step down into the water, Melody put a fist to her mouth. She was overcome with the beauty of her little brother, and not for the first time. Pastor Tuttle stepped to one side and offered his hand to Bobby. Bobby smiled, turned his head left and right, drawing out the moment for full effect. He looked heavenward, then reached down to take the pastor's hand. That was when it all went wrong.

The microphone slipped from the pastor's hand and splashed into the water. Pastor Tuttle yelped, and disappeared. Bobby's beautiful face contorted. His neck snapped back like someone having a seizure. Melody's mother broke the stunned silence, screaming, "Let go. Let go! *Let go!*" She didn't need a microphone to be heard. Bobby jerked, spasmed, fell back onto the hard tile steps. Time passed, though Melody would never know how much, and the sound of a bleating ambulance grew louder until it was deafening. Sunshine poured down the aisle of the church as a pair of paramedics rushed in.

The congregation remained in the pews, some standing, some slumping forward, but Melody's mother moved. She sprinted through the door Bobby had entered earlier and reappeared in the baptismal pool, where she sank down on the top step and pulled Bobby onto her lap. Her skirt, a beautiful linen the color of butter pecan ice cream, gaped open, revealing a glimpse of her lavender silk panties, a disturbing detail that would remain vivid in Melody's memory for the rest of her life. Mama stroked Bobby's hair and seemed to speak to him, though he didn't respond. One of the paramedics appeared and reached for Bobby. Mama reared her head back and hissed. The paramedic stumbled, nearly fell into the water. He looked confused. "Mama," Melody said, her voice too soft to be heard. She spoke up. "Mama, you have to let him go. Let them take him." Mama's lips kept moving; her hands stroked Bobby's face. It was too much, too intimate a display for church, no matter how dire the situation. Melody's face went hot. "Please." She appealed to the paramedic. "Please help my little brother." The paramedic locked eyes with her and she saw that he was scared and very young, but he nodded and pried Bobby from Mama's grasp, checked for a pulse, put his mouth on Bobby's mouth, until Bobby's hands fluttered around the man's face. He lifted Bobby, carried him into the main sanctuary, placed him on a stretcher, and wheeled him down the aisle. A second stretcher carried Pastor Tuttle, who was still and gray and obviously dead. Finally, they came back for Melody's mother, who twitched and cried out some sort of gibberish. No one came for Melody, who was left to wonder what would happen next.

Now Melody walked toward town. Rain clouds gathered to the south, a thick gray mass that hung in the sky like a warning, but the sky above was clear blue. The town smelled just as she remembered, sharp and sweet and smoky. It was the scent of fertilizer mixed with poison exhaust from old trucks. The familiarity of the town was terrifying. She couldn't stop thinking about George Walter and his predictions. History repeats, he'd told her. You are your mother, he'd warned. Was that what it meant to come back here? Was she following in her mother's path as she walked these streets? God, she hoped not. She traveled west, in the direction of Main Street, passing the line of grain bins and an old water tower marked with graffiti. Shabby cinder block houses and ramshackle fix-it shops gave way to wood frame houses, tidy redbrick homes, and whitewashed storefronts. An old man wearing dirty overalls and no shirt sat on the front steps of a shotgun house that had once been painted a cheerful yellow by the look of the strips that hung off the sides and dripped onto the ground. The yard was littered with old tires, bits of scrap metal, and what looked like a brand-new toilet. Melody nodded at the man and said, "Mornin'." The man's head barely bobbed in response. He took a sip from the can wrapped in a brown paper bag that he held between his skinny knees.

The town had not changed, but it seemed to Melody that it had shrunk. Stores were closed at this hour; most wouldn't open at all on a Sunday. In the window of Murray's Department Store, a pair of enormous overalls was on display with a sign reading: ALL SIZES IN STOCK! XXXLARGE AND BEYOND! Abel's Hardware was so crammed with tools and lumber and buckets of paint that there was no room for a window display. Instead, the window contained a thick mangle of garden rakes and push brooms. She walked over to the Ruby Cafe, where she once ate so much fried shrimp and chocolate meringue pie that she later puked it all up right on Mama's good leather shoes. Melody could smell the yeast rolls baking in the back kitchen, the early prep for Sunday dinner. Her stomach rumbled. She hadn't eaten since before the performance last night. She walked on. An old black-and-gray dog slept outside the Trading Post building. When Melody passed, the mutt raised its head and watched her with suspicious eyes.

She knew where she had to go, though it meant visiting a place she'd sworn long ago to avoid. What would George Walter have to say about that? She turned on Church Street with determination. She passed by the imposing stained glass of Immaculate Heart and the large stone entryway of Holy Mary. She passed the revival tent outside Riverside Pentecostal and then kept walking past the Church of Christ and Wesley United Methodist. She would not go so far as Old Glory Baptist, First AME, or Leflore Trinity, and she wouldn't make it to Good Shepherd Lutheran or First Baptist or Ridgewood Baptist. She stopped outside the church she'd not entered since the day she tried to forget: Crossroads Baptist, with its white cross piercing the morning sky, and pale pink tea roses lining the walkway. The early service would begin soon; a few stragglers lingered outside the front doors. She hadn't stepped foot inside the church since Bobby's baptism, and she would not enter the sanctuary now. Instead, she trudged across the damp grass to the area behind the church where the Dumpsters stood, their ugly, gray, necessary bulk hidden from the worshippers. A group of teenage boys with oily skin and gelled hair stood smoking.

The boys tossed their cigarettes when she approached, ducked their heads and swore they were headed right in to hear the sermon. She gave them twenty dollars to drive her home. They let her ride shotgun in an old, rusty Camaro. Rock music blared from a stereo with one busted speaker that cracked and popped beneath the guitars and drum solos. She directed them toward the old county road, where men posted signs advertising farm equipment for sale and where families would set up truck bed storefronts offering homemade jam, fresh boiled peanuts, and whole fruit pies for purchase. The road was deserted on a Sunday morning and the air from the open window was thick with moisture and foreboding. It was a road like every other road in the Delta, straight and seemingly infinite in length. To Melody, it felt like a road traversing time rather than distance. The wide acres of cotton and soybeans, broken up by dense stretches of loblolly pines, were the same today as they had been ten years before and ten years before that. An old rusty cotton thresher leaned precariously at the side of the road and Melody recognized it from years earlier, the only difference a steady advance of kudzu. Nothing changed here, except to be swallowed up by the earth.

She pointed ahead to the small, unmarked dirt road. The

car veered too quickly and Melody grabbed the door handle in panic. The boy steadied the car before it ran off into the ditch. He apologized and slowed down. They wound through a short stretch of heavy wooded forest and dipped into a cool, dark mist before shooting back out into the brightness of the morning. The road beneath turned from well-groomed dirt to a rutted path. "Man," one of the boys said. "I didn't know anyone lived out here. This is bumfucked middle-of-nowhere!" He cut her an apologetic glance.

"You have no idea," she told him. Nowhere sounded good to Melody, but this was definitely somewhere. The sky pressed down, heavy and dangerous; the rain clouds moved closer. The boys dropped her at the end of a long gravel driveway. It was a quarter mile from the road to her front door, but she was glad for the walk. Trees lined the path—pecan and oak, magnolia and maple. The path had not been maintained and tree roots jutted up from the earth. If she dragged her feet, she knew from experience, the roots would snag her toes and pitch her forward. She paused by the old signpost planted by her great-granddaddy. THREE RIVERS FARM, the sign announced, a tribute to the nearby converging rivers that once provided irrigation to the crops: the Yazoo, the Yalobusha, the Tallahatchie. Once the sign had been a shiny, sturdy, important marker, a beacon that proclaimed this was land enough to warrant naming. Now, though, the steel had turned black and the etched letters were caked with grime. No one had bothered to wipe it down and polish it the way Old Granddaddy used to do once a month. No one had so much as aimed a stream of water at it in years. It was probably best. The land could no longer rightly be considered a farm. Nothing useful grew here; nothing was planted, produced, or consumed. Old Granddaddy would be appalled by what had become of his land. Fortunately, as Melody abandoned her faith, she'd abandoned the idea that dead people were hanging out somewhere looking down on her. Old Granddaddy didn't have to be sad or disgusted by the neglect of his land. All he had to do was rot in the dirt, just like the crops he'd once planted.

Melody's father seemed to be rotting while still alive. When Melody was a teenager, her mother often insulted her by telling her she looked "a caution." What she meant was that Melody needed to brush her hair, iron her clothes, put on some makeup, and stand up straight, lest she scare off every available male in the Delta. As if Melody wanted to attract one of the big, flat-faced, slow-moving boys in her high school. "I'm throwing caution to the wind, Mama," she liked to say, just because it pissed Mama off. But when Melody saw her father laid out on the sagging sofa bed, she finally grasped the expression. He smelled of urine or worse. An oxygen tank sighed at the edge of the bed. He was thin; his skin puddled around his bones. Melody's father had been a lot of things, but he had never been thin. She knew, looking at him, that her mother should have called her months earlier. There was nothing she could do, and she wondered if her father would even know her. She barely knew him.

Her brother emerged from the kitchen and stood beside

her. "Bobby," Melody said. She squeezed his arm. "When did things get so awful?"

"I don't know, sis." Bobby pulled away from her. "I reckon when he wouldn't quit smoking two packs a day after his third heart attack."

"You can't blame a man for living," she said. "Or for dying, I guess." She blamed her mother; that's who she blamed.

"The hell I can't." Bobby turned and stomped back into the kitchen.

George Walter's words came back to her: *No one has to do anything in this world. Everything is a choice.* She wondered what her choices were in this situation. Stay or leave, she supposed, but neither seemed likely to lead to anything worthwhile.

She knelt beside the sofa bed, felt her body fold into prayer position. She hadn't prayed in years, could no longer bring herself to talk to someone who either didn't exist or didn't care. Anyway, her father wouldn't put up with anyone praying over him, not even Melody. She touched her father's hair, rubbed the cottony strands between her fingers.

He opened one eye. His pupil dilated. His cheek twitched. Melody felt irrational terror upon seeing that lone blue orb.

"Hi, Daddy."

"Well, I must be dying."

"How do you feel?"

"I feel goddamned awful. What do you think? Aren't you supposed to be touring with the Holy Rollers?"

"I'm taking a little break." No point in telling him she'd offended an entire audience of Holy Rollers and eliminated any chance she might go back. "I'm here to take care of you, Daddy." She pulled the thin blanket up around his shoulders. "Anything you need, you just let me know."

"I need a fucking miracle. Did you pick up any miracles out there with the Bible thumpers?"

"Miracles aren't magic tricks, Daddy. I don't believe I can just pick one up."

"Ain't that the truth, little girl. Ain't that the truth."

Daddy was still there inside the decaying body, and he sounded stronger than he looked. "Well, we've seen miracles in this family before. Maybe we'll get another."

The phone rang. Bobby yelled from the kitchen, "I'll get it!"

"That could be your mother. Tell her I'm doing okay, would you? Tell her you think I look more handsome than ever."

"I'm not gonna start lying, old man." She kissed him on the forehead and rushed to eavesdrop on Bobby's conversation. She had a few things to say to her mother and she intended to say them all. Bobby stood with the phone against his ear. "Hello, hello. . . . *Hello?*"

Bobby had changed in the years Melody was on the road. The delicate, beautiful child she remembered had become a strong, handsome man with a broad chest and biceps that bulged under his cotton T-shirt.

He hung up the phone. "No one there."

"Hey, little brother." Melody touched Bobby's muscled arm. "Someone's been working out."

58

Bobby jerked away, turned his back to her, and rummaged in the refrigerator like he needed something from its cool depths right that minute. His body may have transformed, but he was still her angry, petulant, difficult little brother. He'd drowned his good nature in the baptismal pool.

"You look good. You look strong." Melody did not look good, and she knew it. Three years of diner food and doughnuts had left her as soft and doughy as the food itself.

Bobby pulled his head out of the fridge. His eyes were damp and his jaw clenched. He glared at her. "You left us. Left us. Left me."

"But I'm here now." She reached behind him and pushed the refrigerator door shut, not that there was much in the fridge worth preserving. She began making a mental list of things she would need to do. Go to the store. Clean. Bobby stared at her, gaping. He expected more. "I had a life to live," she said.

"What about my life, sis?"

"You have a life here."

"I have a life sentence here." Bobby looked a bit like the boy he'd been before the baptism; his eyes flashed and his eyebrow cocked. She laughed, too loudly. It felt good to share a joke with her brother, but Bobby wasn't laughing. She cleared her throat, coughed. "Sorry," she mumbled. Bobby stared.

A sound like the rattle of a struggling engine echoed through the house. "What on earth?"

"Daddy," Bobby replied in a voice that made it clear he didn't care.

"Good Lord!" Melody turned toward the living room, but Bobby grabbed her arm and held her tight. "Let go of me!" She struggled, but Bobby was as strong as he looked. "What are you doing? What's wrong with him?"

"He pulled out the tube. No breath, no breath. He does it all the time."

Melody twisted, struggled to wrench free of Bobby's grasp. "Let go of me!"

"Why, sis? What are you gonna do? Save him? Gonna save us all?"

"Goddamnit, Bobby!" The rattle from the next room grew louder, then seemed to wane. Melody shook against Bobby's grip like an animal caught in a trap. "Bobby, quit it. This isn't funny. This isn't a joke." He released her and she stumbled.

"It's a funny bit," he said. "A little bit funny."

She ran into the living room and slipped the tube under her father's nose. His skin felt clammy and his eyes wobbled in their sockets. "It's okay, Daddy," she told him. "It's okay."

Bobby smirked, folded his arms across his chest.

"Shame on you." Melody wanted to slap him hard across the face. "How could you?" And how could Mama leave Daddy here alone with you? she wondered. In Melody's mind, one thing was certain: This was all her mother's fault.

"Hey, sis, he can put it back in himself."

Melody looked at her father. Bobby was right. Daddy wasn't paralyzed. His arms worked and the tube was fastened to the bed in such a way that it couldn't fall outside his reach.

She fell back in the chair next to the sofa bed. "You scared me half to death, Daddy." His lips curled into a slight smile. He closed his eyes. A familiar, suffocating dread enveloped her. This was what it was like to be home.

"Just keeping you on your toes." Her father's weak, raspy voice managed to sound mirthful.

"This is exactly why I stayed away for so long. You're not funny." She turned to face Bobby. "Neither are you." She stood and rubbed her head with her hands. "I'm worn out. I'm going upstairs to take a shower, see if I can find some decent clothes to wear. Then I'll see what needs to be done around the house. This place is a disaster."

"Don't." Her father reached out and grabbed her hand. "Sit down and tell me all about the Holy Rollers."

She flinched. "I came home to help and you're just being mean to me."

"It was a joke."

"It wasn't funny."

He kept hold of her hand. She considered walking out the door and leaving him there with Bobby. The two of them could sit around in this filthy house and make terrible jokes until Daddy died and Bobby fell to pieces. The big problem with that plan, of course, was that Melody had nowhere to go. If everything was a choice, her options were terrible.

She settled into the chair at Daddy's bedside and told him as many good things as she could remember until he released a guttural snore. She was hungry and thirsty and exhausted. Her childhood bedroom was just upstairs, the spot where she'd spent her adolescence dreaming of ways to leave. Now all she wanted was to tuck herself under the familiar quilt and sleep the day away. Instead, she stayed with her father, listening to the rhythmic *pfft, pfft, pfft* of the oxygen tank and the low rattle of his snore. She closed her eyes, just for a minute.

Melody was adept at sleeping in uncomfortable spots. That was the one thing she picked up while touring. While she never slept peacefully, she could get to sleep quickly. So when the front door opened and startled her awake, she didn't know how much time had passed and was momentarily confused about where she was. That the person coming through the door was a tall, handsome black man, confused her even further. She wiped drool from the corner of her mouth, stood too quickly, and fell back. "What? Who? What?"

The man shifted an overstuffed and scratched leather satchel from his right hand to his left. He held his right hand out to Melody, but she just stared at it.

"Who are you?" Her mouth was dry from sleep, her tongue thick and clumsy.

"You must be Melody," the man said. "I'm Maurice."

"Who?"

"I thought your mother would have mentioned me," he said. "Or Bobby."

Melody stood, determined to regain some dignity. No such luck. Her right foot was asleep and she couldn't put weight on it without losing balance. She jiggled her leg, and pinpricks surged through her ankle and lower calf. She sat again, reached down to massage her foot while craning her neck up to see the man. He was obviously no stranger to her family, but he was still a stranger to her.

"Or your father, for that matter. How you doing, Mr. Mahaffey?"

Daddy snapped his eyes shut when she glanced down. He smiled, just barely.

Melody was furious. Why did her family persist in keeping secrets from her? First her father's illness and now this strange man. She hadn't been home a full day. What other surprises were they hiding? She found her voice. "What in God's name is going on here? Who are you? You can't just barge in here without even knocking. It isn't right."

"I'm the nurse from the hospice center."

Melody stared. That explained nothing.

"Maurice? I'm here to take care of your father?" He clearly thought she should know him.

"*I'm* here to take care of Daddy," Melody said. "It's the whole reason I'm here."

Maurice knelt beside the bed. He listened to her father's heartbeat and pulled a syringe from his satchel. He looked comfortable, as if he'd spent a lot of time at the house, and with her father.

"Just how long have you been coming here?"

"Three weeks," Maurice said. "And don't worry, there's plenty for you to do. I'm only here to make sure he isn't in any pain and to switch out the oxygen tanks. I told Mrs. Mahaffey that if she was going to leave, someone would have to be here to help out. We help people stay comfortably with their families. The family members have to do their part."

Melody heard the disapproval in Maurice's voice. "I'm

perfectly capable of handling things," she said, though she didn't feel at all capable.

"Good." Maurice filled a syringe and thumped it with his middle finger. "I know this isn't easy."

Growing up, Melody's family never had domestic help. Mama did not allow strangers in the house, said they would snoop and pry. Mama was always hiding something.

"What is that?" She pointed to the syringe.

"Pain medicine."

"I thought you said he wasn't in pain."

"Well, he will be if he doesn't get his medicine. You call the shots now, though. Want me to skip it?"

The man was rude. Melody couldn't imagine her mother put up with such insolence.

"You can't talk to me like that." Melody's voice shook. "You don't know Mama. You don't know me."

"No, I do not." Maurice worked his jaw around as if to swallow something bitter. "All I know about your mother is that she up and left her dying husband. All I know about you is that you're an Elvis fan."

"What?" The man was crazy. "What does Elvis have to do with anything?"

"Your shirt," Maurice said as he plunged the needle into her father's arm.

Melody looked down, realized she was still wearing the extra-large T-shirt she'd bought at the train station. "You know I'd be happy to call the hospice center and have them send over someone with less attitude."

"Good luck," Maurice said. "Before me, there were three other nurses and none of them lasted more than two days. I'm your last option. If you fire me or if I quit, Mr. Mahaffey will have to spend the rest of his days in a hospital and he seems particularly dead set against that. Pardon the phrasing."

"No goddamned hospitals!" her father barked.

Bobby ran into the room, heavy footsteps banging against the wood floors. "Maurice. Maurice!" He grinned wildly.

Melody shushed him, but he didn't acknowledge her. He threw his arms around Maurice, who didn't flinch or push him away, but embraced him.

"Hey, there." They hugged like brothers who hadn't seen each other in a year. Melody could not have been more shocked. How had her brother, her difficult and damaged brother, become so friendly with this stranger? And why did Maurice allow it? It was unprofessional, wasn't it? But why should Melody care? She did care. She stood watching them embrace and she felt alone. No one had pulled her that close since the humiliating encounter with Chris.

They parted and Maurice smiled at Melody. His teeth were beautifully white.

"Sorry to get off on the wrong foot." We can go over everything that needs to be done whenever you're ready. I'm here twice a day, midmorning and early evening. Sometimes I stop in again late at night just to be sure he's sleeping okay."

Bobby grinned. "Sometimes he sleeps here."

"Well, it's such a long drive."

"Oh, for heaven's sakes, it's fine." Melody rubbed her

eyes with her palms until she saw stars. She smelled something ripe and unpleasant and realized it was her. She stank. She was exhausted. She was sick of dealing with this man. He had a job to do and she would let him do it. "If someone had just mentioned you before you walked in the door, I wouldn't have been so startled. I'm not sure why you were such a big secret."

Bobby laughed, then tapered off into giggles.

She sighed. "I'm just worn out. I need a shower and a long nap."

"We can go over things when I return this evening."

"Stay for dinner," Bobby said. "Melody's a good cook."

"I don't want to be any trouble," Maurice said.

"No trouble." That was a lie. Melody hadn't managed to feed herself in a solid day, and she was in no mood to whip up a feast for company. She doubted there was anything worth cooking in the house, and the kitchen was filthy. A trip to the store would chew up half the day. She gave up on the idea of a nap, hoped a shower would be enough to revive her. Like it or not, Maurice seemed to be a part of things here. Bobby liked him, and her father seemed comfortable with him. If anything, Melody felt like the outsider. Besides, what Bobby said was true. She was a good cook. She hadn't prepared a whole meal in years, but she didn't for a second believe she'd lost her touch in the kitchen.

Chapter Eight

Obi prided himself on being strong and independent. Other men needed women to care for them, but those men were weak. A man who couldn't cook for himself or dress himself or acquire the things he needed was no man at all in Obi's mind. And yet, when in trouble, he ran to his mother. She was not an ordinary woman, but she was a woman nonetheless. He swallowed his shame and tried to take comfort in the joy that Liam expressed upon seeing his grandmother.

Liam snuggled on her lap. Morning sun shone through the windows in defiance of gray clouds gathering on the horizon. Obi sipped a strong cup of hot coffee, grateful for the bitter jolt and the comforting weight of a porcelain mug in his hands. The light of day and the retelling of last night's events left him feeling sick and exposed.

Pisa ran her fingers through the boy's hair as she talked. Her given name was Sally, but for years she'd called herself Pisa. It was an old Chickasaw name and she thought it lent her more credibility than an ordinary American name. Pisa's home smelled sweet, a mixture of fruit and sugar, clove and sage. She turned berries into jams and jellies that she sold at a roadside stand for far more than they cost her to make. Her primary business, though, was as a spiritual guide and a healer for white women. Pisa claimed to have cured more than a few people of diseases doctors couldn't touch. Pisa arranged for the women to sweat in a lodge, ingest hallucinogenic plants, and walk in circles for a day or more before being delivered to her. She then sat with the women and revealed a bit of their future, though never too much. She told them just enough to satisfy their craving for knowledge but not enough to terrify them or keep them from coming back. She made them gifts of healing herbs and she chanted over them in a language they didn't understand. For all this spiritual fulfillment, she charged them what she knew they would pay. The women who came to her were wealthy and bored, so Pisa had plenty.

"This is big trouble," she said.

"I know, but it was just an accident."

"There is no such thing. You have to hide for a while. You need to get off the river and go somewhere safe."

"Can't we stay here?" For the first time in years, Obi wanted to sleep under his mother's roof, just for a night or two until he figured out a plan.

Pisa wouldn't allow it. "Once they figure out who you are, they'll come here looking for you. It's too easy to track people nowadays. The girl will identify you. She'll describe your truck, describe Liam, describe you with that cut on your face and someone along the river will point the finger at you to avoid any trouble for themselves."

Obi remembered the look in Samuel's eyes. No one on the river owed him a thing, and they had their own secrets. They wouldn't want the law poking around. But he also remembered the look in the girl's eyes when she said she would be in trouble with her father. She seemed more worried about that than about the boy on the ground.

"Maybe she won't tell anyone," he said. "She was young and scared. She wasn't supposed to be there."

"What about the other boy? The one who ran away?"

His mother was right. His only hope was to hide and wait for things to pass, hope that things would pass. It was like facing the social worker all over again. It was like that time when Liam was a baby and they'd almost lost him, only this was worse because back then Obi hadn't understood how much he loved Liam. The thought of losing him then was scary, but the thought of losing him now was unbearable. He would do anything to protect Liam, even if they had to run forever, even if he had to kill twenty men. He'd hurt Liam once. He wouldn't do it again.

To this day he was ashamed of how he'd hurt his son, of how his temper got the best of him. It was Eileen he'd been angry with, but it was Liam who suffered. In the end, it made Obi a better man, a stronger man.

He'd been weak back then, sleepwalking through day after terrible day. One day he came home from work exhausted, filthy, and covered in the sharp stench of burning metal. All he wanted was to shower, eat some kind of supper that hadn't been zapped in a microwave, and sleep. His joints ached, his eyes burned from staring at the welding torch flame, his feet and legs were as heavy as the steel beams he'd spent the day moving. He heard Liam's cry before he opened the door. He'd stepped into the tiny, cluttered mess of a house and peeled off his work boots. Liam's screams grew louder. He kicked his boots to one side and unbuttoned the heavy denim shirt he wore to protect his skin from the torch flames and the sun. He shimmied out of his jeans and stood there in the laundry room in his underwear and a T-shirt and a pair of mismatched, holey socks. Even though the house was filthy—the kitchen table scattered with unidentifiable crumbs, the sink crowded with crusty plates and mugs, the living room floor a circus maze of plastic toys and shoes—Eileen would not allow Obi to tromp through the house in his work clothes. She insisted he strip down to his underwear before crossing the kitchen and walking down the short hallway to the bathroom where he could shower away the filth of his workday.

On that day, Obi wanted a shower more than he wanted to check on his screaming son. If the boy was crying, he was alive. Obi figured a few more minutes wouldn't kill the kid and, anyway, he'd been busting his ass all day; Eileen could do something.

The shower steam rose up and cleared away some of his frustration. He lathered his face and hair and stood beneath the water, turning his head from side to side to stretch out the kinks in his neck. Liam screamed and screamed. Obi wrapped a towel around his waist and went to his son. He lifted Liam to his chest and the child's cries turned into a series of soft hiccups against Obi's skin. He felt the heavy, soggy weight of his son's diaper and smelled the putrid scent of the boy's waste. "Goddammit, Eileen." Obi cleaned Liam and changed his diaper. He washed his face, mopping up the tear-streaked cheeks and clearing the trail of snot from Liam's upper lip.

When he was done, he sat Liam down in the living room and went to look for his wife. Eileen was passed out in the bedroom, an open bag of greasy chips spilled out beside her. She looked almost peaceful, her red curls splayed across the pillow. Obi wanted to love her, had loved her once, but she had turned into someone he could barely stand. He shook her until she opened her glassy eyes and stared at him. "Get up," he demanded.

"Leave me alone." She turned her back to him and slung an arm across her face. Obi grabbed the arm and yanked her to her feet. She was a small woman and easy to lift.

"I said get up." Obi steered Eileen's limp body through the house. He forced her to look at the mess. "I work all day. I shouldn't have to clean the house, clean up Liam, when I come home at night."

"You don't know what it's like being here with him all day."

Eileen's voice was like a mosquito buzzing in Obi's ear. He gripped her shoulders, shook her hard.

"Stop it." She cried, "You're hurting me."

"Well, you're killing me. I can't live like this." He steered her to the living room, where Liam slumped over a toy truck. He pushed the truck back and forth, but not as if he cared about it. "Look at your son."

"Our son," Eileen said.

"Our son. Look at him. He's not even dressed. He was

sitting here in a filthy, stinking diaper when I came home. He was screaming."

Eileen shoved her hands against his chest. "That's all he does." She spoke through clenched teeth. "He pisses and he shits himself all day long. And he screams. That's it. He doesn't do anything else. Why should I bother putting clothes on someone who is just going to piss and shit all over himself? Answer me that."

"He's a baby," Obi said.

"He's a year old!" Eileen yelled. "He doesn't talk and he doesn't care about using the toilet and he still isn't walking. When does he stop being a baby and turn into a god-damned human being? You're never here and you don't know what it's like to live with an animal all day long."

Obi slapped her. It wasn't the first time, but it was the first time he'd put any force behind it. Eileen balled up her fists and punched his bare chest. The towel around Obi's waist slipped to the floor and he stood there, naked, fighting with his wife in front of his son. He flung her away. "You make me sick."

Eileen fell, her knee coming down hard on Liam's left arm. Obi heard the crack of the bone as it snapped in half. Liam looked at him, his pink, moist mouth a gaping question and then, suddenly, a scream.

"Look what you've done!" Eileen yelled at him. "This is your fault."

Obi pushed Eileen away and knelt beside his son. Liam's arm hung limp and at an unnatural angle.

At the hospital, the doctor glared at him when he took Liam off to X-ray and set his arm. A plump woman with weary eyes asked a lot of questions. She made notes on a clipboard and said she would send someone to their home to make sure it was a safe place for a child. "Standard procedure." It didn't feel standard.

Eileen left them. Obi didn't know where she had gone. He didn't look for her. The social worker visited once and then showed up a few weeks later, unannounced. That was the beginning. A terrible beginning, but perhaps a necessary one.

"You need to get rid of your truck," Pisa said. "I have a car you can take. It's old, but it runs and the plates are current."

"I need a truck," Obi said. "We have so much stuff to carry."

"It's a big car. Most of it will fit. Decide what's important and leave the rest. I'll have someone drive the truck into a lake. They won't find it for months or years, and by the time they do, it'll be rusted and untraceable."

"Can't we just let it sit? Maybe I can come back for it when this blows over." The truck was solid and reliable. Obi knew how to fix what needed fixing. He knew just what kind of terrain the truck would handle. Liam slept on the vinyl bench seat on rainy nights. The bed of the truck was his workbench and their card table.

"Don't hang on to things that don't matter, son. I've tried to teach you that your whole life."

"I can't believe this is happening," Obi said. "The boy came at me with a knife. Liam was right there. I had to do something."

"The boys are guilty of crimes," Pisa said. "I can see that. They have done bad things, but that won't change what you did."

"Is he dead?" Obi asked. "Did I kill him?"

Pisa closed her eyes and bowed her head as if she were praying. She rocked back and forth and was silent for so long that Obi wondered if she had drifted to sleep. Finally, she spoke. "Don't ask questions for which there are no answers, son. Curiosity kills more than cats."

"Where should we go?"

Pisa stroked her chin, touched a mole on the right side of her face and plucked at the wiry hairs that sprouted there. "I know a place. Let me draw you a map."

Chapter Nine

Geneva had a thirst for prophecy, even as a child. Sometimes, when the preacher of her childhood was droning on
over a particularly dry bit of scripture, Geneva would play
a game. She would open her Bible at random, close her
eyes, and let her index finger travel down the cool, onion-
skin pages until she felt compelled to stop. Then she tried
to read the future from whatever verse she'd found. It was
at least as accurate as her horoscope in the newspaper and
far more interesting. In Geneva's experience, damnation
lurked everywhere. Even now, in the cool morning air as
she squatted and peed between rows of young cotton, she
was overcome with a strong sense that things might go to
hell at any second.

"Let's get moving," she said to the woman who was shaking out the wool blanket. She might as well have spoken
to one of the cotton bolls for all the reaction she got. These
women, the guides, seemed to delight in being as abstract
and mysterious as possible. And unhurried. Not one of
them ever seemed to hurry, no matter how badly Geneva

needed to see Pisa. She'd never been more desperate than today, but to admit that might just inspire this woman to waste the better part of the day walking Geneva in circles across the Delta.

"I know, I know," Geneva said. "In time."

"That's right." The woman stuffed the blanket into a satchel. "Patience is a virtue."

"If only I gave a damn about virtue," Geneva muttered.

The woman turned her back to Geneva and lifted one hand into the air. She looked like she was testing the direction of the wind. "Be like the river," she said.

Geneva stared at the woman's back, waiting. Surely there was more to her advice than that. When Geneva was convinced the woman had turned to stone, she swung around and pointed an accusing finger. "Rivers know this: There is no hurry. We shall get there someday."

She was quoting someone, obviously, but Geneva wasn't sure if the quote was biblical or historical or literary. Frankly, she didn't care. As long as someday was today, she would flow along.

She followed the woman across the cotton field and through a patch of thick forest. It was familiar and strange at once. Soon enough, they emerged from the trees and Geneva spotted the familiar house. The river flows on, she thought. I am the river. She was a solid fifty yards from the house when she saw Pisa step out onto the front porch. The woman never changed. Geneva would recognize that squat, sturdy body, the long dark braid, the flowing dress from a million miles away. She was the same at thirty as at fifty. She'd be the same at 110 and Geneva figured she'd live that long. Pisa's hands moved like playful birds when she spoke. She spoke now to a man and a small child, who followed her onto the porch. Geneva had never seen men in that house. It was a female place, full of female energy.

The woman leading Geneva stopped and put an arm out like a barrier. "Let's wait."

Geneva resisted the urge to tell her that rivers might slow, but they didn't wait. She watched Pisa hand the man a package, then kneel to hug the child. She helped the child into the passenger seat of a dusty gray hatchback. The man climbed in behind the wheel. The car pulled away and Pisa stood watching until the dust trail behind it settled. When the car disappeared, Pisa's shoulders sagged and she walked back into the house. Pisa had never looked less powerful. Maybe coming here was a mistake. Maybe Pisa was just an ordinary woman, prone to disappointment and grief.

The guide pressed Geneva forward. They climbed onto the front porch and stood amid the hodgepodge of junk: clay figurines of jackrabbits and wolves, a pair of warped handmade cane rocking chairs, wind chimes hanging still and silent in the calm of the morning, pots filled with herbs for cooking and for healing. Fresh pine, lemon balm, and something that made her crave seafood filled the air. "Give me a moment." The woman rapped on the door and stepped inside. Geneva smoothed her hair and waited.

The woman emerged, jiggling a set of keys in her palm. "Pisa is ready for you now."

The river has arrived, Geneva thought as she stepped into the cool mouth of the house. Pisa grabbed her hands and pulled her in close. She inhaled the sweet clove scent of

Pisa's hair. Pisa held on to Geneva's shoulders and stared into her eyes. Pisa's skin, the color of a faded red oak, showed few signs of age. The faintest web of lines surrounded her mouth and eyes. Her hair, shot through with silver threads, hung long and black in a single braid down her back. She wore a dress much like Geneva's, a faded cotton sack that skimmed across her strong, generous body.

"So much." Pisa's voice quivered. "So much is happening for you."

Or *to* me, Geneva thought.

The women sat on a woven rug and faced each other in silence for what seemed like an hour. Geneva leaned in, impatient for Pisa's words. Finally, Pisa spoke. "Your husband is very ill. He will die, but that's not news. We all die." Pisa laughed and tilted her head.

She sighed, glad to see that Pisa still had the gift. "When will he die?"

Pisa gave her a long look. "I can't tell you that. It's too much to know. I will give you a bouquet of healing herbs to burn at his bedside and some words to say. They will ease his transition."

Pisa closed her eyes and swayed a bit, trancelike. "I sense that your daughter has returned home."

"Well, thank goodness." Geneva was mostly thankful that Pisa's gift seemed to be strong. How else could Pisa know about Melody? "I asked her to come home and take care of Bruce, but I wasn't sure she'd come," Geneva said. "That girl doesn't care a lick about what I need."

"She is at a point in her life where it is good to be a bit selfish. You remember being that young. She needs to figure herself out before she can move forward, but she is home now. She has just arrived and it is good that she will be there for her father. It will be good for her and good for him and good for Bobby, too."

"And good for me."

"It will be difficult for you."

Geneva didn't doubt that. Pisa had predicted Bobby's accident and given her the words that saved his life. She gave her absolution and filled her with power and strength after her mother's horrible death. If Pisa said it would be difficult, Geneva would just have to bear it.

Pisa turned her eyes toward the ceiling, let her gaze track along a path that only she could see. She seemed to be slipping into a trance but, quick as lightning, she snapped her head down and clapped her hands. "I have wonderful news."

"You're kidding." Geneva couldn't fathom receiving wonderful news.

"Bobby will find love. It will not last, but it will be real. Better to have loved and lost, right?"

Geneva laughed. Pisa must be kidding. Bobby rarely left the house and showed no signs of being able to hold down a job. What kind of woman would want such a man? How would he even meet a woman?

"You doubt me." Pisa grinned at Geneva.

"It's seems pretty unlikely. He's never been the same since . . ."

"Since we saved his life?"

"Yes." Geneva paused, careful not to offend Pisa. "I know. I'm grateful. We saved his life, but I can't help thinking we might have let some part of him drown. He has no drive, no ambition."

"Ambition is not everything."

"No. Not everything, but it's something. Something important, if you ask me."

Pisa took Geneva's hands again. "Have I ever told you about my son?"

Geneva figured Pisa had sprung up from the ground fully formed and unburdened by anything as ordinary as family.

"He's a wonderful man. Strong and fierce. He has a son of his own." Pisa's voice dripped like tree syrup, like she was trying to sell Geneva something. "There's been a spot of trouble and he needs a safe place to stay. You have so much land."

Was Pisa really asking Geneva for a favor? Maybe Pisa realized Geneva's wealth was drying up and she would no longer be able to pay for these pilgrimages. She'd barely scraped together the fee for this one. Even so, she didn't much care for the idea of a strange man in her house. She was nursing a glut of trouble at home already. No sense inviting more.

Pisa kept right on talking like she could hear Geneva's thoughts. Likely she could. "He is perfectly happy to camp outside. He prefers it. He will cause you no trouble. He can help you with things that need doing."

Geneva could spin a list a mile long of things that needed doing. Bruce stopped fixing stuff around the house years ago. She was a deadbeat housekeeper and Bobby couldn't be bothered to wash his own dishes. When things needed doing, Geneva ignored them for as long as she could and then broke down and called someone. Plumbing, carpentry, electrical work: it wasn't cheap. She'd been letting things go for some time now. Money was tight as a dress at a shotgun wedding. She had insurance for that hospice nurse, but it would run out soon. If Bruce didn't die within the next three weeks, she might have to kill him. It wasn't out of the question.

"Is he good and handy?"

"Oh yes," Pisa said. "He can fix almost anything. Plus, of course, I would consider this a personal favor."

Geneva liked the idea of Pisa being indebted to her rather than the other way around. She agreed with a quick nod. Pisa pressed a package of gifts on her, a basket full of fragrant herbs with directions to burn some and to tuck some into Bruce's pillow. She passed along two magic chants for when he was in pain and when he wasn't. She wrote down a blessing for Bobby and one for Melody. She handed her a jar of blackberry jam and a pot of clover honey.

"I knew I could count on you," Pisa said. "We'll get you back to your car within the hour. You can meet him there."

Geneva sighed. "Well . . ."

"You are going to that man." Pisa's voice, which had been so happy and light, turned thin and accusing.

Geneva braced herself.

"No good will come from seeing him. I warned you last time."

"You warned me," Geneva said. "But nothing bad happened. I love him."

"Love is just a feeling. It is easy to feel love when you do not see someone very often. It is harder when the person is with you every day."

"He loves me. I deserve to be loved, don't I? Is it really so much to ask?"

"It is," Pisa said. "Love is not rational. You are not rational when you cry love." She flicked a bit of lint off her dress.

Geneva pushed her hair back. It did no good to argue. "This is the last time. I won't see him again, but I can't just spin off the planet and disappear."

Pisa wagged a long bony finger in Geneva's face. "If you go to him, trouble will follow. There will be death."

"You're the one who said we all die," Geneva said. "You can't blame death on me."

"There will be terrible consequences. You have no idea the amount of violence that will be set in motion. You must go straight home." Pisa's eyes flashed.

Pisa had never gotten so wound up before. Geneva figured she was worried about her son. "I'll call home and set everything straight. Don't worry."

Pisa slapped her palms down on the floor between them. She leaned in and put her nose just a few inches from Geneva's face. Geneva saw her own reflection in Pisa's eyes. She saw a glint of brightness followed by a rolling darkness, like storm clouds descending. Geneva pulled back, but could not look away.

"You are the one who should worry," Pisa said. "Heed my words. You must go home. You must go now."

Chapter Ten

Melody was having a hell of a bad time. Her father was cranky and needy, her brother had disappeared again, and all she'd managed to eat was a handful of crackers that may have been previously nibbled on by a rat. There was a ragged hole at the bottom of the cellophane wrapper and a few suspicious black pellets in the box, but it didn't stop her from cramming a handful of salty crumbs into her mouth as she fetched her father's lunch. And that was another problem. Her father was existing on a liquid diet of nutrition shakes that were advertised as tasting like a delicious milk shake. He hated them.

Melody held the straw up to his mouth and coaxed him along. "Just a few more sips." She wiped a dribble of the chalky white liquid from his chin. "Mmmm, it's good." She hated the condescending tone in her voice, but she felt like she was feeding a baby, and her voice betrayed that.

Her father wasn't amused. He spit out the straw and a stream of thick, sticky liquid sprayed across the bed and splattered across Melody's arm. "It's goddamned awful, little girl. You drink it."

Melody slammed the can down on the table beside her father's bed and wiped her arm roughly with a ragged paper napkin. The napkin shredded and tore, sending linty bits flying. The smell and the texture of the spilled drink reminded her of the time she'd eaten too much homemade peanut brittle at the school harvest fair and woke up in the night to vomit hot chunks of it onto her cotton gown. The drink was supposed to provide the vitamins, minerals, and calories Daddy needed, but without all the hassle of chewing and digesting actual foods. He was supposed to consume three a day, but Melody was having a hard time getting him to suck down one. She tasted the drink.

It was nothing like a milk shake. It certainly was not delicious. Melody thought it tasted like badly set Jell-O mixed with cough syrup. No wonder he spit it out. "Fine, Daddy. Don't drink it. You're right, it's goddamned awful. I'll head out to the store in a bit and find shakes that taste better." She hoped they made shakes that tasted better than this one.

He glared at her, then sighed; a long, rattling breath that vibrated through his body. "I don't feel so good, little girl."

"I know, Daddy. I can see that." Her head throbbed and a dull pain spread behind her eyes. The handful of rat-crackers had done nothing to sate her hunger, and she still needed sleep. It was wrong to be annoyed with Daddy, but she couldn't help it. She'd done the right thing, she'd come home and was trying to be a good daughter, but it was so hard. Even when her father was well, he was difficult. Sick, he was impossible.

He closed his eyes. She cleared the straw and the nasty

drink from his bedside, took a few gag-inducing sips of the drink with the idea that any nourishment would be better than none, then turned off the lamp and stared out the front window. Menacing clouds gathered in the distance; the sky above the house was a hot, hazy, silver shade of blue. Wavy heat warped the horizon and made the dogwood trees seem soft and fuzzy. The air pressed in heavy and tangible with the promise of rain. It smelled electric, like a wall plug gone bad. She wished the storm would move more quickly, bring on the cooling rains, wash away the bugs and the misery. She yanked the curtains closed, aware that her motions were too vigorous for the task. The curtain rings screeched across the metal rod and made her teeth ache. Dust rained down on her shoulders. She sneezed. Daddy moaned.

Melody's mother had always been a god-awful house-keeper, but it seemed she'd completely given up now. Bobby was no help. Melody thought they'd screwed up with Bobby. They shouldn't have coddled him after the baptism. He took no responsibility for anything. Dusting, for example, was not beyond his capabilities, and yet there was a thick layer of dust on every surface.

"Bobby!" she called out, walking into the kitchen. The least he could do is help her clean. If she was going to shop and pull together dinner for his new best friend Maurice, then he could damn well push a broom. No response. No sound of rustling from upstairs. She squinted out the kitchen window, scanned the property for some sign of him.

She rubbed her head. It was just past noon. Maurice would be back at five. There was so much to do that she didn't know where to start. The kitchen floor was sticky and black with footprints. The sink needed a good scrubbing to rid the porcelain of tomato stains and scuff marks. The upstairs bathroom where she'd showered was particularly unnerving, with dark scummy patches lining the tub, mildew packed deep between the tiles, and a toilet that looked like it hadn't been cleaned in weeks. Melody fantasized about leaving, just turning the house over to nature. It wouldn't last a year, not on this damp, humid, rotting piece of godforsaken earth. The land was supposed to be valuable, but Melody doubted they could give it away in its current state.

Melody's father often said this land was one of Mama's finest attributes, certainly the one that recommended her for marriage. Beauty was fleeting, but property was forever. Old Granddaddy had farmed cotton here until he died. Mama inherited the property and her father's wealth, which was already waning. Melody's father was no farmer, but he tried to keep the cotton in production. Then he'd turned over the land and put in soybeans. It would be bigger than King Cotton and would make them all rich, but her father hated tending the fields. He was too lazy even to oversee the laborers he'd hired to harvest the beans, and the crop rotted on the vine. He had more luck raising catfish. The tanks filled with living, swimming whiskered fish pleased him in a way that plants in a field never could. He raised catfish for more than seven years, joining the regional co-op that sold Delta catfish to restaurants, grocery stores, and catering services.

As a child, Melody rode along in the pickup truck as he drove from tank to tank, inspecting the stock and talking to the workers about yield per feed and other things she didn't understand. When Melody was thirteen years old, the Tallahatchie, Yalobusha, and Yazoo rivers overflowed during a season of heavy rainfall and terrifying weather. When the water rose, the catfish tanks overflowed. The fish swam toward freedom. Daddy stood waist-deep in the rushing waters, trying to catch his catfish with a net. He looked like a fool. The local newspaper reported on men who'd put out lines in the middle of Howard Street and caught enough catfish to feed their families for a year. The farmers threatened to search the freezers of suspected fish poachers and prosecute anyone found hoarding an excess of the sweet, white fish. It was all bluster. Daddy didn't have enough money or patience or drive to repair the tanks and to restock. They sold off the equipment that was useful, but much of it still lay rotting and rusting behind the house. After that, Daddy worked on and off at various jobs—light carpentry, house painting, fishing guide—but he never enjoyed work or made any real money. Melody knew her father hadn't been happy, stuck out here in the middle of nowhere with a wife who was more than half crazy. Still, he chose to marry Mama and to live on this land. Melody was born into it and had no say in the matter.

She filled the kitchen sink with hot water and dish soap, and threw open the cabinets. There was little worth saving. Just like the crackers she'd eaten earlier, everything seemed to be infested with droppings or mealworm larvae. Mold overtook the lone loaf of bread. Roaches scurried out when she pulled down a sack of pretzels. She bit down hard on her tongue to keep from screaming. She scrubbed every dish and glass in hot water, draining the sink and refilling it again and again. She wiped down the breakfast table with water and ammonia and stacked the clean dishes there while she started on the silverware. She was elbow-deep in suds and covered in grime when she heard her father's choking cough. He sounded like a man rattling apart, and she knew the filth was not good for his lungs. She went to check on him, wiping her damp hands on her T-shirt.

"You okay, Daddy? What can I do?"

Her father waved weakly and trembled between deep, echoing coughs. She put her hand on his chest, thin and hollow beneath her palm. His lungs heaved and struggled to force out whatever poison had taken root. After a long spell, the coughing wound down and his head flopped from side to side on the flat pillow. His sheets were drenched with sweat, and the smell of urine reached her nose.

"Daddy?"

"Yeah?" His voice was surprisingly strong.

"Shouldn't you be in a hospital?"

"Hell no," he barked at her. "I am not going to spend my last days in some goddamned hospital with a bunch of strangers. I am staying right here, little girl. Don't go trying to force me out of my house."

"Settle down, old man. No one's forcing you to do anything."

"I looked after you and your brother your whole goddamned life. You want to ship me off to a hospital. I won't go. I'll kill myself first."

Melody tugged on the hem of her T-shirt. "No one's shipping you anywhere. No one's gonna make you do anything you don't want to do." She smiled at him. "Stubborn old man."

"I hate hospitals. Damn things are packed with hypocrites and liars and self-righteous bastards. 'Bout as bad as a church, maybe worse. You remember what that hospital was like when your brother—"

"Of course I remember," Melody said. "How could I forget? Don't worry. You can stay right here and suffer at home. The rest of us will suffer right along with you. That's the way it's supposed to work, right?" She reached out and stroked his forehead. It was cool and damp. "Okay, let's get you some fresh clothes."

She pulled clean sheets and a fresh blanket from a plastic bin beside the bed. She supposed Maurice was responsible for the relative tidiness of this room. She stripped off her father's gown and removed his heavy, dank diaper, avoiding his eyes as she ran a damp cloth around his groin and over his shriveled penis. The task filled her with shame. When her father was clean, she pulled the dirty sheets off the corners of the bed and rolled him from side to side. He was thin, but she broke a sweat trying to move him without hurting him. There was so much to deal with: his oxygen tube and his fragile bones and the way he struggled to breathe when she rolled him over.

"Little girl," he said. "Getting old is a damned awful thing."

She snapped a fresh sheet over him and pulled the blanket up to his chin. "It beats the alternative, Daddy." She touched his forehead. It was cool beneath her palm. "It sure as hell beats the alternative."

Melody knew damn well why her father wouldn't go to the hospital. After Bobby's baptism, that's where they'd ended up. He was right; it was awful. Full of hypocrites and liars and self-righteous bastards. Melody's father was an ornery old man, but he was no fool.

After the baptism, one of the church deacons drove Melody to the hospital. He prayed with her in the car in the hospital parking lot, but Melody knew God was not listening. She didn't need God in that moment, she needed her Daddy, but when she called home from a pay phone in the hospital lobby, he didn't answer. Melody felt completely alone, abandoned by her heavenly father and her earthly father at the same time.

A nurse led her through an endless succession of motion-sensitive doors to a cold, bright room where her mother lay propped like royalty in a bed full of pillows.

"Mama." Melody took her hand. It was cold and dry as reptile skin. "Are you okay, Mama?"

"I saved him." Her mother smiled and closed her eyes. "I saved my baby and he's going to be just fine."

That seemed unlikely. Melody couldn't get the image of Bobby's distorted face out of her head. "Really, Mama? Are you sure?"

"Oh, honey, yes." She peered at Melody from beneath heavy viper lids. "I cannot do it again." Her mother's voice sounded gravelly, like when she drank too much whiskey. "I'm too weakened and I will not be able to do it again. Do you understand?"

Melody understood perfectly. Bobby was worth saving, but Melody was on her own. Melody fumed. She thought, I wouldn't save you either, you old witch. I wouldn't pull you out of a lake. What she said was, "I can take care of myself."

There was a window in the room, and the view was nothing but flat, brown earth stretching on forever. Melody felt smothered by the vast emptiness. "I'm gonna call Daddy. Somebody needs to talk to the doctor, figure out what we should do for Bobby."

"He'll be fine." Her mother settled back on the mound of white pillows. "My baby's going to be just fine."

Melody found the doctor in the hallway. "I did not say he'd be fine." The gray-haired woman with a face full of soft doughy wrinkles flipped through a pile of papers on a clipboard. "My dear." The doctor looked at her. "Your brother is lucky to be alive. Electric shock is very serious. His heart is fibrillating. That means it is fluttering rather than beating. A fluttering heart cannot do the job of pumping the blood through the body and to the brain. It's the brain we must be concerned about now."

Melody's own heart seemed to beat more solidly in her chest when she heard those words. "Can I see him?"

The doctor nodded. "In a moment, dear." She gestured to a woman standing a few feet away. "This is Mrs. Mc-Neil. She's one of the social workers on our staff." The woman joined them. She was short and round and gray as the roly-poly bugs Melody and Bobby plucked off over-turned stones in the creek bed behind their house. She

91

took Melody's hand and stared at her with an earnestness that left Melody feeling like a lab specimen. "Please call me Margaret. And you are Melody?"

Melody nodded, confused. Why couldn't they just take her to Bobby? What did this woman want from her?

"I have some questions about your mother. Do you mind?"

"Mama? Oh, she's fine," Melody assured the woman. "She's just a touch dramatic."

The social worker laughed but didn't seem amused. "I think it's a bit more serious than that, don't you? She seems to think that she saved your brother's life with some kind of chanting spell. She seems to believe that she's some sort of magical being, a witch or something."

"She's not a witch," Melody said, though she often thought of her mother as a witch or actually as a bitch, but she was still too young to allow herself that word. "That's ridiculous."

"I'd like to hear about how things are at your home. Are you happy? Is there anything you'd like to talk about?"

Melody yanked her hand from the woman's grip, balled it into a hard fist that she held stiffly at her side. She imagined sending the fist into the woman's fat face. "Things at my home are none of your business." She wanted to squash the woman beneath her shoes the way she had squashed the roly-poly bugs. "I'd like to see my brother now. Can someone please take me to see Bobby?"

The doctor nodded. The social worker reached out and touched Melody's arm. "I just want you to know that I'm here. Nothing you could tell me would shock me. If you want to talk about anything at all, you call me." She pressed a small card into Melody's hand. Melody crumpled the card and let it fall to the ground between them. She smirked at the round woman, aware that she was acting like a brat. She didn't care.

"Take me to Bobby." The doctor and the social worker exchanged a look. These women thought they were better than her, better than her mother. Maybe they were, but Melody wasn't going to give them the satisfaction of acknowledging their superiority. She lifted her chin and raised her voice. "Take me to see my brother this instant."

Melody's father was in Bobby's room. She buried her face in his chest like a child. Her anger at the women and her mother melted. He hadn't abandoned her, after all. God might be a mirage, but her father was real.

He rubbed her back. Her father smelled of tobacco, stale alcohol, and leather. "I tried to call you." Melody sniffed, but did not cry. She wouldn't give anyone the satisfaction of seeing her cry.

"What in the hell happened?"

The doctor spoke up, explained again about Bobby's fluttering heart.

"Mr. Mahaffey," the doctor said. "May I have a word with you about your wife?"

"My wife?" Daddy planted a kiss on the crown of Melody's head and pushed her down into a chair at Bobby's bedside. "I'll handle this." Melody knew then that she didn't need God and she sure as hell didn't need her mother. Daddy would take care of everything.

The doctor explained about the chanting and the delusions. She recommended a mental health evaluation. She spoke in the soft, caring tones of a grandmother, but her soothing bedside manner did not impress Melody's father one bit.

"You think my wife is crazy, is that it?"

"We don't like to use the word 'crazy,' Mr. Mahaffey."

"You don't? What word do you use? I just want to make sure I'm using the right goddamned terminology when talking about my wife. *My* wife."

"Mr. Mahaffey, I just think that this kind of unusual behavior warrants some attention. We can help her."

"Are you a religious woman?"

"I'm a scientist, but I'm not without faith."

"Do you pray?"

The doctor nodded. "I do. I do pray. When they brought your son in this morning, I said a prayer for him."

"Then maybe you should be evaluated by your mental health professionals. Talking to some invisible man in the sky? That's not crazy?"

"But, Mr. Mahaffey—" The doctor's voice rose.

Daddy cut her off. "How the hell is your prayer any different from my wife saying a few words over her own son? Because the words are different? Because she has the guts to say 'em out loud instead of being ashamed and whispering them in her head? What makes you so almighty goddamned superior?"

The doctor's chin wobbled. She hugged the clipboard to her chest. "I didn't intend to offend you, Mr. Mahaffey. I was trying to help."

"You want to help?" His voice boomed off the cold tile. "You work on getting my boy out of this hospital and back home. I'll worry about my wife."

Two weeks later, Bobby was released from the hospital. His fluttering heart had stabilized and begun to beat in a normal, healthy rhythm. The only visible damage was a purple burn on his right hand and forearm. His face was beautiful as ever, and his body, grown thinner, worked as it was supposed to work. Bobby could walk and eat and talk and live, but something was missing. Bobby was changed. When he talked, his words twisted and fell flat. His eyes, still beautiful, had lost their shine. Bobby, Melody knew, had left something vital behind in the cool, blue baptismal waters.

The scientific explanation was this: anoxia-based brain damage. Bobby's brain was starved for oxygen for several long minutes, and some of his brain cells did not survive. The lack of these cells left him confused, impatient, and irritable. He struggled with simple concepts, confused common words. It became clear in the months and years following the baptism that Melody's brother was never going to fully recover. Melody's mother would not discuss Bobby's shortcomings, preferred to pretend that her favorite child was just fine. If Bobby, clumsy and slow, broke a plate or a mug, Mama blamed Melody for not watching him more closely or helping him or just doing the chores herself. Melody's father was on her side, though. He wouldn't stand up to her mother. No one would do that. But he treated Melody more gently, as if she, too, were damaged by the events of that terrible day.

* * *

She was damaged. So was he. Melody would not force her father to go to a hospital now. She would do what it took to keep her dying father at home. She'd change his diapers and wipe the drool off his chin. She'd deal with being spit on when he grew sick of his nutrition drinks. She'd let him curse and fuss and whimper, and moon after Melody's mother, who'd left him there to die. She'd shop and clean and cook. On that spooky ride to the train station, George Walter told her everything was a choice, that no one had to do anything in this world. Fine. She *chose* to care for her father. She *chose* to be nice to Maurice. She *chose* to deal with Bobby. She *chose* to do all of it, but then she would do one more thing. The very minute her mother returned, Melody planned to stage a good old-fashioned come-to-Jesus soul-cleansing confrontation. It was, she thought, the only choice.

Chapter Eleven

Obi left his mother's house with a box packed full of sweet preserves, homemade bread, herbal tea, peanut butter, and a plastic container full of spice cookies. Obi and Liam each wore a braided necklace woven with herbs that smelled of clove and sage and sulfur. It was not necessarily a pleasant scent, but neither did it stink. Pisa said they would get used to it soon and smell nothing at all. The necklaces were supposed to provide protection. Obi retrieved the old Winchester from behind the seat of his truck anyway. He appreciated his mother's gifts, but he didn't intend to rely on her. He'd managed to pack their tent and most of their supplies in the car. They left behind some clothing. It would be too hot for long sleeves or coats for quite a while. He struggled to adjust to the car, to its unfamiliar musty scent, to the brakes that responded with the slightest tap of his foot. He felt cramped and low to the ground and he longed for his truck. His cheek, sliced open by the same knife that slid into the boy's throat, throbbed underneath the poultice his mother had applied. The map she'd drawn for him lay unfolded on one knee. It was simple and would take no more than two hours, even staying to the farm roads and off the main highway.

"Daddy," Liam said.

"What is it?"

"Are we in trouble?"

Obi didn't like to lie to Liam, but he said, "No, we're not in trouble at all."

"Did you hurt that man?"

"No." Obi's stomach ached. "Of course not."

"Don't feel bad," Liam told him. "Grandma will take care of us."

It was the worst thing Liam could say. That his own son should look to someone else to keep him safe made Obi feel small and useless.

During the dark time after Eileen left, Obi tried to do the right thing. He bathed Liam for the first time and shopped for diapers and clothes. He read to him at night and told him stories about his ancestors. He came to understand how hard it was to take care of another human being, but also how important. Liam began to respond to Obi in new ways. He smiled when Obi came into a room. He laughed at Obi's stories, and Obi understood Liam might not speak much, but he understood plenty. It was hard to work all day and come home and do all the housework at night, but it was better than fighting with Eileen.

When Eileen first disappeared, Obi called in sick for a few days and realized he would have to make some arrangement for Liam while he worked. There were hundreds of day care centers to choose from, and Obi found one he could afford. Soon after entering day care, Liam began to walk. Then he began to talk. He never babbled or chattered like some of the other children, but he said just enough to get what he needed. Obi discovered that Liam was right on track with the other children when it came to potty training. Eileen had been pushing him to learn too much too soon.

Liam learned to tell Obi when he was hungry or thirsty or hot or cold. Soon he asked to "go potty." He imitated the other children and he went from being a baby to being a human being in a matter of months. How surprised, how happy Eileen would be if she could see Liam walking and talking and out of his diaper, but Eileen did not return, and the woman who came from the government seemed to care more about the state of the house and what was or wasn't in the refrigerator than she did about Liam's progress. She left warnings and written instructions about nutritious food programs, court dates where he needed to appear, proper clothing for a boy Liam's age. Obi tried to explain that he couldn't do it all. He couldn't work and shop and clean and go to court all at the same time. "You have to find a way," the woman told him. "Or we'll find someone who does have the resources to care for your son." Obi knew a threat when he heard one. They began living along the river shortly after Liam's third birthday.

The sound of rushing water and the smell of a dying campfire became Liam's lullaby, the juicy smash of wild berries and freshly shot game were breakfast, lunch, and supper. They played games, collected bugs, and bathed in the fresh spring waters of a dozen lakes. Obi never touched the boy in anger, never raised his voice or allowed even the smallest hint of frustration to creep into his interactions with Liam. His whole life was devoted to raising the boy to be a man, a man of dignity and honor and instinct.

Now Obi feared he'd jeopardized everything. If it was "standard procedure" to look into a boy who'd had his arm broken, what was the penalty for knifing a man in front of him? If they caught him, he would go to jail and they would take Liam away. Obi resolved to stay free at any cost.

The road beneath him was rutted and bumpy. In the truck, Obi would not worry about it, but the car rattled as if it would fall apart, and so he drove slowly, easing the car past the farms and the wide-open spaces of the Delta.

Pisa had assured Obi there was plenty of land where they were headed, but what he hoped for was water, some creek or stream he could cast a line for fish and a place to wash up. Living off the land was no hardship so long as there was fresh water.

"When will we get there, Daddy?"

Obi looked at the map, traced one finger along a line that represented the road they were on, and glanced at the speedometer. "In about an hour and a half, I think."

"What's it like?"

"What's what like?"

"The safe place."

That's what Pisa called it, but Obi doubted there were any safe places left for him. He knew his mother would persuade the woman to let them camp on the land. His mother could sell anything to anyone at any time. She'd made a living selling gullible women words and herbs. Still, it would be a safe place only if they could somehow live undetected. The woman would have to keep her mouth shut and, in Obi's experience, most women weren't great at keeping secrets.

"I don't know what it's like," Obi said. "I think it'll be like most of the other places we've stayed. There will be trees and grass and probably squirrel and rabbit."

"And a house?"

"Yes," Obi said. "But we won't be living in the house. We'll live just like we always have. You and me and no one else."

Obi reached into the backseat and found one of the cookie tins Pisa had packed for them. He set the tin between them and pried off the lid. The scent of ginger and cloves filled the car. Liam dipped his hand in and brought one of the cookies to his mouth.

Obi pushed the gas pedal. He hoped the car was as sturdy as his mother had promised. The sooner they got to this new place, the sooner it would stop being a mystery. He grabbed one of the cookies for himself and took a big bite of the chewy, spicy sweetness. Then he lied to his son again.

"Nothing's changed," he said. "You'll see."

Obi found the place easily enough, though when he'd first turned on the dirt road, he thought his mother's directions were wrong. He drove slowly on the rutted, gravel-strewn road, through a long, dark stretch of pine forest without seeing any sign of habitation. Finally he came around a curve and saw the house. It had once been a fine house; he could see that. It rose up from the land, two stories of cedar plank beams and a huge porch that wrapped all the way around. There were oak trees and a line of fragrant magnolias out front. The lawn was grown wild, full of thorny weeds and grass as tall as Liam. He bypassed the gravel driveway and stayed on the long dirt road that wove around behind the house. He passed an old blue pickup truck that looked as if it hadn't been driven in years, an aluminum johnboat, and a three-wheeler that was missing a wheel. The dirt road ran out at an old tin shed behind the house. He drove on across the open field, toward a line of pine trees. The field was littered with sharp objects, and Obi swerved to avoid them. He wanted to settle far enough away from the house to avoid being spotted from those large windows, but close enough to keep an eye on things.

He hoped there would be a vegetable garden on the land, but nothing useful grew here. He could tell just by the rich, fecund smell and by the patches of wild blackberries and raspberries he spotted as he drove that the dirt beneath them was fertile. There was plenty of room for summer squash and tomatoes, pole beans and peas, corn and a peanut patch. What was land for if not to provide sustenance?

"Who lives here?" Liam rubbed his eyes. He'd napped for the last twenty minutes, and his hair stuck to his forehead in a damp mass.

"Crazy people," Obi told him. "People who don't know what they have."

"Bad crazy or good crazy?"

"We'll see." Obi tried to teach Liam the difference between people who were harmless but chose to live outside

102

the norms of society as they did, and people who might bring danger to them regardless of how normal they seemed to the rest of the world. "Everyone's crazy in some way," he said. "Until we know for sure, though, I think we'll just keep to ourselves."

"I wish we could have stayed with Grandma."

"Really?" Obi studied his son. It was unlike him to express a connection to another person, to express any desire for a home. "Why?"

Liam pulled something from his pocket and worked his hand around it.

"Whatcha got there?"

Liam opened his hand and Obi saw the fish eye, a milky gelatinous orb flecked with lint from Liam's pocket.

"Where did you get that?"

"Mr. Sam."

That dinner with the deer and the bucket of fresh fish seemed like something that had happened in another lifetime, but of course, it was just last night.

"Do you think we'll ever live inside?" Liam asked.

"Do you want to?"

Liam shrugged. "I don't know. I don't remember."

"But you like our life now, right? Because I remember when we lived inside and we weren't as happy as we are now."

"How do we know we're happy?"

Obi reached the line of pine trees and saw that it would be easy to pitch the tent in the shade, that the trees would provide good cover for them. They wouldn't be invisible, but so long as no one ventured too close, Obi thought they'd be well camouflaged. He looked back toward the house, figured they were about half a mile from the back porch, though it was difficult to gauge distances on this flat land. If it weren't for trees or buildings, he could see forever. "Well, I guess if we aren't sad, then we're happy, right?" He stepped out of the car. A creek burbled nearby. It was a good sign. "And water. Clean water makes me happy. Just listen to that."

With the deer jerky he'd smoked and cured, the bread and cookies and peanut butter and preserves from his mother, and his own supply of cornmeal, flour, sugar, maple syrup, and powdered milk, they would live just fine. Liam tumbled out of the car and ran into the trees, following the sound of the creek. Obi followed. Liam knelt down to scoop water to his mouth. There would be squirrel in these woods and probably deer. There might be wild turkey. He could hunt for meat just as he had along the river.

He pulled the old canvas tent from the trunk and assembled the poles, stretching the fabric across the metal rods and pounding the stakes into the ground under a shady circle of trees. Clouds were rolling in, dark clouds that would bring rain. The air smelled like smoldering steel, a big storm brewing.

"I don't think I'm sad," Liam said. "But I don't think I'm happy either."

"Let's explore a little." Obi said. "Before it starts raining. Can you smell the rain?"

Liam sniffed and nodded. He placed his fish eye on the dashboard of the car and climbed onto Obi's back, peered over his shoulder. Obi strode out toward the house, but not in a direct line. He stopped by a pair of sage bushes near the shed and dropped Liam to the ground. Liam plucked wild berries from the vines grown up alongside the shed and popped them in his mouth one by one. In moments, his hands and lips stained dark purple. Obi rubbed his son's red curls. He noticed a cloud of dust rising up in the distance, a vehicle on the road to the house. Obi waited until the dust settled and walked on, forging a crooked path to stay behind the rusted tractor and old vehicles and out of the line of sight of anyone who might be watching from the house.

He crouched behind the old truck parked out back, signaled that Liam should be quiet. He wanted to get a sense of the place, but there was not much to see and he wasn't comfortable exploring any further in the light of day. The curtains on the windows did not move and he saw no shadow in their winking panes. It was not just the land that was neglected here. The porch sagged and there were dangerous gaps where boards had rotted away. The roof needed new shingles.

Back at the campsite, the flap to the tent was untethered and the grass around the car was trampled. Someone had rifled through their things. He set Liam down, opened the car door, and pulled his rifle from under the seat. He nudged the barrel of the gun through the slack opening of the canvas tent and poked his head in after. Obi let out a long slow sigh of relief. The tent was empty.

When Obi was satisfied no one was hiding in the trees, he took inventory of their supplies. Everything seemed to be in place, though the tin of cookies on the front seat of the car seemed a bit emptier.

"Daddy." Liam ran his hands across the dashboard. "My fish eye is gone."

"Are you sure you didn't drop it?"

Liam's lip quivered and his eyes welled up. "I put it right here." He slapped his hand on the dashboard. "I put it right here for later."

What kind of person would dig through all their stuff—food, tools, supplies for making fire, blankets and clothing, his rifle; who would dig through all of that and decide the one thing worth taking was the dirty eyeball from a dead fish?

"Don't worry about it, son." He scooped Liam into his arms. "There are plenty of fish in the world and they all have eyes. We'll get you another one soon."

"But I liked that one."

Obi tried not to laugh. He knew Liam was serious, but he also knew that the boy wouldn't remember the eyeball tomorrow.

"I tell you what," Obi said. "How about we wash up in that creek and I'll make us some dinner. How does that sound?"

Liam sniffled and rested his head on Obi's shoulder. "Now I'm sad."

Obi patted his back. "I know, but this is a small sadness. Trust me." He pulled a piece of the deer jerky from a sack in the backseat of the car and handed it to Liam. The boy stuck the hard meat in his mouth and sucked and chewed on it while Obi pulled out the ingredients to make a pan of biscuits. A good supper and a good night's sleep were what they needed. Tomorrow, he could explore.

Chapter Twelve

Geneva drove down Highway 49, past small towns that offered up nothing but a steady dose of coffee, booze, and religion to the farmers and musicians who paced up and down the Delta in their old cars and rust-spotted trucks. The kernel of fear planted by Pisa's warning took root and sprouted into a full flop sweat. She rolled down the window and cranked the air conditioner to high. A bank of dark clouds swelled heavy in the sky. Just like Pisa's eyes, she realized. She ought to whip the car around and drive home, but she was not one for doing what she ought to. At Shellmound, she pulled into the One Stop to fill the tank.

The gasoline stung her nose. She leaned against the car and studied the field of cotton across the road. When she got home, she would sell some land. Crazy to hang on to it. Nothing had been farmed there since Melody was a tot. Few years back, a man came looking to buy up most of it; for what, she didn't even ask. She just slammed the door in his face and refused to answer the phone. That land was what her father had left her. She never thought she'd give it up. Now she couldn't believe she'd kept it for so long.

What good was a bunch of land that produced nothing? Bruce's medical bills were strangling her. Keeping up the house was hard enough, and she wasn't about to let go of her house. It was the only thing in the wide world that was truly hers. No bank owned any part of it. She'd been born there, right on the bed that she and Bruce had shared for the past twenty-six years. She had every intention of dying there.

She drove on, slurping the dregs of a gas station iced tea through a plastic straw. Fields of soybeans and cotton stretched out as far as she could see. The beans were low and planted in even rows, thick green leaves beginning to carpet the land. The cotton stood taller, brown and scrubby at this time of year. The air smelled sharp, a mixture of fertilizer, diesel fuel, and impending thunderstorms. The radio faded in and out, but from what Geneva could gather, there was a storm moving in from the Gulf. Rain, high winds, possible tornadoes, flash floods. Well, they were always warning of something. If they weren't bitching about a drought, they were hollering about the rain. "You can't please anyone," Geneva said to no one at all. She pressed her foot down on the gas pedal and sped up to keep ahead of the storm.

Fat drops splatted on the window as she pulled into the parking lot of the Jolly Inn. Shaped like a cross laid flat, the motel was small and squat. An office and lobby ran east to west in the center, and a dozen rooms stretched out north to south on either side. She entered the lobby through the back entrance—the pool entrance, though the pitiful swimming pool hadn't held water in all the years she'd visited. The air-conditioning sent goose bumps up her arms. Geneva touched the silver bell on the counter.

Atul emerged looking haggard. His face sagged so heavily that his skin threatened to slide right off the bone, like skin off a chicken. His hair, normally combed back and gleaming with exotic oil, hung across his forehead, dull and uncombed. His hands trembled as he slid a key off the board behind the desk. "I tried to call you."

The front door swung open and a young couple with two noisy children entered the lobby. Geneva took the key, attached to a plastic fob stamped with the number 215. She left Atul to deal with the rambunctious family and climbed the stairs on the outside of the motel. The room was like any other. A horrid brown and orange polyester spread covered the bed. Underneath, she knew, were scratchy sheets made of a cheap cotton-poly blend. No matter how much she complained, Atul never upgraded the quality of the sheets. She splashed cold water on her face in the tiny, fluorescent-lit bathroom.

Geneva never had much cause to stay in motels before she met Atul. Even when they had money, they didn't travel. As a child, she'd read books about children who lived in apartments in New York City or flats in London or even big hotels in Paris. The books were illustrated with tall buildings and sidewalks full of people. She had wanted to go, to see what it was like in a busy city. Her father said she was welcome to go on her own dime when she got older, but he had no intention of taking her anywhere. "It's not the city I hate, it's the goddamned people," her father told her. "They think they're better than us because they talk faster and go to school past the point when they ought to be earning a living. Let me tell you something, just because a person talks fast doesn't mean he thinks fast. A wall full of fancy degrees don't make you smart. I have dealt with more than my share of overeducated, fast-talking northern fools. You're better off here."

By the time Geneva was old enough to do anything on her own dime, she was married with children and had dealt with her own share of overeducated fools. Her father complained about the uppity northerners, but Geneva knew a good many overeducated fools with southern accents. Nonetheless, her wanderlust faded into memory. Something powerful tied Geneva to this flat, fertile, downtrodden area of the world, much as it had tied down her father. The idea of traveling too far away left her breathless. Who would she be in a small apartment? On a sidewalk? In a crowd? She no longer cared to find out.

Melody wasn't afraid to leave, though. She didn't feel the tug of the land the way Geneva did. It was for the best. Somebody ought to venture out and see what the rest of the world offered. Melody resented Geneva for not being a better mother, but she ought to be grateful. Who would Melody be if she'd been raised up by a dull, ordinary housewife? Not a girl who traveled from city to city, playing music and sleeping in a bus, Geneva figured. Not a girl with so much freedom.

She used the phone next to the bed to call home. Might as well talk to Melody, find out how Bruce was doing. As usual, there was no answer. Pisa's son would be there soon, and Geneva felt like she ought to warn Melody. Well, what's

111

the worst that could happen? If Bruce was well and vertical, he'd shoot a strange man on sight. Melody wasn't so rash. Bobby probably wouldn't give a fig. She'd be home soon enough.

The doorknob jiggled. Atul stepped into the room and closed the door behind him.

"What is it?" Geneva said. "What's wrong?" She stood and pulled Atul close. Underneath his normal spicy scent, something rank wafted up. Fear. She ran her fingers across his fine linen shirt. "Tell me."

"Chandra," he whispered. His face crumpled like a used tissue.

Of course. His daughter, nineteen years old, riding a full scholarship to Ole Miss, and yet somehow managing to cause trouble.

"What about her?"

"It is all my fault. She is home for the summer. She said she wanted to go camping with her friend. I let her go even though I knew better. She said if I did not let her go, she would stop coming home to visit. She said she was not a child and I could not keep treating her like one. We had already fought about so many things."

This surprised Geneva. It wasn't like Atul to fight with his daughter. He doted on her—too much, in Geneva's opinion. "What sort of things?"

"Little stuff, not important." His shoulders heaved. "She came home from that college wearing makeup and with her hair cut short. She wore shorts and T-shirts like an ordinary girl. She told me that everyone dresses this way. I

112

hated it. I said her mother would be ashamed. I told her she could not go anywhere with friends who led her to such bad decisions, but then I was afraid I would lose her and I could not stand that. I should never have said that about her mother."

When Chandra was thirteen, her mother was mowed down by a car just outside the motel. The driver didn't stop, left her to bleed out like a slaughtered hog. Sheriff's deputies ran down the driver, but never charged him with anything. An accident, they said. Your wife should not have been out walking alone after dark. This, despite the fact that the man spent the four hours before the accident drinking himself blind at a roadside bar. By the time they caught him, the other men at the bar insisted he'd had nothing stronger than RC Cola for hours. The man was wealthy. He owned several restaurants in Greenville. The next month, the sheriff's office got a whole fleet of new patrol cars, and the promise of fresh tamales every Christmas. It was the way things worked, but Atul wanted to believe life was fair. Geneva knew better.

"Mira was always proud of Chandra."

"Of course she was." Geneva pressed her lips to Atul's sweat-soaked forehead. How was she supposed to break it off with a man who was already broken? "Chandra knows that."

"She came home in the early morning. It was pitch-black out. She was nervous and shaking. She would not talk to me. She would not eat. Finally, she said that she had seen a man kill someone. It was one of those dangerous men who live on the river, and she said he killed a boy about her age."

"Which river?" If she drove three miles in any direction, she'd cross a river.

"I am not sure. She would not talk about it. She said she was afraid the man would come after her."

"When did this happen?"

"It is still happening. It will never end."

"Everything ends." If she'd wanted to deal with a hopeless man, she could have stayed home. "Where is Chandra now?"

"I called you, but your son answered the phone. I didn't know what to say or how to ask for you."

"When was this?"

"Today. This morning."

She'd been on the road to see Pisa. "Well, I don't know what I could have done anyhow." Geneva didn't know what she was supposed to do now. She didn't have much time here. There were plenty of troubles waiting for her at her own home. "Is Chandra home alone?"

"No, no. She is with her aunt in Indianola. She needs the comfort of a woman. I could not protect her, so what good am I? I sent her off into danger."

This was the problem with having children, Geneva thought. It was sure to end in disappointment. She had failed her own children even with the help of Pisa's magic chants and potions. She'd managed to save Bobby's life, but not his spirit, and she'd pushed Melody away, thinking it would make her stronger. Instead, it only made her more resentful. "Atul, I'm sorry, but you'll work it out. Chandra needs to go see the sheriff."

"She is too afraid."

"Even so." Geneva knew it was a terrible time to leave him, but it was time. "We can't keep doing this. I have to take care of my family. I came to tell you that. I can't stay. I'm sorry."

He grabbed her and pushed her down on the bed. "You cannot leave me. Not now."

He pinned her with his body. His strength surprised her.

"Atul, I have to get home tonight." She struggled beneath him.

"You would abandon me now? I thought you loved me. What am I going to do? What am I supposed to do about all this?" His face hovered just inches over her own. Every word rained down moist and warm on her skin.

"Talk to Chandra." She lay still beneath him, not wanting to agitate him further. Was this the violence Pisa had warned about? Would her gentle lover turn against her, try to hurt her? "Tell her to go to the sheriff."

"The sheriff does not care about me. No one cared when Mira was killed, and they will not care about this." He wailed. His body shook against hers. How could she leave him like this?

"Look." Geneva shifted her hips from side to side, but he didn't budge. "I know the Muskogee county sheriff. We went to school together. He's a good man. Fair. Chandra can talk to him. Tell him the truth."

"What does that mean? Tell the truth. When has she lied?"

His sharp hipbones ground painfully into her own. Now she was having trouble breathing. "All I'm saying is that she needs to tell someone what happened, where it happened, at what time. They're going to ask a bunch of questions and she needs to answer."

"Those men who live on the river. They are desperate and dangerous."

"Not all of them." None of them had ever held her against her will. She had expected Atul to crumble and cry when she said she was leaving. Instead, he turned his body against her, the same body she'd loved so much for so many years. She took shallow sips of air.

"You will go with me to the sheriff."

"No." Her heart beat against Atul's chest. There was no hiding her fear. "I'll call him. I'll let him know that you'll stop by first thing tomorrow morning."

"You must go with me. I will not go alone." He grabbed her wrists, yanked them up above her head until her shoulders burned.

"You're hurting me," she said between clenched teeth. "And you're being ridiculous."

"Then I am ridiculous. I am a ridiculous man. An unloved man."

"You are hurting me."

"You are killing me," he said in a flat voice that scared her more than if he'd screamed.

"I love you. You know that I do," she reassured him.

"If you loved me, you would stay."

"I'll take you to the sheriff's office in the morning, but then I'm heading home. You can't imprison me, Atul. You can't force me to stay with you."

Atul stared at her, and Geneva saw the same storm rolling in his eyes that she'd seen in Pisa's. Was she going mad?

Maybe it was the lack of oxygen. Did he intend to sleep on top of her all night long? When she'd given up hope that he would ever move, he rolled off. She coughed and took a few long, deep breaths. He kept hold of one wrist.

"You're going to stay?"

"Just until morning."

"I'm sorry." He released her wrist and rolled away from her. "I need you."

Geneva lay still. Pisa was wrong. Atul was scared and upset, but he was not a violent man.

Chapter Thirteen

Melody unpacked sacks of groceries. She dripped with sweat, and her clothes clung to her skin like flypaper. She wished the clouds in the distance would roll in already and dump some rain. The woman on the radio said a big front was coming, and they were in for a gully washer, possible flooding. She hoped so. Anything to break the god-awful heat.

Her father was sleeping—peacefully, it seemed—and she took a moment to examine his pale skin, his flattened cheeks, and the bruised pockets of his eyes. He barely resembled the father she remembered. He looked like a bad, deflated imitation of himself.

The grocery store had been packed with folks laying in supplies for the weather. People liked to be prepared. Melody knew better. There was no preparing for weather. A strong storm could be death and destruction or it could be a cleansing force. Melody desperately wanted to be cleansed. Life on the road had left her sluggish and bloated. It felt good to be shut of that life. George Walter's dire predictions ran through her head. She wished she could stop thinking about the crazy man who'd given her a ride to the station, but his warnings haunted her. He was wrong about one thing, though. She wasn't leaving behind anything that she would miss. She just had to figure out what came next.

She sang softly as she filled the fridge with fresh milk, eggs, juice, fruits, and vegetables, then unpacked a case of the new nutrition drink for her father. The man at the grocery store swore this drink would taste better; she hoped he was right. She shoved a soft, squishy carton of ice cream into the freezer. She sang an old Carole King tune, one of her favorites: *I feel the earth move under my feet / I feel the sky tumbling down.* It felt good to sing for no one and for no reason, except that she felt like singing. She ran a mound of blackberries under the sink tap, picked off a few stray leaves and stems, dumped the berries into a bowl, and dusted them with sugar. She chopped onions until her nose ran, patted fat pork chops dry with paper towels, then dredged them in seasoned flour.

It was good to prepare a meal, to do something useful. She looked forward to eating. She'd scarfed down a pack of Nabs on her way back from the grocery, could still taste the orange crackers and peanut butter between her teeth. This feast would be a great improvement over the road food she'd been shoveling in her mouth for the past three years. She was sick of diner food and vowed she would never again eat a casserole held together by cream of mushroom soup.

She shook a pot of butter beans on the back burner, turned down the heat to a low simmer, and set to making cornbread—real cornbread with buttermilk and oil and egg, none of that sweet stuff from a box. For sweet stuff, she was fixing a cobbler. She stirred the batter with a wooden spoon and sang louder. She never heard Maurice enter.

"This smells delicious," he said.

Melody managed to hang on to the bowl in her hand, but dropped the spoon on the floor as she spun around. Her face went hot. How long had he been standing there, listening to her sing? "You scared the life out of me," she said. "You're always sneaking into a room. Make some noise, for God's sake."

Maurice picked up the spoon, washed it, and ran a dish towel over it before handing it back. "Sorry. My mother always said I was too light-footed. She threatened to strap a bell around my neck like a cat."

He had changed clothes since the morning and was now dressed in a pair of dark fitted jeans and a starched button-down oxford shirt, blue pinstripes on cream. She, on the other hand, wore a pair of too-tight gym shorts and an old pink sorority T-shirt imprinted with a kickline of faded ladybugs. It was all she could find in the chest of drawers in her old bedroom. Or at least it was all she could find that would actually slide up over her fat ass. She'd tried to pull on a pair of linen trousers, but they were much too tight. The gym shorts were hideous but stretchy.

She gestured toward the stove. "Pork chops and onions, butter beans, cornbread, and blackberry cobbler with ice cream for dessert." She hoped he ate cobbler. He looked like he could still fit into his clothes from high school and might be the kind of person who shied away from butter and sugar. "Do you like cobbler?"

"Are you kidding? I love cobbler. It's probably my favorite food. I wouldn't trust a person who didn't eat cobbler."

"That's a wise policy." She laughed and stabbed the spoon into the air. "Death to the cobbler haters!"

Maurice looked around the kitchen. "Can I help?"

"Oh, fear not. I know it looks like a great big mess, but I've got this under control."

Maurice nodded. "Bobby said you could sing, but he didn't tell me you could *sing*. I mean, woowee, that's quite a voice.

Melody did not want to talk about her voice. It just led to thinking about her ruined career. She turned to pour the batter over the berries. "How's Daddy doing?"

"Bobby told me you were in a band."

"It's nothing." She wiped her hands on a dish towel. "I was in a band. Now I'm not."

"Their loss," Maurice said. "You don't even need a band. You could just stand in the middle of a stage and sing, and people would come from miles around to hear you, I bet."

"Well, you'd lose that bet." She slammed a pot down on the stove.

"Sorry," Maurice said. "Your father's fine. I'll turn him right before we eat, and once again before I leave tonight. That'll get you through to tomorrow. Save you a bit of trouble."

"Thank you." Melody forced a smile. "There's some tea in the fridge, if you want it. Also I picked up some beer. I wasn't sure what you drank. *If* you drank. I'm sure Daddy has a bottle of whiskey stashed somewhere. Help yourself."

"Tea's fine. Thank you." A whisper of cool air ran across Melody's skin when Maurice opened the refrigerator.

Bobby burst through the back door. A gust of wind followed, and Melody inhaled the cool, metallic scent of the coming rain. Bobby looked around at the activity in the kitchen as if he didn't quite trust what he was seeing. "What's going on?"

"Where on God's green earth have you been?" Melody shook a spoon at him. "You've got to quit disappearing on me. I need your help around here."

Bobby glared at her. "I help. Don't say I don't help. It ain't fair! I do everything more, everything more. I do more. I do everything."

"Don't say 'ain't.'" Melody crossed over and slammed the door shut behind him. "You're letting in bugs." She felt Maurice watching them, judging them.

"You've been gone," Bobby whined. "You don't, you don't, you don't know what all I do."

"There's no evidence you do anything useful." She hated the sharp tone in her voice and turned to apologize. Bobby's hair was a mess, full of twigs and dirt. He was working something around in his hand.

"What have you got there?" Melody grabbed for him. "What have you got there in your hand, Bobby?"

Maurice stepped forward and held his own hand out toward Bobby. "Let's see." He looked genuinely curious.

Bobby dropped something into Maurice's outstretched palm. Maurice let out a shriek and dropped the thing on the floor. He wiped his hand on his jeans. "Oh, Lord— what is that slimy thing?"

Bobby laughed. "I found it."

Melody picked up the small gelatinous orb, held it lightly between her index finger and her thumb. It was dirty and disgusting and looked as if it might have been alive not so long ago. She dropped it into the trash.

"Hey!" Bobby lunged at her. She slapped him away.

"Can't you see that I've just spent a whole day cleaning this place? I can't believe you dragged that filthy thing in here while I'm cooking dinner. It's like you don't have any sense at all." Melody ran her hands under hot water and squeezed soap onto her palms. "Get washed up. We're eating soon." Bobby stomped out of the kitchen.

"Sorry," Melody said to Maurice, who was now washing his own hands. "Sometimes Bobby is just a little off. I'm sure you've noticed."

Maurice wiped his hands on a paper towel. "He's fascinating, isn't he?"

"Fascinating" was not the word she'd use to describe Bobby. "Infuriating" was more like it. "He wasn't always like this. You should have seen him as a kid. He was just beautiful. So smart."

"I'm going to go check on him," Maurice said. "Make sure he's not upset."

"Don't worry about it. He'll get over it. He'll be fine."

Maurice left the kitchen, and Melody heard him walk up the stairs. It was weird, this concern Maurice had for her brother. Even weirder that Bobby seemed to like it, though Melody remembered a few other odd relationships Bobby had had with strange men. He'd been particularly close to the special education teacher at the high school, hanging out at his house after school and eating dinner with the creepy old man. Melody asked Bobby what he did over at Mr. Pimentel's house, and Bobby just shrugged and said the man was helping him with schoolwork. "You can tell me if he ever does anything you don't like," she assured him. "Go to hell," Bobby told her.

Melody pulled the cornbread from the oven just as Daddy started in on a loud coughing fit. She set the hot skillet on the stovetop and ran out to check on him. His cough rattled, so deep that Melody's own chest ached.

Maurice was already there. He cleared away a wad of crumpled, blood-streaked tissues.

"He's bleeding."

Maurice nodded. "It's normal enough. He's coughing up blood."

"That's not normal," Melody said. "How can that be normal?"

Maurice gave her a look.

"What he's telling you, little girl, is that I deserve it. Brought it on myself." He coughed again, pounded his chest with a weak fist. "This is what happens when you smoke all your life."

"Don't blame yourself, Daddy. It's not your fault."

"I 'spect it is," he said between coughs. "I'm not stupid, little girl. I know what caused this. I'm just real sorry you had to come home and see me like this. Better to remember your daddy as the wild, strong man you always knew."

"Don't flatter yourself," she said. "You were never all that wild."

"I don't know what you're cooking, but it sure smells good."

Maurice ran a damp cloth over her father's forehead. Bobby clomped down the stairs. He wore a plaid oxford shirt and a pair of dark jeans. It looked like he and Maurice were shopping at the same store. His hair flopped over his forehead in a mass of black curls. He looked like the brother she remembered, handsome and fastidious. "You don't do everything around here," he said. "Maurice does plenty."

Maurice snapped fresh pillowcases onto the pillows. "She's cooking dinner. That's not nothing."

Bobby smiled. He could still charm with that smile.

"Yes, and supper is ready," Melody said. "Is it all right if we just help ourselves from the stove? It'll keep me from dirtying every dish in the kitchen." Bobby put an arm around her shoulder, hugged her close to him. Perhaps he was not quite so impossible as he seemed.

She poured tall glasses of sweet tea and they piled their plates high. The doorbell rang before she could take a bite. She pushed back from the table. "Eat," she instructed Bobby and Maurice.

She couldn't imagine who would be at the door. They lived too far from town to attract solicitors or missionaries. Daddy had long ago chased off any well-meaning deacons come to bring them back to the church. They had no friends.

She didn't know whom to expect, but she sure as hell didn't expect to see Chris on her front steps. Her face turned hot, just as it had that night in the alley. She gripped the door handle so hard her hand went numb.

"Why?" She stared at him. "Why on earth are you here?"

"You are a hard person to track down. I've been all over the county. Someone told me that you lived in the house in the middle of nowhere. You should put your name on the mailbox or something. I thought I was lost and then, suddenly, a house." He looked around as if he were discovering a foreign land and didn't want to miss anything. "I never pictured you out here in the country."

She stepped onto the porch and pulled the door shut. The moist heat of the evening hit her like a force. Sweat broke out on her bare legs and upper lip. "Everyone who needs to find us, finds us just fine." The porch was soft beneath her bare feet, the wood rotted and worn down. Wisteria vines crept up the railings like sinister arms working to pull the house down.

"I heard about your father. I'd like to help."

The sky was luminescent, gray clouds turning silver in the sunset. Wind stirred the warm air, moist and lilac scented. Trees swayed; oak leaves and pine needles reached out, as if grasping for the same prize. "Shouldn't you be halfway to Florida by now?"

"I was fired."

"Fired?"

"I aired your, um, profanity on the radio. It was a live broadcast. We're supposed to air all live broadcasts on a five-second delay, but I didn't. It was a Christian concert. I thought, what could happen?"

She plucked at the clinging hem of her shorts. "Well, now you know."

"Yes."

"I don't know what you expect me to do about it." She thought about the way Chris had run from the alley and how ashamed he was to be caught with her. She wasn't about to feel sorry for him. She grasped the door handle. "Go home, Chris. Marry your fiancée. Get a new job."

"We broke off the engagement. I've been trying to tell you that for months." Chris stepped closer, put his hand over hers on the door handle. The touch sent a spark through her arm. "We prayed about it. Marriage was not what God had planned for us. It was what everyone expected of us, but it wasn't right."

Melody envied Chris's ability to pray and make decisions, his confidence about right and wrong. She was just bumbling through life. She looked past Chris. In the waning light, the land didn't look so bad. The rusted-out vehicles and the overgrown gardens seemed almost beautiful, wild and untamed and free. "Well, what do you want? Do you want me to call the station and apologize?"

"I don't want my job back."

"You've come all this way. You're all the way out here in the *country*." Her voice was sharp with sarcasm. "You must want something."

Chris tightened his grip on her hand, stepped closer, put his face right in front of hers, so close that she could feel him exhale against her lips, smell the sharp, grassy scent of his body. "I want your voice. Rather, I want you to use your voice. I have an idea. . . ."

She was dizzy with so much closeness. "I think my singing career is over, don't you? I can't imagine the Christians would welcome me back after I poisoned their ears with such profane language. I know Joy won't have me back."

"Joy!" Chris rolled his eyes and threw his hands in the air. "Who cares about Joy?"

"Joy cares about Joy," Melody said.

"Exactly. Look, I told you before, you could have a great solo career. You were always better than that band. They won't last five minutes without you."

Melody wished she didn't feel so flattered by Chris's compliment. "I can't deal with this right now. Daddy is sick. He's dying. I can't think about anything else."

"You don't belong here." Chris spoke with conviction. He acted like he knew Melody, even though they'd never shared more than one sordid alleyway encounter.

"This is my home. If I don't belong here, I don't belong anywhere." The truth of that statement hit her hard.

"I have a friend in Memphis. He has a recording studio, runs a small Christian label, does a bit of soft pop crossover. I told him about you. He's interested."

"I can't just leave," Melody said. "And even if I could, how am I supposed to go solo after what I said? In front of a bunch of *Christians*? In front of a bunch of Christians with *children*? My God, you lost your job because of my big mouth. I think I've burned my bridges."

"I don't think so." Chris rubbed his palm across his stubbled chin. "We just have to script the right narrative. Write a new story."

Melody brushed a persistent mosquito from her upper arm. "I don't even know what that means."

"Redemption acts are big right now." Chris leaned in. "All you have to do is repent. Publicly, of course. I'll help you with what to say."

"Well, I could certainly use some help choosing my words," Melody said. "But this isn't going to work."

"It's good PR. We'll set up some interviews, talk about the stress you were under because of your dying father—"

"No!"

"But, Melody."

"No! I'm not using Daddy's illness as an excuse. That's sick!"

"It's not an excuse if it's true."

"I'll tell you what's true, Chris. Daddy is dying and my life is a mess. I have no idea what I'll do with my future, but I know what I have to do today."

"The future comes whether you plan for it or not, Melody."

First George Walter and now Chris. Prophets everywhere. "I have to go." She turned to open the door. "Sorry you came all this way for nothing."

Chris grabbed hold of her shoulder. "God brought us together for a reason."

"That's bullshit, and you know it." He opened his mouth to speak, but she barreled on, holding up her hand to keep him from interrupting. "You can't possibly be shocked by my language at this point. Anyway, God didn't bring us together. Our jobs brought us together. That's not divine intervention, that's just life."

"I'm not asking you to lie. I can call some spiritual leaders. We'll work to build you back up as a strong voice for God."

Melody pictured a dozen scary white-haired men in flowing robes looming above her, chanting for her lost soul.

"We'll build up a set list that emphasizes forgiveness and humility. I can help you craft the message. We'll set up radio interviews, and television."

Melody had very little experience with television. Her mother forbade them to turn the set on, said she couldn't bear the "infernal racket." Melody wasn't even sure the old set in the house still worked. Chris didn't know her. He imagined she could repent, but she wasn't sorry. He imagined God would save her, but she didn't believe there was a God.

"What you did is nothing in the big scheme of things. When people understand about your father, your family problems, they'll be dying to forgive you and to listen to you." His voice rose and he talked faster. "There's money to be made. That would help your family, wouldn't it?"

"I thought money was the root of evil," Melody said. "I thought it was easier for a camel to get through the eye of a needle than for a rich man to enter the kingdom of heaven."

"If you obey and believe, the Lord will grant you abundant prosperity. It's right there in the Bible. Abundant prosperity."

Melody snorted. "I don't buy that."

"You don't buy the word of God?"

"Look around. Look at all these people who obey and believe and struggle all their lives just to put food on the table. Where's their prosperity? This area is full of those people. Why is God punishing them?"

Chris stared down at his hands. "Maybe they don't truly believe."

"Maybe I don't either." Melody opened the door a crack, careful to keep her voice low in case Daddy was sleeping.

"But you love music," Chris said. "You're so talented."

"I have to go."

"Will you think about it? Pray on it?"

"You are wasting your time."

"God has a plan for you, Melody. I'm not giving up on you. God won't give up on you, either."

She slipped inside and shut the door on him. It was rude. She should have invited him in and offered him a pork chop, but she couldn't stand the thought of exposing him to the spectacle of Daddy dying in the living room, of Bobby's unpredictable behavior. She didn't want to share awful truths of her life.

"Who was that?" Daddy asked.

"No one," Melody said. "Don't worry about it."

In the kitchen, Bobby and Maurice were cleaning their plates. "Sorry," Maurice said. "We waited for a while."

"Who was at the door?" Bobby sounded as if he were accusing her of something.

"Just someone I used to know. No one important."

"I heard a man's voice."

"Who wants cobbler? We've got ice cream."

Maurice stood and took his plate to the sink. "You eat. We'll take care of dessert. We'll get some of these plates cleared away."

The beans were cold but good. Melody ate a few bites and broke off a hunk of cornbread. She sliced into the pork, but the smell of it turned her stomach, and the gray flesh made her think of death. She scraped the food into the trash, her appetite gone. She looked out the kitchen window. It was nearly dark. Everything as far as she could see was colorless and flat.

"This cobbler is perfect." Maurice dipped a spoon into the bubbling dish. The batter rose up around the berries, which generated a thick, sweet syrup. It was dark and crunchy on top, golden and tender in the middle. How reassuring to know she could dump a bunch of ordinary ingredients into a dish and, in just an hour, transform it into something wonderful.

"I want lots of ice cream." Bobby pulled the carton from the freezer. "I wonder what that man and little boy are going to eat tonight."

Melody pulled the ice cream scoop from a drawer. "What man? What little boy?"

"The ones camped out by the creek."

"Our creek?" She took the carton from Bobby, pried off the top. It wasn't the first time vagrants had squatted on their land. Daddy always handled it, approaching the men with his shotgun at his side. Most of them were running from something, wives or girlfriends or someone they owed money or the sheriff. They moved on without argument, not wanting more trouble. Daddy was in no shape to handle it now, of course. "A little boy? How little?"

"Really little," Bobby said. "Tiny." He drew the word out until it had four syllables rather than two.

"About how old?"

Bobby held his hand about three feet high. "This old."

"Are you sure, Bobby?" Maurice touched Bobby's arm. Bobby smiled and nodded. "I watched them today. They put up a tent. I hope they don't get wet."

The land was a funhouse of rusty equipment, expired chemicals, sharp bits of metal, and half-empty jugs of poison. If some man decided to trespass and got hurt, that was one thing, Melody thought, but a little boy was another matter. She peered out the kitchen window toward the far edges of the land. The nightfall masked any movement or shadow.

"Well, they can't stay here," she said. "This is no place for a child. Never has been." She knew from her own childhood that danger lurked around every bush, behind every tree. It was a miracle that she and Bobby had survived. There were plenty of close calls: the nest of cottonmouths Bobby almost stepped on after a bad flood, a rusty nail that punctured Melody's foot, a fishhook that dug deep into Bobby's palm, numerous bouts of poison oak. They came of age in a flurry of tetanus shots, ACE bandages, and Mama's odd-smelling salves. They knew what was out there. A strange child would not know of the dangers hiding beneath the overgrown weeds.

"I don't see anything." Maurice said. "How much of this land is yours?"

"We have about five hundred acres," Melody said.

Maurice let out a low whistle. "That's a lot of land."

"More trouble than it's worth." Melody quoted Old Granddaddy. "Land is only useful if you plant it or build on it."

Maurice stirred melting ice cream into his cobbler. "I'll go out there and look around tomorrow when the light is better."

"Don't worry about it," Melody said. "It's not your job."

"I don't mind."

Bobby sat at the table and shoveled gobs of cobbler and ice cream into his mouth. Blackberry juice stained his chin. His hands were sticky with ice cream. He seemed to have lost interest in the squatters. "How did the boy look?" Melody asked. "Did he seem scared?"

Bobby spoke with his mouth full. "He looked normal, like a normal boy."

"Maybe I should call the sheriff," she said. "What if the boy was snatched?"

Bobby helped himself to more cobbler. "Father. He seemed like a father."

"I think we should check it out before we call anyone," Maurice said. "They might just be camping. No need to cause trouble for them."

"I guess it can wait until tomorrow." She ate a few bites of the cobbler, was pleased to find that it tasted just as good as it looked.

"You did all the cooking," Maurice said. "Why don't you let Bobby and me clean up?"

"That's okay." Melody turned on the hot water to fill the sink. "Just check on Daddy before you leave."

Maurice insisted on cleaning. He told Melody to relax, that he'd take care of her father and the kitchen. After protesting halfheartedly, she left him and Bobby with the dirty dishes. She was so tired. It was hard to believe she'd left Memphis just that morning. In the living room, she sat beside her father's bed. "Daddy?" she whispered. His eyes fluttered open and he blinked at her. "How are you feeling? Can I bring you anything?"

"That boy at the door," he said.

"Chris?"

"He likes you."

"No." She picked a bit of lint from the blanket across his chest, an old, thin bit of cotton. "Are you warm enough?"

"Does he have money?"

"Who?"

"The boy."

"Chris?"

"That's who we're talking about, isn't it?"

"I don't have any idea if he has money, Daddy." Melody's voice rose. "What difference does it make?"

Her father grinned, a wicked grin that exposed his soft, gray teeth. "Because it's just as easy to fall in love with a rich man as a poor one. It's a hell of a lot smarter to marry the rich one." He laughed. It was something he'd said to her many times, as if Melody had a steady stream of men knocking at her door.

"I'm not falling in love with anyone, Daddy. I'm not getting married."

"You're not getting any younger."

Melody chewed on the cuticle of her thumb until it was loose enough to rip off. Blood pooled around the nail, and she sucked it clean. "None of us is getting any younger, Daddy. None of us."

"You're right about that, little girl. Just remember, when I'm gone, you'll be on your own. Someone is going to have to care for your brother. He sure can't take care of himself."

She pressed her bloody thumb inside her palm. She didn't know what she'd be doing in the future, but she damn sure wouldn't be doing it here. "Mama will take care of Bobby."

"Little girl, she ain't here."

"She'll be back. She always comes back." Whether we want her to or not, Melody thought.

"I took care of you, didn't I? Didn't I do my best for you, little girl?"

He reached for her hand. She held him with a loose grip, afraid the slightest pressure would crush his fragile bones.

"I taught you everything I knew, didn't I?"

That was true. Melody's father taught her lots of useful things and plenty of useless ones, too. She knew how to work a rod and reel, and could shoot as good as anyone. She knew if you were going to hunt with a flask of whiskey, you should wrap it in electrical tape to keep the shine from spooking the deer. He took her hunting when she was just nine years old, told her to sit still on the wooden stand and wait. She sat in the cold morning air while her father sipped from his tape-wrapped flask. She couldn't stand it anymore; she pulled a Nancy Drew mystery from the front pocket of her overalls, cracked it open so carefully she couldn't have made a sound. Even so, he snatched the book and flung it through the woods. "Let's go." He climbed down the ladder and started packing up the truck. He was angry, but so was Melody. "I hate you," she said. Nancy Drew's father never blamed her when things went wrong. He bought her clothes and a blue convertible, and Nancy didn't even have to deal with having a mother. The injustice was too much for young Melody. She dumped her orange vest on the ground and ran through the woods. She zigged and zagged through the trees, hopped over dense underbrush. She ran until her legs turned to pudding and then slumped against a tree. Her head simmered beneath her forest green hunting cap. She pulled it off, wiped her runny nose on her sleeve. Then there was a loud crack. Bark and dirt rained down. She screamed. Her father broke through the trees. It was like being in a dream. Her father's eyes were crazed, his face flushed. He lifted her off the ground with one arm and ran a rough hand across her head and chest. His lips moved, but Melody couldn't understand him over the rushing fear in her ears. Another man appeared, dropped down from the trees. The man was pale and shaking, and couldn't stand. He kept falling to his knees. Her father set her down, turned, and punched the man hard in the face. His nose spurted blood. They left the man there, bleeding and alone. She rode out of the woods in her father's arms, drinking in his smoky, sour scent. For years, she would tell the story of how a man mistook her for a deer in the woods and how Daddy came to her rescue. "Thank God that man was no kind of shot," her father would say. "You'd have been terrible eating."

Now she held his hand, cupped as if it were still cradling her head all those years ago. "You taught me plenty, Daddy," she said, though he was sleeping. "You taught me plenty."

Chapter Fourteen

Obi was antsy, and couldn't sleep. He knew, just knew, someone was going to come along and threaten them soon. Even the air smelled ominous, hot and metallic. Fat drops of rain fell on and off through the night. A big storm was coming, but Obi did not fear the weather. He feared the person who snuck around and went through their things. He feared the people in the house who didn't have the good sense to grow food on all this land. More than anything, he feared the consequences of his own actions. The law would come for him, and then Social Services would take Liam. He could lose his son because of what happened with that boy by the river. If he lost Liam, he lost everything.

Liam slept beside him now, hands folded beneath his cheek. Obi laid one hand on Liam's head and the other on his rifle, which he'd kept close as a lover all night long. The boy didn't stir. Dawn would break soon. Obi crawled outside the tent, pulled on his boots, and stared up at the sky. Clouds muted the moonlight and blocked the stars. He stood still in the quiet morning air until his eyes adjusted to the darkness. The rifle rested in his left hand, barrel down. His memory called up a wooden cane he'd carried around as a child. The cane was his grandfather's, carved from one long piece of knotty pine, twisted but balanced. It was stained and polished a pale green–gold, the color of grass in the fall. He wondered what became of that cane. He'd like to give it to Liam as a talisman.

He picked out shapes in the darkness. A smoky scent from last night's fire lingered on his clothes. Liam would sleep for a while longer and would not be afraid if he woke to find Obi gone. Obi often hunted or gathered wood in the early morning while Liam slept. Liam knew Obi would always return before the sun was high in the sky.

Obi headed toward the house. He could be there in minutes if he walked briskly in a straight line, but he crept slowly in the darkness, on the unfamiliar land. The land was littered with hazards, but Obi was sure-footed. He lacked his mother's gifts of healing and seeing, but he could read the land. He reached the back porch as the gray mist of dawn began to rise.

Obi climbed the rotting porch steps. He could fix this porch. All he needed was a bit of lumber and some time. He peered through a window, confident no one would be awake and staring back at him at this hour. Someone had left a light on over the kitchen sink. A pile of dishes dried on a rack. A sturdy white-and-blue wrought-iron table and matching chairs sat in the center of the kitchen; a refrigerator and freezer stood against a wall. The countertop was lined with small appliances: a coffeemaker, a toaster, an electric mixer, a blender, a ceramic spoon rest. Dull, ordinary things. Obi moved on.

He looked into another window and saw the dining room with its long, polished oak table and chairs. A tall cabinet made from the same oak as the dining table stood against the wall. The cabinet was lit up on the inside, each shelf with a spotlight like a cabinet at a museum. The light shone off stacks of blue-and-white plates, teacups, and saucers. Obi knew nothing about china, but it looked like a valuable collection.

He moved around to the side of the house where the windows were smaller. The rooms were dark, and there wasn't much to see anyhow—a laundry room, a half bath, some sort of storage room, a den filled with books.

By the time Obi got around to the front porch, a gray and muted light shone through the clouds of the eastern sky. Curtains covered the large front windows, but the heavy drapes didn't quite meet in the middle. Obi shielded his eyes with his hand and squinted into the small space. The room was large and shadowy. He could barely make out one piece of furniture from another. He turned away from the window and scanned the front yard. Nothing but weeds and dead grass in the raised beds bordered by rotting logs. What a waste.

Obi left the porch and circled around to the back of the house again. The bedrooms would be upstairs, he knew, and he considered climbing a live oak that would give him a clear view into one of the upstairs rooms. He wanted to see what these people looked like, to take their measure. He gave up the idea as too risky when he realized he wouldn't be able to climb and keep his rifle at the ready.

He walked back toward camp. After he'd taken about a

hundred long strides, he turned around to look at the house once more. He saw movement in one of the upstairs windows, and a light was on that hadn't been before. A man with dark hair stared down at him. Obi had the feeling this man was watching him all along. A hard kernel of fear settled beneath his breastbone. He hugged the rifle closer. A fat drop of rain came down on Obi's shoulder, then another on his forehead. He hurried back to the tent, back to Liam.

Liam, still groggy, walked out into the wet morning and relieved himself against a pine tree. From the car, Obi retrieved the tin of spice cookies his mother had given them and two leftover biscuits from the night before, plus the jerky and a container of mixed nuts. Liam ate and they listened to the rain. It was going to be a dark, dreary day. Obi wondered if the nearby creek contained any fish worth catching in the rain. He decided against it, mostly because he doubted he'd be able to get a fire going if he did catch anything. They would make do with the cans of deviled ham and Vienna sausages, peanut butter and crackers Obi kept with him for days like this one. Neither Obi nor Liam minded a bit of rain. It kept things cool and, on the river at least, the fishing was always best after a hard rain. No one ever died from getting wet.

The hardest thing about a rainy day was how it seemed to slow down time. On a sunny day, Liam would dig holes in the dirt and help Obi fetch water and they would build a fire for cooking or for warmth. They would fish or Obi would hunt for squirrel or turkey, often with Liam by his side. On a dry, sunny day, hours passed without effort, and

Obi and Liam would be exhausted and ready for sleep come nightfall. Even if there was a good, soaking rain in the afternoon—and often there was—it was just an excuse to rest for an hour or so. When the rain started like this, though, first thing in the morning, it would continue for hours or even days. He hoped the tent wouldn't flood. If so, they'd have to sleep in the car.

Liam finished eating and stretched out on his back. He rested his head on his hands, and Obi could see how the boy was going to look as a man. "Did I ever tell you about my grandfather?" Obi asked Liam. "About your great-grandfather?"

Liam shook his head and Obi smiled. The story came to him fully formed, though he had no clear memory of being told the story himself. It must have been the memory of his grandfather's cane that brought it back to him. As soon as he began to speak, he could hear his mother whispering the story into his ear, and Obi knew she must have done so when he was no bigger than Liam.

"Your great-grandfather was a white dog. He looked like a man when the sun shone, but at night he became a large white dog with silver eyes and a soft, pure coat. White animals are rare and powerful." Obi glanced at Liam to make sure he was listening. The boy's green eyes were bright with interest. "White animals are hunted for their skins. A woman married in the skin of a white deer will have nothing but luck and prosperity with her husband, and she'll have children who are strong and smart and bring her happiness. The tail of a white fox provides protection. A feather plucked from an all-white rooster brings wisdom. Men who become animals are even more rare, and men who become white animals are the most powerful men of all.

"Your great-grandfather was a white dog. He was a great hunter because he could sniff out prey where other hunters had to rely on their eyes. He was loyal and kind, but also fierce when he needed to be. When he was young, he learned to read and write, even though plenty of boys did not learn such things at the time. He went hunting with his father. His mother taught him which plants he could eat and which would make him sick. At night, he roamed for miles and miles. He scavenged through the woods and made friends with the wolves who lived there. The wolves hunted at night, and your great-grandfather helped them find food. He knew how to get into the barns of his neighbors and where the chickens roosted. The wolves ate well every night, and every morning, the people in the houses with the barns and the chickens would be angry about the stolen livestock. The men put heavy doors on the barns to keep out predators, but still their animals disappeared. Some nights, all the men would agree to keep a lookout and to kill any predators who trespassed onto their land. On those nights, your great-grandfather warned his wolf friends and they stayed far away from the men with the guns.

"One night, one of the men decided to stay up through the night and keep an eye on his livestock. He decided to keep his plan a secret, because whenever the men discussed their plans as a group, the predators did not come. This man, a smart man, had figured that the predator was not an animal, but one of the men who lived in the village.

This man loaded a gun and sat in the darkness of his barn, waiting for the door to open and for the thief to show himself. Night came on and the moon, which was no more than a sliver that night, rose up into the sky. This man waited, quiet and patient. He had already decided he would wait for as many nights as it took to catch the thief.

"When the night was as dark as it would ever get, the door of the man's barn pushed open. The man aimed his gun, but he was so surprised to see a white dog in the doorway he barely noticed the pack of wolves coming in behind. The eyes of the white dog seemed familiar to the man, and the beast had somehow opened the barn door like a human. The dog looked the man in the eyes, saw the gun in the man's lap, and began to howl in warning. The wolves streamed out of the barn, their jaws packed with all the chickens they could grab. The man regained his senses and aimed the gun at the howling dog. He shot as the dog turned and ran away. The bullet hit the dog, hit your great-grandfather, in his right leg. He howled in pain, and a white hawk, the largest hawk the man had ever seen, flew down from the sky and carried the white dog away.

"When your great-grandfather awoke the next morning, a man again, his leg throbbed where the bullet had hit him. The hawk was no longer a bird, but a woman just about the same age as your great-grandfather. She told him she had plucked the bullet from his leg with her sharp beak and packed the wound with healing plants to stop the bleeding and ease the pain.

"Because of the bullet, your great-grandfather always walked with a limp, but he didn't mind, because the bullet brought your great-grandmother to him. At night, when he was a dog and your great-grandmother was a hawk, they would travel as far as they could together and as they traveled, they played a game. Your great-grandmother would find beautiful limbs high in the trees and she would drop them into the woods. Your great-grandfather would fetch the limbs and run ahead until morning. During the day, your great-grandfather carved the limbs he'd carried the night before into sturdy, straight sticks. Together they placed the stick in the ground, and they would travel in whichever direction it leaned. After many, many nights, one of the sticks stood straight up. It did not lean to the east or the west. It did not point to the north or the south. On that day, your great-grandparents knew they were home. They built a house and soon they had your grandmother. Your great-grandfather continued to carve the branches from the trees. He lived to be a very old man, and the limp from the bullet grew worse as he grew older. He used the sticks he carved as walking canes during the day. At night, he still became the white dog but he no longer roamed. He stayed by your great-grandmother's side, loyal and true. And she stayed with him, always protecting him from danger."

Liam looked up at his father like he expected more. "That's it," Obi said. "That's the story of your great-grandparents."

The rain poured. The ground beneath the tent was turning to mud. It was the middle of the day, but it could just as easily have been night. No sunlight broke through the dark sky.

Liam scratched a mosquito bite on his ankle. "No," he said. "I don't think that's true."

Obi laughed. "And why not?"

"Because sometimes I dream about the white dog and he doesn't limp at all."

Liam reached for a sleeve of crackers and a jar of peanut butter. He dipped one of the crackers into the jar and brought it to his mouth. Crumbs scattered across his chest and onto the sleeping bag. "Tell me something else," he said. "Something true."

Chapter Fifteen

Geneva listened to the rain splat against the pavement outside. Even from the motel bed, she could see it was going to be a gray, dreary day. No light shone through the window. Atul slept beside her, one leg kicked out from under the thin, cheap sheets. He looked like a child. Hard to believe he was the same man who'd pinned her last night. Hard to believe there was a side of Atul she hadn't seen before. What other surprises was he hiding? She would never know. Their time was up. Already she'd stayed too long. Pisa told her to go straight home, and now it was a new day. Dread, that was what she felt. Dread for what was coming, and for everything she didn't know.

She should have listened to her father. He'd told her Bruce was not a man worth marrying. He said she'd regret it. How she hated it when other people were right. Still, even though their life together was one disappointment after another, when she learned Bruce was dying, she felt something vital ripped from her gut. When the doctor laid out Bruce's long list of illnesses and said he might not live a month, she lashed out at him. "What do you know? There are bigger forces working here. You can't predict everything with your medicine."

The doctor admitted he didn't know anything for sure. "Then stop spreading lies," she told him. "I have witnessed miracles. I won't be a slave to your science." Now it was nearly a month later, and Bruce was still alive. Nothing about the month felt miraculous.

This is what the doctor told her: Bruce had cancer in his lungs and liver, emphysema, coronary atherosclerosis, high blood pressure, diabetes, and a few other things she couldn't recall. She hadn't even known he was sick until she found him collapsed by the shed, that dreadful shed. She hadn't wanted to know.

She slipped from bed and closed herself into the tiny bathroom, where she scrubbed her face with a rough cloth and a bar of soap that smelled like lemon drop candy. She ought to head out this instant, before the rain picked up and before Atul decided to try to keep her here against her will. Also, she really didn't want to get involved in Chandra's problems. Geneva didn't trust the girl. Chandra played innocent for her father, but Geneva recognized a streak of deception in her. No telling what really happened by the river. Better to keep out of it, let Chandra deal with her own problems.

The door to the bathroom creaked loudly when she pushed it open. "Come back to bed," Atul said.

She slipped her feet into her sandals, bent to straighten a strap caught under her heel. "I have to get home." She avoided his eyes, not wanting to see the violence bubble up again.

"You said you would help me. You said you knew that man, the sheriff." Atul's voice rose in an annoying whine that put Geneva in mind of mosquitoes. Would he sting her next? Take her blood? Probably.

"I'll take you to the sheriff, but then I'm gone. You can't keep me here, Atul." No one can keep me, she thought.

"How do you know this man?" Atul's voice was sharp and accusing.

"He's an old friend. We went to school together." In fact, there was a time she might have married Randall, but no sense telling Atul that. She'd broken Randall years ago, back when she was not much older than Chandra. That's what he told her when she said she was marrying Bruce. "I'm broken," he said. "I'm in pieces." As she knew he would, he'd pulled himself together and married an average, pretty woman. They raised two average, pretty children. Yet Randall never got over Geneva. The few times they'd crossed paths over the years, he'd looked at her with those moonstruck eyes, called her Genie. When she needed him, he was there. That time she'd poisoned Bruce, an incident that got blown way out of proportion in her opinion, Randall was the one who'd convinced the judge she was fragile and not dangerous.

"Chandra needs to come with us." Geneva picked up her purse and checked to make sure her keys were in the front pocket. "She really should have reported this right away."

"She was scared," Atul said.

By the time she was Chandra's age, she'd been scared plenty. She was just about Chandra's age when she lost her own mother, something she still didn't like to think about.

Chandra needed to learn that fear could be the source of great power. Chandra needed to go see Pisa.

They drove out into the wet morning. Atul insisted on riding with her, even though it would be a far sight quicker if she didn't have to take him back to the motel later. He was afraid she would abandon him. It was a reasonable fear. She parked the car in front of his sister's home. "Turn it off," he said. She killed the engine. He took the keys from her and walked up the front steps, where he pressed a door-bell. Geneva saw a curtain flutter in one of the windows, but it might have just been a breeze or a trick of the light. He knocked. Knocked again. The door remained shut and Atul returned to the car. His hair dripped with rainwater. "She isn't home."

My ass, Geneva thought. "It's seven o'clock in the morning. Where could she be?"

"My sister works at the hospital. She often goes in early."

"I'm talking about Chandra. That girl is in there sleeping or ignoring you. You need to go in and get her."

Atul returned to the front door, knocked again, and then banged on the door with the side of his fist. The curtain moved. It was no trick of the light. Geneva got out of the car, followed Atul up the front walk.

"Atul, this is ridiculous." She reached past him and tried the door handle. The door flew open. "There—" Geneva gestured at the entryway. "—go get her. I'll just wait here in the rain."

From where she stood on the front porch, Geneva saw an overstuffed floral sofa worn thin along the arms, a shelf filled with an ungodly number of ceramic cows, and an empty brass umbrella stand. She could use an umbrella right about now.

Atul walked past the cow display and disappeared down a dark hallway. Rain fell harder now. It would get worse before it let up. She should have listened to Pisa and gone straight home. Now she'd be stuck driving in the rain, and it would take twice as long.

Chandra skulked out behind Atul. She wore a pair of baggy blue shorts and a gray T-shirt with OLE MISS scrawled across the front in red letters, a navy baseball cap pushed down low over her forehead, a pair of plastic flip-flops on her feet. This generation seemed to believe flip-flops were actual shoes and not just something you slipped on to avoid getting foot fungus at public pools. Geneva led the sorry procession back to the car, flinching at every *slap, slap, slap* of the dreadful flip-flops. Chandra slid into the backseat and sat slumped down, arms folded across her chest, jaw clenched.

Atul slid into the passenger seat. "She doesn't want to do this. Maybe we should let it go."

Geneva glanced at Chandra in the rearview mirror. "Your father says you saw a man kill someone. Is that true?"

"What do you mean, is it true? Do you think I'm a liar?"

Geneva cranked the car, pulled away from curb. She wanted to reach back and slap the girl, yank the stupid hat off her head, and tell her to sit up straight. Instead, she drove. The rain fell in large, heavy drops. Geneva turned on the windshield wipers. "Your father says you were out by the river. Which river?"

"The Tallahatchie, I think." Chandra said. "I don't know, maybe the Yazoo."

"What were you doing out there at night? It's not safe."

"I was camping," Chandra said. "I went for a hike and I got turned around and was out later than I expected."

Geneva did not believe that for a second. Chandra didn't look a bit like a girl who camped or hiked. There was nothing robust or outdoorsy about her. If anything, she looked sickly and pale. "Alone?"

"With a friend from school," Chandra said. "But I was alone when it happened."

"Where was your friend?" Atul twisted around in his seat to look at his daughter.

"See, I knew this would happen. I knew you would get mad."

Geneva turned the car onto Highway 49. She increased her speed and flew past a tractor taking up the southbound lane. She barely avoided a head-on collision with a pickup truck traveling north. The driver of the pickup laid on his horn and raised his middle finger as they passed.

Chandra screamed. "Oh my God, she's going to kill us all!"

Geneva's stomach clenched. She had a flash of the three of them dead and bleeding on the side of the highway. She thought of the storm she'd seen in Pisa's eyes and then in Atul's. She slowed down and turned the windshield wipers up a notch. The road felt slick and unsteady beneath her.

"You can tell all this to the sheriff," Geneva said. "You don't have to tell us."

"I would like to know where your friend was when all this happened," Atul said. "You told me that you were going camping with Debbie. I knew I should have met her before I let you go. I don't know anything about this girl or her family. You go to college and you come back with no hair and you wear clothes that look like they were plucked from the garbage and you don't talk to me and you disappear for days. I won't have it. I won't have a daughter of mine behaving like some common American slut."

Geneva turned off the highway. The car bounced across railroad tracks. She bit her tongue, tasted blood.

"You can't make me do anything," Chandra said. "I'm twenty years old. I'm an adult."

"You're a child," Atul said. "You are behaving like a child."

Geneva pulled into the alley behind the county jail. Three trustees stood outside smoking cigarettes. "Lock the doors." They walked past the trustees who nodded at them and blew smoke in their faces. Inside the building, Geneva shivered. She pushed her rain-soaked hair back and led Chandra and Atul down the dreary hallway to the main office. She'd spent a bit of time here when she was arrested for poisoning Bruce. She knew that the door to the left led to a dozen cells where inmates sat waiting for trial dates or transportation to a larger facility.

She told Chandra and Atul to wait for her, gesturing toward a row of plastic chairs underneath a wall full of Wanted notices. Atul sat, but Chandra stood looking nervous as a trapped rat. A deputy who looked no older than Bobby sat behind the only desk in the room. He looked up when they came in. "Wutcha nee?" The man's cheeks were bulging and he could barely speak around the wad of chewing tobacco in his mouth. He spit a brown stream into a coffee mug, and removed the wet wad from his mouth with a practiced scoop of forefinger and thumb. "What do you need?"

"I'm looking for Randall." Geneva pulled herself up tall and peered down on the insolent deputy. "Is the sheriff in?"

"Not today." The deputy shoved the tobacco back into his mouth and resumed typing on an old computer.

Geneva adjusted her skirt, just to give her hands something to do. "Can you give him a call? I need to speak with Sheriff Randall."

The deputy rolled his eyes and scooped the tobacco out of his cheek again. "If you need something, you'll have to deal with me. Otherwise, I need to finish up this paperwork."

"There's no need to be rude," Geneva told the man. "And, if you don't mind my saying so, you shouldn't be chewing tobacco if you can't even talk to people while you do it. It's a disgusting habit."

"Look, lady." He dropped the wad of tobacco onto a piece of plain white paper. A wet, brown stain bled out around it. "I'm trying to quit smoking. Up until about a month ago, I could smoke right here at this desk. Now, all of a sudden, it's a nonsmoking building. It wasn't my idea, but there you go. I don't really care for this chewing tobacco and I'll grant you I don't quite have the hang of it, but it's the one thing that is keeping me from climbing the damn walls. Can you understand that?"

"I suppose I can."

"All right, then. The sheriff's daughter is getting married this week. He's got all sorts of family in town, and he left me strict instructions not to bother him unless it's a genuine emergency. Is this a genuine emergency? 'Cause if it's not, you're gonna have to deal with me."

Geneva looked over her shoulder at Atul and Chandra. Of course it wasn't an emergency. The girl didn't even want to be here. She glowered at Geneva. Her eyes were glassy and red, her skin sallow to the point of jaundice. She looked like she'd been on a bender. Geneva turned back to the tobacco-chewing deputy. "We need to report a crime. Sheriff Randall is an old friend of mine. If he can't help me himself, I'll count on you to act on his behalf."

The deputy stared at her. She was afraid he would pop the nasty wad back in his mouth and ignore her. Instead, he stood up and offered her his hand. It was the same hand that had been digging around in his mouth since she walked through the door. "Buster Boggs."

She stared at the hand, the spit-stained forefinger a shade darker than his other fingers.

He laughed. "I don't reckon I'd shake that hand, either." He wiped the nasty digit across the thigh of his pants. "All right, tell me what the problem is."

Geneva waved Atul and Chandra over. Boggs pulled out chairs for them and settled back into his own chair behind the desk. He rested a pencil on a yellow legal pad. "What happened?"

"My daughter witnessed a murder," Atul said.

Boggs looked at Chandra. "Is that true? When did this happen?"

"Saturday night," Chandra said. "I'm not sure about the

time. Maybe ten? Maybe midnight? Near where the rivers come together."

Boggs scribbled on the legal pad. "Why didn't you come to us then?"

"I was scared."

Atul leaned forward. "We don't trust you. You did nothing when my wife was killed. You don't care about us."

"Whoa," Boggs said. "What's this about your wife?"

Geneva touched Atul's hand. "It was years ago. A car accident." She turned to Atul. "That was in Tallahatchie County. These people would not have been involved."

"Okay, okay," Boggs said. "I'm sorry about your wife, sir, but let's get back to the business at hand, so to speak." He turned to Chandra. "Why don't you walk me through what happened. Start at the beginning."

Chandra looked at her father. "I was camping with a friend."

"Friend's name?"

"Debbie," said Atul.

"I need her whole name," Boggs said. He looked at Chandra.

"I don't want to get anyone in trouble," Chandra said.

"No one's in any trouble," Boggs said. "But I am going to have to speak to everyone involved."

Chandra looked down at her lap.

"Tell him," Atul said. "What is the matter?"

"It's just that . . ." Chandra kept her head down. She spoke so softly Geneva had to lean in to hear her. "I wasn't with Debbie."

Atul stood. "What do you mean? You said you were going camping with Debbie. You told me you were with Debbie. Now you say you were not? What is the truth?"

Chandra looked up, her face pale and tear streaked. "I was with friends, but they are boys and I knew you wouldn't let me go."

Atul slapped Chandra across the face. "You filthy whore."

"You are the one who's filthy," Chandra said. "You think I don't know that you cheated on my mother with this woman?" She pointed at Geneva. "You think I don't know that she's married? That she has children?" Chandra shouted, her voice thick with anger.

"I am your father."

"Big deal. It isn't all that difficult to get someone pregnant."

"This is what you learn in college? To speak to your father like this? To spend the night with boys? I am sending you to live with your grandparents in Mumbai. You think I am strict? Wait until you spend a few months with your grandmother. You will be lucky to leave the house. You will not date. She will choose a husband for you. That is, if she can find one who will accept a woman of such loose morals."

"Atul!" Geneva touched his arm. "She's not a child. You have to let her make her own decisions. This is America."

Atul spit on the floor in front of her, a wad of stringy, yellow mucus. "That is what I think of America."

"Okay, okay." Boggs came around the desk and wiped up Atul's spit with a wad of tissue, as if cleaning up bodily fluids were something he did every day. "Let's all just calm down. Let's all just take a minute and calm down. Sir," Boggs said to Atul. "I understand that you're upset, but you can't be slapping people right here in the sheriff's office. If it happens again, I'm going to place you under arrest. Do you understand?"

Atul held his arms out, wrists together. "Arrest me. I don't know how things could be any worse. You might as well arrest me."

Boggs looked at his wad of tobacco with longing. "Why don't you go get a cup of coffee or something while I talk with your daughter? It might be easier if we could talk in private."

"I am going nowhere," Atul said.

Geneva checked her watch. "Is there a phone I could use?"

Boggs pointed to the phone on the counter at the entrance to the office. "Dial nine."

Geneva dialed the number to her house and turned her back on the three of them. She put a hand over one ear to drown out their conversation. The phone rang and rang, but no one picked up. It was just after nine in the morning. Where could Bobby and Melody be at this hour? She hung up and pretended to study the Wanted posters. Chandra had shocked her with the news that she knew about Atul and her from even before her mother had died. She wondered if Atul's wife had known about them, as well.

"That's quite a story," Boggs said. "We don't have a body. No one's been reported missing."

"But I saw it happen." Chandra pouted, crossed her arms like a spoiled child.

"All I'm saying is that it would be a hell of a lot easier for me to investigate if I actually had a victim, or if I knew where to look for one. The details seem a little fuzzy."

"I was scared," Chandra said. "I just ran away. I didn't have a map. I didn't check my watch."

Boggs leaned forward, folded his hands on top of the legal pad. "Now, I'm not insinuating anything, but I need you to be honest with me. Were you all using any illegal substances?"

Atul exploded. "We are not going to sit here and be insulted. I cannot believe you accuse my daughter of doing drugs. You do not have a body, so she must have been on drugs? Is that it?"

"Look, mister, I'm just asking her the same questions we would ask anyone under these circumstances. Now, we've had no reports of a murder, and no one has reported anyone missing, but in the past two weeks, we've had a real significant increase in burglaries and vandalism. We've had boxes of cold medicine swiped from local pharmacies. A woman was raped and beaten on Saturday evening, the same night this alleged murder took place, and not too damn far from the river where your daughter thinks she might have witnessed this murder. We didn't find any body, but we did find a good supply of marijuana and what looks like the start of a big batch of methamphetamine in an abandoned camper out by the river. And the description we got from our rape victim matches the one your daughter just gave us of her friend. So I'm not accusing anyone of anything. I'm just trying to get to the truth."

Geneva watched Chandra and knew that Boggs had hit

on something. She was lying, either for her father's sake or to protect herself. Whatever she'd learned in her first year of college, it wasn't going to be enough to pull one over on Deputy Buster Boggs. Geneva had underestimated him; he was sharp as a blade.

"Atul," Geneva said. "I really think it would be better if you let Chandra talk to the deputy alone. You're making her nervous."

"I know what I saw," Chandra said. "That man cut Reese's throat. He did it right in front of his kid, right in front of that little boy."

Geneva coughed. She felt like she'd swallowed a jagged shard of ice. How many men traveled around with little boys? Hadn't Pisa said there was trouble? Geneva realized she might be harboring the criminal on her land, and she still hadn't reached Melody to warn her about Pisa's son. This was what happened when she ignored Pisa's advice. After all these years, she ought to know better.

"I believe a private conversation is what's called for," Boggs said.

Geneva wished she'd never brought Atul and Chandra here. What would Pisa do to her if she put her son in danger? What could she do? Geneva could never figure out just how powerful Pisa really was. Were her gifts mostly about predicting the future, or did she actually set things in motion? And what about her son? Was there really just a bit of trouble, or was her son a murderer? Not that murder wasn't sometimes justified. Geneva knew good and well that some people needed killing. She didn't trust Chandra. The girl could hardly open her mouth without lying. Any boy she was running with was bound to be trouble.

"I have to leave soon," she told Boggs. "We'll just get a cup of coffee, give you a bit of space."

"That'll do. Give us a half hour or so."

As they left, a shrill alarm buzzed through a gadget on Boggs's desk. He punched a button and the noise quieted. "Weather alert," he said. "Big storm moving in."

In the alley, the trustees were gone. Rain came down in sheets. A big storm, indeed. "I wonder if I have an umbrella in the car?"

"What difference would it make?" Atul said. "Water is not the enemy." He sulked, furious at Geneva for taking him away from his daughter.

She drove into the rain, navigating the half mile to the bakery by memory as much as by sight. It was the same place she'd met her lawyer after she poisoned Bruce. Her windshield wipers slapped furiously without improving her visibility an ounce. She gripped the steering wheel and leaned forward, tried to bring the road into focus. All she saw was a wet, gray scrim of rain and sky. The car seemed to be skimming along a river rather than rolling along the road. This was not Geneva's first flood. She doubted it would be her last.

"You came to me in a storm like this," Atul said.

She remembered. Thirteen years ago, she'd seen Pisa and was heading home when the rain began to fall. She pulled into the Jolly Inn to wait it out. Atul was there alone, his wife and daughter off visiting relatives. When she entered the lobby, soaked and shivering, Atul made her sit, wrapped her in a large, clean sheet, and brought her a cup of tea spiced with ginger and cloves. She told him she only needed to rest for a few hours, to wait for the storm to let up. He gave her the key to a room. "You must shower and put on dry clothes. You will be sick if you do not."

"Oh, I don't want to be any trouble," she'd said, though she enjoyed the fuss he was making.

"This storm is not going to let up today. You cannot continue on in this weather. You will shower and put on dry clothes and then eat with me. I am all alone here, and there will be no customers today. Not unless there are other mad women driving around in the rain."

They stayed up late, talking and playing blackjack. She wore his wife's clothes while hers dried. She hadn't set out to seduce him, but the storm kept raging and he kept bringing her good things to eat and drink. What was she supposed to do? She stayed for three days. "You will come back to me," Atul said when she left him that first time.

Bruce had said he could smell Atul on her. Maybe he could. They fought. Bruce demanded to know his name, but Geneva denied, denied, denied. She taunted him. In a fit of fury, Bruce flung her mother's antique water pitcher. He aimed to hit her, but she ducked and the crystal shattered against the wall. It rained down in sharp, dangerous shards that matched her mood. "You'll regret that, darling," she told him. "Just wait and see."

A few weeks later, she fetched what she needed from her father's old shed. The smell was the same as it had been all those years before, sharp and sour and raw. She put a spoonful of rat poison into her mixing bowl and whipped up a batch of Bruce's favorite cookies, oatmeal with butterscotch and chocolate chips. She made a clean batch for the kids. "These are for you," she told Bobby and Melody. "But these are just for Daddy." Bruce gobbled the cookies. He had no knack for moderation.

It was nearly a day before the sickness set in. Geneva worried that she hadn't used enough, or that the poison was too old to be effective. But just as she'd given up watching him, his nose started bleeding. His gums leeched pink onto his toothbrush. His piss splashed rust-colored into the toilet. "I'm dying of thirst," he told her. "I'm too tired to move." He begged Geneva to take him to a doctor. How could she refuse? Urine samples, blood samples, too many questions. The doctor had seen it all before. Rat poison was common and people were careless, he said. He shot Bruce full of vitamin K and prescribed activated charcoal to absorb any remaining poison in his system. The law required that he lecture Bruce about wearing gloves, washing his hands, keeping children and animals away from treated areas. All the while, Geneva stood in the corner of the room, waiting like a hawk on a branch. She watched Bruce's face, so full of frustration as he insisted he hadn't touched any rat poison.

It took him longer than it should have to work it out. God knows, she didn't marry him for his smarts. He was running down a list of everything he'd done in the past forty-eight hours. When he got to the cookies, he fell silent. He stared at Geneva. She stared right back at him. "You did it," he said. "You tried to kill me."

"You broke my water pitcher," she told him.

The doctor called the sheriff, though Bruce told him not to bother. He said he would handle it himself. Geneva had been grateful to be led away in handcuffs. Better to be locked up than to go home with Bruce at that moment.

She'd spent a few bleak months in a mental hospital where no one, as far as she could tell, was actually crazy. It was a dumping ground for folks who couldn't conform, and Geneva knew she was not a misfit in the dingy gray hallways of the hospital. Even so, she had no intention of going back. By the time she came home, plump and slow from the drugs, Bruce had forgiven her. Or maybe he'd just remembered what she was capable of doing when pushed too far. Either way, she came and went as she pleased, and saw Atul as often as she wanted. Now it seemed her brazen betrayals might catch up with her. Pisa had warned her about consequences. "The universe will find balance. Wrong will be set right."

She pulled the car into the bakery parking lot and watched the rain fall. Was the universe seeking balance by punishing her now? As she sat there in a parking lot in the middle of a storm, things were happening beyond her control. Chandra was telling her story to Deputy Boggs, Pisa's son was camped out on her land, her daughter was home after three years on the road, her son was alive but not well, her husband was dying, her lover sulked. If she could go back and start over, she'd listen to Pisa. Yes, she would. Now she had to push forward. She had to see it through.

Chapter Sixteen

Melody was dead tired but slept badly. She dreamed she was being hunted by a pack of hungry wolves. To protect herself, she tossed small children to the growling beasts. She woke before dawn in a sweaty nightmare panic. At least she wouldn't have to lie there and pretend to sleep, as she did on the road. Even in good times, Melody slept poorly, suffered from hellish dreams, and woke before sunrise. When she was sharing a tour bus or cheap hotel room with her bandmates, she couldn't just get up and get on with her day. Now, in her family home, she was free to roam at all hours. Everyone in her family woke early, and it was normal to find one or all of them prowling around the house before daylight.

She decided to make good use of the time by searching for clues of her mother's whereabouts. In her parents' bedroom, she pulled everything she could find from the closet and chest of drawers. She piled it all on the bed and sat cross-legged in a mess of dusty boxes and old photo albums. The first box, an old cardboard boot box, overflowed with yellow newspaper clippings, nearly all of them featuring

Melody's mother wearing some sort of fancy white dress and, often, a tiara. She was the Maid of Cotton, Miss Junior Miss, Miss White Forest Senior Year, homecoming queen, prom queen, and, of course, a young bride. All of it just reinforced Melody's belief that beauty was more important than substance to most people. How else could her mother, selfish and crazy as a loon, have ever become so popular? Melody moved on to a huge album. A spider skittered out from between the pages, and she brushed it off the bed with a shudder. The book was filled with photographs. Melody flipped through the snapshots. Familiar scenes flooded the pages: her father holding a big catfish, her mother laughing at something off camera, Bobby as a toddler, Melody as a teen. She didn't want familiar scenes from the past; she wanted something that would lead her to her mother today. In the past, Melody was too timid or too young or too awed by her mother to tell her how she felt. Not anymore. Now she couldn't wait to find her mother and tell her that she was selfish, insane, and mean as a snake. Someone had to say it.

She heaved the album aside and pulled out a small box. It was a child's keepsake box, with a slot for a key. She pried it open without much force. A lemony scent filled the room, and a few bits of brown and green flecked out onto the quilt, a dried plant from an old corsage or a clipping from the wishing bushes out back. Mama had brought the wishing bushes back after an unexplained disappearance. She never told Melody or Bobby where the bushes had come from, just that they should plant them and make a wish. She'd disappeared a dozen times over the years, always without notice and never with an explanation. Once, just once, she took Melody along.

At ten years old, Melody was awkward and miserable. Melody did not yet know that most ten-year-old girls were awkward and miserable; she imagined she was unique. She spent the first week of summer vacation sulking because her best friend, her only friend, abandoned her for a group of girls who specialized in whispered insults, haughty superiority, and cruel giggling. One girl, the leader, had a grating, nasally voice that carried even at a whisper. "Gawd," the little brat would say when Melody climbed from the bus in the morning. "Is *that* whatcher wearing today?" Or, as Melody shuffled through the cafeteria line, "Y'all know I'm not one to judge, but if I was to get fat, I don't reckon I'd help myself to a piece of cake. That's just me." While Melody was glad to be done with school for a few months because it meant a break from the relentless cruelty, she was already dreading the next year. Summer offered her no opportunity to make things right or make new friends. Melody's family lived so far out of town that summer meant three months of isolation. While other kids went swimming and ate snow cones and played baseball, Melody was stuck out on her mother's useless land. She spent the last week of the school year plotting ways to set things right, but then she heard her former best friend whisper "white trash" when she walked into math class. She was doomed and she planned to spend the summer sulking. Her mother told Melody she had no intention of spending her days with a mopey, depressed, ungrateful child. Melody imagined her mother had spent her own youth surrounded by friends who couldn't get enough of her great beauty. How could she understand what it felt like to be plain and unpopular?

One early morning, her mother woke her and said they were going away for a few days. Melody, still half-asleep, asked a few questions and tried to pack a bag, but Mama pushed her into the car while the sun was barely beginning to peek over the horizon. "We're going to see someone," Mama said. "Someone who might be able to help you."

She drove Melody to a house that seemed to stand alone at the edge of the world. The house was surrounded by cottonwoods and live oaks. The trees sparkled, prisms and bright blue bottles hung from the branches. Women appeared and disappeared, and Melody couldn't tell them apart. They wore loose cotton dresses and no makeup. Melody thought they seemed exotic. There were no men. A couple of the women tended a plot of fragrant herbs and flowers that seemed to pulse with butterflies and ruby-throated hummingbirds.

Mama spoke with one of the women while Melody stood underneath a tree, picking at a scab on her right knee. It was a habit Mama deplored, but it took her mind off the fact that she needed to pee. They had left so quickly she hadn't gone before getting into the car, and now, in this strange place, she didn't want to ask. The woman her mother spoke with approached Melody. Melody stopped picking at her scab and stood up straight. "You are having some trouble with your friends?"

Melody looked at her mother, who nodded. "They aren't my friends. They're mean." Melody pulled at the hem of her T-shirt, bit her lower lip, shifted from foot to foot. "Well, one of them *was* my friend. I don't think she is now."

"Friends come and go," the woman said. "But you are stuck with yourself."

Melody hiccuped, but refused to cry, even though it seemed an awful and cruel thing to say.

"Your mother is going to take you to meet someone. She will help you, but only if you want help, only if you trust her, only if you really believe."

Melody had no idea what the woman was talking about, but she nodded.

"Good girl," the woman said.

The woman took her inside the house and instructed her to change into a dress that was laid across an old ladder-back wooden chair. Melody slipped the cotton sheath over her head and rubbed her hands across the fabric, feeling the soft, vibrant warmth of the dress. It smelled of sage and cinnamon. The room where she changed was small, and the only door led back out to the hallway and the woman. She knew there must a bathroom somewhere in the house, but she didn't get a chance to ask. Mama emerged wearing a similar dress and led her back outside.

"We'll forgo the ceremony," the woman said. "She is still too young."

Her mother seemed disappointed, but didn't argue. They followed the woman across the open field, and Melody's opportunity to ask for a restroom vanished. They walked for hours. The sun shifted positions in the sky above them, tracing an arc of brightness that seared her skin and left her dizzy. Prickly grass and hard-packed dirt scraped against the soles of her bare feet. A swarm of chiggers attacked as she trod through a patch of overgrown weeds, leaving behind itchy red welts. Melody scratched her ankles until they bled, but neither Mama nor the strange woman seemed to care. By the time they reached the little house with the wrap-around porch, Melody was desperate. Her face and shoulders were singed a bright pink and her tongue felt thick and useless inside her mouth. Her bladder felt ready to explode.

"Here we are." The woman's voice was bright and song-like, as if she'd just awakened from a refreshing nap. Melody shivered despite the heat. She followed the woman up the front steps, carefully placing her feet in the very center of each wooden board. Her legs felt limp and unreliable. The world shifted like a reflection in pond water. Her brain felt swollen inside her skull.

Another woman appeared beside the first woman, or maybe she was just seeing double. No, this new woman was shorter, with dark hair that she wore in a long braid down her back. Her face was like the bark of a tree worn smooth by harsh weather. Her hands were surprisingly soft and gentle as she stroked Melody's hair.

When the woman touched her, Melody floated toward the woman's soft, generous bosom. She fell gently forward as a warm pool of liquid spread between her legs and the world went dark.

Even in the darkness, she was aware of things happening. The women rushed around her. One of them held a bundle of fresh-smelling leaves under her nose. Another fanned her face. Melody smelled something ripe and gamey. The scent grew stronger and something moist swiped across her face. A tongue? She opened her eyes and saw a gray coyote slinking out the back door. By the time she was fully awake, only the women remained. Mama was angry and demanded she apologize. The women said everything was fine. Melody had ruined something important, though she hadn't understood what. Later, when Melody was back in her own clothes and seated beside Mama for the drive home, she tried to ask about the coyote.

"That's ridiculous," Mama said.

"I saw him," Melody insisted.

"I'm humiliated enough. Don't start making up stories."

Melody didn't mention the coyote again, but the next year when the girls teased her or ignored her or made hateful comments, she summoned the memory of the coyote and she felt stronger. She'd not thought of the coyote in many years, but the memory of his scent came back to her now in this box of her mother's things. She missed him.

She pulled a manila envelope from under the box with the herbs. Unlike most of the junk in her mother's room, the envelope was new and not covered in dust. Inside was a handful of newspaper and magazine clippings, clippings that weren't yellow with age. There was a picture of Melody with the band in an advertisement for a concert in Fort Lauderdale. There was a calendar listing from Nashville, a short article about a festival in Chattanooga. There were a few photocopies of flyers and promotional materials. Her mother had gone to some trouble to gather these clips, Melody knew. "Well, fuck you," she said aloud. She knew she should be happy to find evidence that her mother cared about her life, but the pile of clippings just fueled her anger.

It was typical of her mother to stuff all evidence that she cared into an envelope stashed in the back of a closet. Melody crumpled the papers and photos into a wad and tossed them across the room. She wasn't going to find anything. If she wanted to confront her mother, she'd have to wait for her mother to return. As always, her mother was in charge.

Rain clattered against the roof, sporadic and then more steadily. There was no real sunrise, just a bare lifting of darkness. Melody blew her nose, left the dirty tissue on her mother's bed, and went downstairs to check on her father. His sheets needed changing, as did his pajamas. He blinked at her, helpless and ashamed. She slid a fresh pillow beneath his head and began the process of stripping and cleaning him. It was amazing how quickly she'd become used to seeing her father in a state of naked humiliation.

"Daddy, where is Mama?"

"Wherever she wants to be." He laughed and his body spasmed. She tossed aside his pajamas, soaked through with sweat.

"You're her husband. I wouldn't let my husband just disappear."

"You don't know what you'll do, little girl. I'm not so easy to live with. She needs some space."

Melody shook her head. "She's a terrible wife. It isn't right." She ran a wet cloth over his body.

"Everything is not right and wrong, little girl. You're old enough to know that now."

"She shouldn't leave you here when you need her. She shouldn't leave you when you're, when you're . . ." She trailed off.

"Dying. It's okay, little girl. You can say it. I'm dying."
He grimaced. "One thing I know about your mother, you
sure as hell don't want to force her to be somewhere or to
do something she doesn't want to do. Bad things happen
when Genie is unhappy."

Bad things happen no matter what, Melody thought.
"Let me massage your legs, Daddy. Then I'll get you some
breakfast."

"I don't want those awful drinks anymore. Bring me a
shot of whiskey. Bring me a goddamned bottle of whiskey."
His laugh turned to a cough.

"Your whiskey days are behind you, old man."

"Don't worry about your mother, little girl. She'll be
home. This is her land. She's never let me forget that." He
closed his eyes. "It'll be your land when she's gone."

"Dear God, I don't want it." Melody piled the soiled
clothing in a plastic bin. "What on earth would I do with
it? Anyway, Mama's too mean to die."

"Don't talk that way about your mother."

"I don't know why you defend her." She pulled one of
the humiliating adult diapers onto her father.

"Neither do I, little girl. Neither do I." He grinned at
her. "Where do we stand on that whiskey? Would you deny
a dying man a little pleasure?"

"Yes. Yes, I would." She massaged his legs, careful not
to bruise the fragile skin. She rubbed cream around his
knees and ankles the way Maurice showed her. The phone
rang.

"Bobby!" she called out. "Will you get that, please?"
Bobby didn't respond. She didn't know if he was still sleep-

ing or already out roaming the land. "Well, they'll just have to wait." If it was her mother, Melody thought, it would do her good to wonder where they were.

By the time she finished dressing her father, she was sweating. The rainy morning made even the interior of the house more humid than usual. She brought Daddy one of the new shakes from the refrigerator, along with a straw. "Strawberry, this morning. These are supposed to taste better." She propped another pillow underneath his head, helped him sit up. He took a sip, made a face, and pushed the can away. She pushed it back. "No. You have to drink it, Daddy."

He glared at her and turned the entire can upside down. The thick, sticky, pink liquid splashed on the blanket and spread over his clean pajamas.

"Damn it, Daddy!" She grabbed the can. Her head ached, and the smell of the drink made her nauseated. "I'm not dealing with this right now. You can sit there with your breakfast in your lap."

He whimpered pitifully, but Melody ignored him. She gathered the bin of soiled clothes and sheets. "I'll have to do twice the laundry now. Is that what you want?"

"I want," her father said. "I want."

"I want, too," she snapped. "I want plenty."

Melody found Bobby on the back porch. She stepped out into a puddle and noticed that the porch roof was leaking in several spots. "Didn't you hear the phone ringing? Why didn't you answer it?"

"Checking on the boy," Bobby said.

Melody had forgotten about the man and the little boy Bobby mentioned the night before.

"The man came to look at us," Bobby said.

"What do you mean?" Melody peered out into the rainy morning.

"He was looking at us," Bobby said. "Just the man, not the little boy."

"He came here?" Was the man planning to rob them? Or something worse? "That's it. I'm calling the sheriff. We can't have strange men prowling around while we sleep. And no one should have a kid outside in this weather."

"Maurice said he'd talk to them. He said we should wait."

"Maurice is not a part of this family." She regretted how harsh she sounded, but she couldn't seem to summon any patience. "If this man robs us blind, Maurice won't care. If he breaks in and murders us while we sleep, Maurice won't give a damn."

"He will, too!" Bobby yelled.

Melody stepped back, surprised by his anger.

"He would," Bobby said. "Know don't you, know don't you. You don't know him."

"I'm calling the sheriff." She ducked into the kitchen and let the screen door slam. A labored rattling sound came from the living room and she knew her father had pulled out his oxygen tube again. "Don't you dare do that to me right now!" she yelled. "I won't put up with it." She listened until his breathing leveled out, then picked up the phone.

A man answered on the third ring. "Sheriff's office."

"Hello. Is Sheriff Randall available?"

"Nope. He's not in. Can I help you?"

Melody chewed her ragged thumbnail. She had hoped to speak to Sheriff Randall. "Can I leave a message for him?"

"Yep," the voice said. "You sure can, but he won't get it until next week. If this is urgent, you'll want to deal with me. If it's an emergency, you should call 911."

Melody considered her options, but the man on the line kept talking. "Look, I'm here all alone and I'm taking a statement right now, so if I can help with something, let me know. Is there a crime in progress?" He sounded impatient.

"It isn't an emergency," Melody said. "I can call back later."

"Much obliged," the man said.

Melody heard the front door open and went out to greet Maurice. He slipped off his wet shoes. She pulled the blanket from the bed. "I was just about to strip this bed. Daddy spilled his shake this morning."

"It's really coming down out there." Maurice draped a rain jacket over a chair near the door. "I'll take care of the bed. It isn't the first time," Maurice said. "There's a guy outside. Says he's a friend of yours."

Melody left the bedclothes and went to the door. She stuck her head out and saw Chris, grinning and holding up a white paper bag. "I brought cinnamon rolls. There's this bakery just off the highway that makes the best cinnamon rolls you ever tasted. A woman at the motel told me about it. People around here are so nice."

Melody knew the bakery he was talking about. She'd gone to school with the owner's son. The boy was not nice at all. He was a bully and a thief, but even he knew how to say "please" and "thank you" and "yes, ma'am" and "no, sir." People often made the mistake of confusing good manners with kindness. "I figured you'd be home by now."

Chris waggled the greasy paper sack. "I'm getting soaked out here."

A rumble of thunder traveled across the sky. "You're going to want to get on the road before the storm hits."

"I think it's a bit late for that."

"This is nothing," she said. "You wait and see. The roads will flood and you'll be stuck."

Chris cocked his head and lifted up the white paper bag like an offering.

She sighed. "Fine. I was just about to make coffee. She strode past Maurice and Daddy without a word. In the kitchen, she measured out coffee and ran water into the pot. "It's gonna come a flood. You don't want to be here when the water rises, I promise you that."

"I talked to the general manager at the radio station this morning," Chris told her. He set the bag of cinnamon rolls on the table.

"Are you getting your job back?"

"I don't need that job. God has a different plan for us."

"There is no 'us,' Chris. Get that straight."

Chris opened the bag, and the scent of cinnamon mingled with the brewing coffee. Melody pulled out a clean plate and set it on the table.

"The FCC is investigating your profanity. Well, the station's airing of your profanity. They may fine the station. They may fine the band." Chris placed the cinnamon rolls on the plate. "Of course, it might not amount to anything. Hard to tell."

The coffeemaker hissed. Melody pulled a mug from the cabinet and poured a half cup before the pot was done brewing. She sipped the warm bitterness, sat down at the kitchen table, and looked at Chris. "How much?"

"Could be a few thousand, could be ten thousand. I don't think it would be more than that."

Once again, Melody regretted squandering three years of her life traipsing around with a terrible band. She had no marketable skills and meager savings. It would not take much to leave her flat broke. She refilled her mug and filled one for Chris. "Why are you telling me this? I can't do a thing about it." She pulled a pint of cream from the fridge and set it on the table.

Chris started in again with his speech from the night before, his plea about Melody's potential solo career, her voice, her talent, her story. She held up her hand to cut him off, but he kept right on talking. He told her his friend in Memphis could record a demo next week. "We're ready," he said.

"Well I'm not ready," Melody said. "I've got my hands full here."

Chris wouldn't listen. He kept talking, spouting more nonsense about redemption and forgiveness. Melody was stunned that anyone could be so dense. When she couldn't stand another second of his babble, she slammed her hands down on the table between them. "Chris!" She shouted to be heard. "You're not listening to me. I can't drop everything and go to Memphis. Even if I could, I don't have enough songs to record an album."

He sat back and smiled as if she'd agreed with him about something. "We'll record what you have, and you'll write some more."

"Writing a song isn't like scribbling down a shopping list."

"So we'll hire some writers, option songs from other musicians."

"I can't think about this right now," Melody said. "Daddy is so sick. He's dying."

"But you have to think about it now," Chris said. "Soon it will be too late."

"Too late for what?"

Chris leaned forward. "I'm working on a series for a new cable channel. A Christian channel. We'll profile people who were down and out until they turned away from sin and found redemption. I call it *Salvation Hour.* What do you think?"

She thought it sounded dreadful. Melody wasn't so desperate that she would look for evidence of miracles on cable television, and she doubted anyone else would, either. "I don't need salvation."

"Everyone needs to be saved."

"I don't." She bit into a cinnamon roll, and the gooey, sweet dough filled her mouth. She swallowed, but a film of grease and sugar remained on her tongue. "I hate television, all that noise and nonsense. I hate those TV preachers most of all."

"If Noah were alive today, he would spread the word of the flood by using the airwaves. Moses would broadcast the Ten Commandments to the masses. It's our duty as Christians to share the gospel."

"That's not my duty." She pushed the cinnamon roll away.

"Melody, I need you. Some of these people we want to feature don't look so great. Bad teeth, bad skin, bad hair. It would be fine for radio, but this is television. I need a few people who are camera-ready. The audience will love you."

Melody, sitting there in the same faded T-shirt and shorts she'd worn yesterday, now splattered with her father's nutrition shake and dusted with cinnamon sugar, did not feel camera-ready. "You're not listening to me, Chris. I haven't been redeemed. This isn't some story you get to write for me. I have no faith. If God exists, and I'm not saying he does, I don't like him very much. He seems like an asshole."

"You don't mean that."

"Daddy is in pain. Mama abandoned us. My brother was destroyed by the church. God hasn't done a damn thing about any of it."

Chris kneeled beside Melody, put his arm around her. "God wants your life to be a testament to his grace, but you have to ask for it. 'Remember the Lord your God, for it is he who is giving you the power to make wealth.'"

Melody pushed him away, stood and paced across the kitchen. "The only people getting wealthy off God are the preachers. They get richer and we get poorer."

"Wealth isn't always about money," Chris said.

Melody snorted. "Wealth is always about money to

the goddamned preachers." She rinsed her coffee mug and stared out the window at the rain. She filled a clean mug with coffee and took it out to Maurice. She felt desperate to escape Chris's fervent pleading.

She set the coffee on the bedside table and gathered up the soiled sheets. "I'll start another load of laundry," she said to Maurice. She tilted her head at the mug of coffee. "Do you want cream or sugar? I wasn't sure how you liked it."

"This is fine," Maurice said. "Thank you."

"He hasn't eaten anything," she said. "I tried to get him to drink one of the shakes, but he wouldn't. He just dumped it out all over the bed."

"Mr. Mahaffey," Maurice said. "Is that true? Are you refusing to eat?"

Daddy's hands flailed up, as if he were trying to shoo Maurice away.

"Can't we give him real food? What harm would it do to give him something that tastes good?"

"He won't keep it down," Maurice said. "That's why we started the shakes in the first place. His stomach can't handle it."

"Then do something else. Put in one of those feeding tubes."

"I'm right here," her father barked. "Don't talk about me like I'm not here. I can hear every goddamned word you say. No tubes. I don't want you sticking one more thing in my body."

"Calm down, Mr. Mahaffey. No one's inserting a feeding tube. We talked about this, remember?"

"Well, I didn't talk about it," Melody said.

"Why don't you bring him a glass of water?" Maurice prepped one of his needles. "I'm going to give him a little extra medicine for the pain."

"What exactly are you giving him?"

"Morphine." He might as well have said "cranberry juice" for all the inflection in his voice.

"Don't people get addicted to that?"

"Yes," Maurice said. "People do."

"Well, aren't you worried about that? Daddy, aren't you worried about it?"

Maurice plunged the needle into her father's thigh. He made a note in a small notebook he kept by her father's bed and discarded the needle into a red plastic box with a locking lid. "I'm not worried about it," Maurice said. "How about that water?"

"What if I'm worried about it? Does anyone care what I think?"

"Look." Maurice lowered his voice and stood close to her. "It doesn't matter. Can't you see that? He isn't going to turn into a junkie. He isn't going to be here long enough for that."

"But . . ." Melody wanted to say something sharp and hurtful, but there was no point. Maurice was right.

"I'm sorry," Maurice said. "I know it's difficult."

Right then Melody wished she believed in something. It would be a relief to be one of those people who could just pray and feel better. Melody was tired of feeling hopeless and alone and pissed off at the world.

Chris came into the room, holding a glass of water. "I couldn't help overhearing." He handed the glass to Maurice.

"We should take turns praying for your father so he is constantly being lifted up. It might help his pain, bring some comfort."

Melody glared at him, but it was too late.

"Little girl, if I sniff anyone praying over me, I won't be the only one dying in this house."

"No one's praying, Daddy." She turned to Chris. "What are you doing?"

"I'm trying to help."

"Get this praying asshole out of my house! Now!"

"Calm down, Daddy. No one's praying." Melody pushed Chris back into the kitchen. "What is wrong with you? What in God's name are you trying to do to me?"

Chris stumbled. "I offered to pray. Is that such a terrible thing? Isn't that what God asks of us?"

"You have to go," she said "You have to leave right now."

"God knows you are suffering. He'll forgive your faithlessness."

She pulled a glass from the kitchen cabinet, filled it with tap water, and drank it down. She filled it again. Her hands shook.

"I can help," Chris said.

"I don't want your help. I don't want your prayers. I don't want your God. It's all a lie."

"A lie? When your father dies, do you really believe he'll turn to dust? Do you believe that's all there is?"

Melody hurled the water glass at him. He ducked and the glass shattered on the floor behind him. "Get out!" she yelled. "Get out of my house!"

Chris inched his way toward the door. "You don't know

what you're saying. You'll come around." He stepped out into the rain, and Melody slammed the door behind him.

Maurice stepped into the kitchen. He looked sheepish, and she knew he'd overheard everything. "Your father's sleeping. I'm going to go find Bobby."

"You know, it's not your job to take care of Bobby," Melody said.

"I'm worried about him out in this storm." He left by the back door and disappeared into the rain.

Melody stared out the back window, but there was nothing to see. Everything was gray and wet and dark. When the phone rang, she jumped. She grabbed it before it could ring again and wake her father. "Hello?"

"I'm calling for Geneva Mahaffey. Is she available?" It was a man's voice, somehow familiar, though Melody wasn't sure why.

"No, she most certainly is not available. May I ask who is calling?"

"Yep. Deputy Buster Boggs with the Muskogee County Sheriff's Department. Mrs. Mahaffey was in earlier with Mr. Nair. They were supposed to return and pick up Mr. Nair's daughter an hour ago."

Melody realized this was the same man she spoke with earlier when she'd tried to call Sheriff Randall.

"Mama hasn't been home today," Melody said. "I don't know any of the other people you just mentioned."

"I'm afraid they might be stuck somewhere. We've got a hell of a flood coming in, and I don't reckon anyone should be out driving in this."

"About that," Melody said. "We're out off of County

Road 240 and the water is rising pretty quickly. My brother said there was a man and a small boy out camping on our land last night. I'm worried about a child out in this storm."

"A man with a small boy, huh?"

"Yessir."

"Did your brother describe the man? Can I talk to your brother?"

Melody stretched the phone cord to look out the kitchen window. All she could see was water, falling from the sky and rising up from the ground. A crack of thunder shook the house. The kitchen lights flickered and died. "Our electricity just went out." She was grateful her parents still had an old-fashioned phone with a cord and no plug.

"Yep, it's out all over the county," the man said. "You gonna be okay?"

"I'm sure I'll be fine." She thought of her father, alone in the dark. "I should go now."

"Listen, if you hear from your mother, tell her to sit tight. Tell her that Miss Nair is fine here until the storm blows over. No need to take any chances."

"Sure." Melody didn't believe she would hear from her mother.

"And, ma'am, that man with the little boy might be dangerous. Don't confront him."

Melody wondered if Bobby was outside confronting him right now. "What do you mean, dangerous?"

"Don't know anything for sure," he said. "Just keep your distance."

She stared at the back door and willed Maurice and

Bobby to come through it. "Mr. Boggs? Are you still there?"

"Right here." The man's voice sounded garbled, as if he were chewing something.

"If you do talk to my mother, would you tell her that we're doing just fine without her? Tell her we don't need her here."

She heard a strange wet sound on the other side of the line. "I reckon I can do that."

"Thank you." Melody hung up the phone. She didn't know who Mr. Nair and his daughter were, but Mama had obviously chosen them over her own family.

She found a bundle of old candles in the dining room and a book of matches. She took one of the tapers and an old crystal candlestick holder out to the living room. Daddy moaned and said her name. His chest rattled. He coughed. He gasped.

"Did I wake you? I'm sorry. We lost the electricity." Melody placed the candle atop the piano and lit it. The soft light was comforting. "Flood's coming in."

Daddy's face was gray and his eyes wobbled. He grasped at her. Something was wrong; something was missing. Daddy wheezed and rattled, but the oxygen tank was silent. She stared at the big silver contraption with its clear tubes leading to Daddy's nose and its big black cord plugged into the wall outlet. No electricity, no oxygen. "Oh, Daddy. . . . Just hang on."

There was a portable tank next to the larger electric tank, but she didn't know how to use it. She had to find Maurice. "Try to relax, Daddy. Don't panic."

"Genie," he croaked.

"Don't talk, Daddy. Save your energy."

"Genie." His voice was barely a whisper.

"Mama will come home, you'll see." She ran to the back door to look for Maurice. She hoped she could find him before her father stopped breathing.

Chapter Seventeen

Obi crept through the rising water. The boy he'd seen in the window was hiding behind a tree, spying on Liam. Rain ran down around them, but the boy didn't seem to mind the wet. Obi was soaked. He'd put Liam in the car and gone out to gather firewood, which he carried now wrapped in a tarp for later. When the rain let up, they'd want dry wood and kindling for a fire. Now he wanted the boy behind the tree to go away. What could he be doing, out in this storm and so far from the house? The boy stood between Obi and his son. It was a bad place to stand. Obi stopped and watched the boy, tried to read his stance and his intentions. He was up to no good; Obi was sure about that. People who lived inside stayed inside when the weather turned bad.

Obi's rifle was slung across his back. He set the bundle of wood down in the rushing water and felt the future warmth it could bring wash away. He moved forward. Water swirled around his legs. It was rising fast. When he was about six feet away from the boy, he saw the car driving toward them. It was not the kind of car that anyone should be driving through several feet of rushing water on a dirt path to nowhere. Obi's first thought was that the cops were coming for him, but it wasn't a police car, not even an unmarked police car. It was a cheap subcompact swerving wildly. If the driver didn't slow down, he'd end up in the creek or wrapped around a tree. Then Obi saw the other option, the more likely option; the car was careening toward his car, and toward his son.

Obi sprinted past the boy behind the tree, who was now waving his arms and shouting. The car skidded and bobbed violently along the surface of the water. It happened during floods. Drivers braked when they shouldn't, turned too quickly, or panicked and gave everything to the strong pull of the currents. Obi yanked open the passenger-side door of his mother's car and pulled Liam into his arms. He ran, his son cradled against his chest, toward the spot where he'd first seen the spinning car appear, because one thing was certain: The car was moving forward fast and it wasn't going to turn back.

Liam wrapped his legs around Obi's waist and held tight to his neck. Obi galloped through the water, racing to put as much distance as possible between his son and the careening vehicle. Liam thought it was a game. "Go, Daddy!" he yelled. Behind Obi, there was a sickening crunch of metal followed by a crack of thunder. Someone screamed. Obi turned to look. The car had crashed smack into the passenger side, where Liam had sat just moments before. Obi stared at the point of impact, and even though Liam was in his arms, he pictured his son in the car, pictured him mangled in the horrible wreckage. His only job was to keep Liam safe. Again and again, he came so close to failing.

The driver of the wrecked car stumbled out, fell on his face into the water, scrambled to his feet, and fell again. A bright gash of blood poured down his face, one spot of color in the gray world. Obi hesitated, not wanting to get mixed up with this man, or with the boy behind the tree, or with anyone, but Liam was more compassionate. "He's hurt. Help him, Daddy."

Obi walked toward the man. He kept one arm around Liam and used the other to pull his gun around. He didn't point it at the man, but he kept his hand on the barrel. The cool metal felt like security. The man stared up at Obi, his eyes glassy and frightened. The cut on his head poured blood across his face, lending him a savage look. Obi suspected the man could do with some stitches.

"Are you okay?" Obi asked.

The man stared up at him. "Am I okay?"

"Can you walk?"

The man struggled to his feet. He wobbled but remained standing.

"Do you live here?" Obi asked. "I think you should go back to the house, call a doctor."

The man shook his head and then winced as if the motion pained him. "I was leaving, trying to leave. The roads—oh, they're terrible."

"You shouldn't be driving in this weather," Obi said.

"I turned back, but I couldn't see. I guess I missed the driveway. I don't know what happened." The man slumped down to the ground again. "I'm very tired."

Obi released his grip on the rifle. "Listen." He dragged the man up to a standing position, keeping his other arm around Liam. "You've got a bad gash on your head. You need to go inside, get a doctor." The man nodded, but he didn't seem to understand. "Can you get back to the house? Will someone there help you?"

"She threw me out," he said. "I was trying to help her."

Obi looked for the boy who'd been spying on Liam. Where could the boy have gone? Obi didn't like losing sight of him. It left him feeling exposed and vulnerable. Finally, Obi spotted him. He was not alone. He walked toward Obi with a tall black man. Neither appeared to be armed, but Obi wished he could grab his rifle. If it came down to it, he would drop the injured man in favor of his rifle, he decided.

"Hi, there," the black man said. "I'm Maurice and this is Bobby."

Obi nodded, cautious.

"This is private land," Maurice said.

"I have permission to be here." Obi tightened his grip on Liam. "My mother knows the woman who owns this land. She said we could camp here."

"You know mother mine, mine, mine, Mama?" The boy who'd been spying on Liam spoke with some sort of stutter. And he wasn't really a boy. Something about the way he moved had Obi thinking he was a teenager, but he saw now that the boy was a man, not so much younger than Obi.

"My mother knows your mother," Obi said.

"She is where? Where is she?"

There was something off about the boy, but he didn't seem to be a threat. At least he didn't seem to be threatening them. Obi was less certain about Maurice. The way he said it was "private land" made Obi wonder if he planned to protect the land from people like him. And yet, Obi could hardly believe that Maurice had any claim on the land. Obi knew the type of women who visited his mother. They were, without exception, white and entitled.

"This man is hurt," Obi said.

"We don't know him." Maurice shook his head like a dog trying to shake off water. "He just showed up to talk to Bobby's sister."

"He shouldn't have been driving. He almost killed my son." Obi struggled to balance Liam's comfortable, familiar weight against the heavy pull of the injured man. "He needs a doctor. At the very least, he needs this wound cleaned out." The man's bleeding head sagged against Obi's shoulder.

"I'm a nurse," Maurice said. "Let's get him back to the house."

Obi shoved the man toward Maurice and Bobby, but the man protested. "No." His voice was high pitched and whiny. "I want to stay with you."

"You can't stay out here."

"We can all go home," Bobby said.

"You can help me," the man said.

"No." Obi's arm was numb from supporting the man's weight, and he couldn't believe two able-bodied men would just stand there and not offer help. Maybe Bobby was a little slow, but there was nothing wrong with him

193

physically. If Maurice really was a nurse, Obi figured he wasn't a very good one.

"You should come with us," Maurice said. "This storm is getting worse. If the levees break, we'll be right in the path of the flood. You don't want your son out in this, do you? This is your son, right?"

Obi thought he heard a hint of threat or insinuation in Maurice's voice. He didn't like it one bit. "We'll be fine." Of course, it wasn't true; they would not be fine. The wreck had destroyed their one piece of shelter. They had no way to travel now except by foot. If the rain kept up, they'd be forced to swim.

"Let's all go home, home, home," Bobby sang. Liam laughed.

"No. We'll manage. Thanks for the offer."

"You need to come inside," Maurice said. "If anything happened to you out here—"

"We would not hold you responsible for anything that happened to us."

"Do you really want to be out in this mess with a child?"

They were stranded and it was raining like the end of the world was near. Obi's options were slim, and he knew it. Liam shivered and huddled tight against him. Maurice was right. The floodwaters were rising, and he couldn't protect Liam from the storm. Maybe he could protect him in the house. Maybe he could protect them both.

"Can I get some help here?" He cocked his head toward the injured man hanging on his shoulder. Maurice stepped forward and hoisted the man's weight. They followed Bobby to the house, a sad parade slogging through

three feet of water. Bobby warned them away from ob-
stacles. "Don't step there!" he shouted, and pointed off to
his right. "Big hole!" And a few moments later: "Old tractor parts up here. Swing wide. Follow me."

Obi respected Bobby's sure instructions. Here was a boy
who'd spent his life on these acres and who knew them by
heart. Bobby's stutter disappeared as he led them across the
land. Obi kept an arm around Liam as they walked, though
he needn't have bothered. Liam wrapped his body around
Obi's torso like a strangling snake, and there was no chance
he'd let go.

At the house, a frantic young woman rushed to meet them.
"Oxygen!" she shouted. "Electricity is out. Daddy needs
oxygen."

Maurice pushed the injured man back onto Obi and
sprinted into the house. The woman followed. Obi and
Bobby stood on the porch, supporting the weight of the
injured man between them, all three of them soaked to
the core. Obi felt shackled. His rifle, slung across his back,
was out of reach as long as he held the man.

The woman reappeared. "He's okay. He's okay." She
looked at Bobby when she spoke, but he didn't respond.
Her chest heaved. Obi felt sorry for her. She had the look
of a woman completely overwhelmed. She let her eyes track
across the sorry group of soggy men.

"Dear God, what in the hell happened?"

"Wreck wreck wreck car," Bobby said.

"This is too much." Her body slumped until Obi thought
she might fold in half. "This is too goddamned much."

"Who are you? What are you doing here?" She looked hard at Obi.

"Your friend here almost killed my son," he said. "We'll be on our way."

The woman reached out and touched Liam's arm in a way that was just a little too familiar for Obi's comfort. "No," she said. "You can't have a child out in this weather. Is this your son?"

"Of course he's my son." Obi kept his voice steady, but he didn't mask his anger. Liam could have been killed, and all they wanted to do was establish paternity.

"Come inside," she said. "Leave the gun. I won't have that gun in the house."

Obi hesitated. She met his eyes. "You won't need it."

She took the injured man's arm, and Obi slid the strap of the rifle off his shoulder. He placed it under an old, rotted wood-slat bench on the porch, close enough to retrieve as soon as he got a chance. He might not need it, but he didn't intend to be without it for long.

It was dark inside and oddly quiet except for the rain on the roof and the whoosh of the wind. The only other sound was a steady *pffft, pffft, pffft* coming from the next room. They stood, dripping, in the kitchen.

"How did this happen?" The woman pulled a chair from the kitchen table, and the injured man slumped into it.

"Wreck, wreck, wreck," Bobby said.

"Wreck, wreck, wreck," Liam whispered against Obi's neck.

"He lost control in the rain," Obi said. "Damn near killed my son. He had no business driving in this storm."

"I forced him out." Her voice shook. She sank into a chair. "I sent him out into this mess. He never should have come here, but I'm the one who sent him out. I saw how bad it was raining, and I sent him out anyway." She sighed. "If everything in life is a choice, then my choices are terrible."

Obi recognized fear in the woman's voice. She was running, too, if only from her own demons.

Maurice strode through the kitchen and opened the freezer. "I need ice. And you should call 911. We need to get both of them to a hospital. That spare tank won't last more than a day."

Obi gathered that Maurice was caring for someone in the next room. His mother had mentioned a sick husband.

The woman went to the phone, and put it to her ear. "Line's down."

Maurice emptied ice trays into a plastic bag at the sink. The woman rushed over and shut the freezer door. She scolded Maurice. "There's no electricity. All our food will spoil."

Maurice put the plastic bag on the man's head. "I needed ice."

The man's head lolled forward. "Ouch."

"Well, don't hurt him," the woman said.

"I'm not hurting him. He has a concussion. We need to keep him awake."

Bobby reached over and pinched the man hard on the arm. "I'll do it," he said. "I'll keep him awake." He pinched the man again.

"That's enough for now." Maurice touched Bobby's arm.

"Just make sure he keeps this ice on his head. It should help with the swelling."

Obi watched all this from his spot just inside the door. Liam squirmed; Obi held him tight. He didn't want any part of these people's messy, complicated lives. He had enough problems. It was one thing to take shelter in a house; it was quite another to get mixed up with people. Obi intended to keep his distance. Liam had other plans. He squirmed wildly until Obi had no choice but to set him down or drop him.

"Oh, you're soaked to the bone, aren't you?" The woman smiled at Liam. She was prettier than Obi had first thought. Liam grinned at her, walked straight over, and crawled into her lap. It took every bit of control Obi could muster to keep from snatching him back. Liam looked all too happy in his new spot. The woman put her nose to Liam's head and sniffed. "We'll get you dried off. I'll bet you're freezing." She wrapped her arms around Liam. Obi froze. To see Liam in this woman's lap, so comfortable and content, disturbed him. He'd thought they were doing okay without a woman, that Liam didn't need a mother. He saw now that he was wrong. Something about this woman called to Liam. She called to Obi, too.

He forced himself to speak. "I'm Obi. That's my son, Liam."

The woman kept her face buried in Liam's curls. "I'm Melody."

"Your mother knows my mother," Obi said. "Your mother told my mother that we could camp here. I'm sorry for the trouble."

Melody raised her face to meet his eyes. "You know my mother?"

She seemed familiar. Her brown eyes were the color of the earth, and her skin was pale and clear as the full moon. He knew her from some other time, perhaps from some other life. "No. My mother knows her. I don't know her at all."

"Well, you're not missing much." Melody expelled a bitter laugh. She sucked her bottom lip into her mouth in a way that made her look like a very young girl. She seemed even more familiar. Thunder shook the house.

Maurice pulled the injured man's head back and pressed ice to the wound. He used a damp towel to wipe away the worst of the blood. The man moaned and then giggled. "That tickles." He pitched forward and vomited on the table, stared at the steaming puddle, and said, "Whoops!"

"He needs a doctor," Obi said.

"No kidding," Maurice said. "Until then, we have to keep him awake. We'll get him to a hospital as soon as the storm passes." Maurice gestured for Bobby. He moved Bobby's hand under his on the ice pack. "Hold this here for me. Be gentle."

Obi noticed the affection between the men, and wondered about the nature of their relationship. Maurice left the room, returned with a large black bag, and rummaged through it. "Here we go." He taped the gash on the man's face, wrapped a length of gauze around his head, took the ice from Bobby, and handed it to the man. "Hold this against your head. That's your job, okay?"

The puddle of vomit on the table began to stink. Melody

shifted Liam off her lap. At the sink, she soaked a dish towel with water. "The pumps must be down. We don't have much pressure." She wiped up the mess on the table and dropped the soiled towel in a trash can. She fetched a larger towel from under the sink and wrapped it around Liam. "We'll have to find you some dry clothes."

Liam pulled the towel around his shoulders. "I like water," he said.

The injured man pressed the ice pack to his face, sat back in the chair, and closed his eyes. "Don't worry. I'm awake."

"How do you feel?" Melody asked.

"Worse and worse," the man said. "Why did I come here?"

"You don't remember?"

"I don't remember why I thought it was a good idea."

"It wasn't a good idea," Melody said.

"I thought I could convince you. I prayed on it."

"Well, that'll teach you."

"Everything has gone so wrong."

"It could be worse." She sat and Liam crawled back into her lap. The towel she'd wrapped around him fell to the ground. "Though I don't know how."

Obi knew how it could be worse. He could be stuck here with these people when the law came for him. It did not ease his mind to see Liam cuddled up with the woman again. He resolved to retrieve his rifle first chance he got. He'd feel better with it close at hand. These people seemed okay. He liked the woman, but he didn't trust her yet. He wasn't ready to trust anyone.

Chapter Eighteen

Geneva's mouth watered when she pushed open the heavy door of the bakery. Yeast, sugar, cinnamon, and comfort filled the air. Rain-soaked, shivering, a painful pulse of fear in her chest, she forced herself to speak to Atul. "What do you want? Let me get you something to eat."

"I am not hungry. The smell of this place makes me ill. Fried dough and hollow pastry."

The woman behind the counter glared at Atul. "We're closing."

"Oh, I just want some coffee and a quick bite of something," Geneva said. "Your rolls are my favorite."

"My rolls are everyone's favorite," the woman said. "There's a flood coming. Haven't you seen the news? I don't want to be stuck here when the waters rise. I have to get home to my family."

Geneva hadn't seen any news, of course, but she hardly needed a weatherman to tell her a flood was coming. "I'm trying to get home to my family, too," Geneva said. "I understand."

"You'd better get moving, then. The man on the news says we haven't seen a flood like this since 1927. We could get fifteen inches of rain before noon. The levees won't hold."

The men on the news were always measuring weather against the Easter flood of 1927. They were always wrong. It was just a bunch of hype in a place where days and weeks and years went by with nothing to report but cotton yields and catfish prices. Every few years, the floods came and riled up the forecasters. Geneva doubted this flood was any different from the rest, but she knew she ought to head home before the roads became impassable.

"I have some cinnamon rolls." The woman slid the sticky buns into a white bag lined with waxed paper. "You can have them."

Geneva opened her purse, pulled out a twenty-dollar bill. It was all she had.

"No," the woman said. "I've already cleared the cash register."

"I should give you something."

"Go home," the woman said. "Go be with your family."

"Let's go." Atul pulled at her arm. "We need to get back to Chandra. I should never have left her with that terrible man."

The woman handed the bag to Geneva. "I'm sorry. I don't have any coffee." She turned off the lights in the bakery and herded them out the door, which she locked behind her. "Y'all drive careful, now."

The woman's car fishtailed as she pulled out of the lot.

The rain fell in a frenzy, falling down and sideways and rising up at the same time.

"We have to go back!" Atul shouted, though he was standing right next to her.

She slogged back to the car, slogged through water that swallowed her calves and licked at her knees. The pulse of fear in her chest grew stronger.

"We have to get back to the station," Atul said. "We should never have left her there."

"Chandra's not a child."

"She's just a girl and we left her there with that brutish man."

Geneva's pulse of fear turned to anger. "She's grown, Atul. That's what happens to children. They grow up." For the first time, she felt a bit of pride for Melody's stubborn independence. At least she could venture out into the world without falling to pieces.

"She is just a girl."

"Fine." Geneva slipped the key into the ignition. The engine groaned but didn't turn over. She tried again.

"Oh, this is terrible. God is punishing us." Atul beat his chest with his fists.

"You're being ridiculous," Geneva said. "It's an old car. Give it some time."

"You are trying to keep me from Chandra. You are trying to stop me from getting back to her." Atul reached over and turned the key again. The car made an angry grinding noise.

Geneva slapped his hand away. "You'll flood the engine.

We just need to give it a minute." She reached into the bag on her lap and pulled out a gooey, soft cinnamon roll, bit into it greedily. Sugar, mixed with the salty yeast of the dough, filled her mouth. Perfect. "Here." She handed a chunk of the pastry to Atul. "This will make you feel better."

He swatted it from her hand. "I said no!"

"You're behaving like a child." She popped another bite of the roll into her mouth. "Like a spoiled child."

"We are going to be stuck here, and you don't even care."

"How can you say I don't care?" She lashed out at him. "My husband is dying. I should be home with him and not here dealing with a grown man's tantrums."

"You don't love your husband."

"I love Bruce."

"No," he said. "You love me. You cannot love us both. If you loved your husband, you would not be here." Atul crossed his arms over his chest and stared out the window.

Geneva turned the key. The engine cranked. She backed out of the parking spot and pulled the car onto the road. Atul knew nothing. Of course she could love two men at once. She could hate them both at once, too. Bruce would understand that. He wouldn't like it, but he would understand. Anyway, marriage was not about love; at least it wasn't about the kind of love Atul understood. Bruce wasn't a good husband or father, but he stuck it out. Anytime Geneva took a notion to leave, Bruce stayed. When she was in the mental hospital, he stayed. When she went to see Pisa and then Atul, he stayed. Geneva enjoyed the luxury of being eccentric and flaky, because Bruce was steady.

He let her be just crazy enough to stay sane, something her own father never did for her mother. She loved Bruce for that. Atul could never understand that kind of love.

She steered the car through the waterlogged streets, skidding to the right and left. The road disappeared beneath her. Rain flew off the wheels, spraying a blanket of mud and leaves across the windows. The floorboard was soaked, and not just because they were dripping. She couldn't see a thing.

"Slow down!" Atul braced himself against the dashboard. "Slow down or you'll kill us."

She laughed. It took so little to frighten him. Bruce wouldn't scare so easily.

"Let me drive," he said. "Stop the car."

She pressed her foot down hard on the gas. The car lurched and swerved. "We have to hurry," she said. "We have to get back to Chandra."

"Stop!"

There were no cars on the road, no farm equipment blocking the way, just water underneath and overhead and inside. The windows fogged over with the heat of Atul's fear and the damp warmth of their rain-soaked clothes. It was like traveling in a steam bath. A stream of water rushed across the road ahead. It was either go through the stream or turn back. She floored it. The car's rear end swerved beneath her, then shot forward. Atul tensed and closed his eyes. Geneva leaned forward, kept the gas pedal pressed to the floor. "Come on, come on, come on," she said. It was like flying. She believed the car would lift off and carry her over the water, carry her home. Instead, hitting the moving water was like slamming into a brick wall. Water engulfed the car. They spun until she couldn't tell which way they'd been driving. Her head yanked back and forth on her neck. Atul screamed. The car flipped and landed on the passenger side in a ditch full of rushing water, mud, and probably snakes. Atul panicked, tried to push open his door. Geneva unbuckled her seat belt and fell down on top of him.

"Get off!" He slapped at her. His nose was bleeding.

"Are you okay?"

"Get off of me."

"I'm doing the best I can."

Geneva's right knee throbbed and her left shoulder ached, but nothing seemed broken. If she could get out of the car, she could walk. Water seeped in around the passenger door where Atul lay pressed against the window.

"We have to get out of the car," Geneva said.

He tore at his seat belt, complained it was choking him. She reached up and pulled the latch to open the driver's-side door. Gravity and the pounding rain made it nearly impossible. She braced herself and kicked the door hard. Rain poured into the car.

"We're going to drown," Atul said.

"No," Geneva said. "We surely are not." She unlatched Atul's seat belt and dragged him up past the steering wheel. He struggled. "Be still." She hoisted her legs out the door and pulled them both out. They landed in three feet of water and stinking muck.

"We've got to get to higher ground," she said.

"We are going to die."

"Stop saying that!"

"I'm bleeding."

"It's a nosebleed. You're going to be okay. We need to climb up to the road. No one can see us down here, and the water is rising fast. If we can get up a little higher, we can flag down some help."

"Who?" Atul flailed his arms around. "Who is going to help us? Who would be out in this?"

"We can walk to the sheriff's office. It isn't that far from here."

"It might as well be in another country. We can swim there, perhaps, but walking is out of the question."

"Fine, we'll swim."

"I can't swim. I don't know how."

"The water is not that deep," she said. "Start walking. It's the only way to get back to Chandra. It's the only way we'll make it home."

They struggled up the slimy embankment, trudged through the muddy, slick water. "Stay on the road." Geneva's words disappeared on a gust of wind, drowned by the falling rain. She thought Atul did not hear her, and she yelled at him again.

"I cannot see the road," Atul said. He stumbled forward like a wounded animal.

She scraped her sodden hair out of her eyes, but she could see only a few feet in front of her. The world was gray and swollen. Her clothes were like tissue paper against her skin, insignificant and fragile. Water invaded every inch of her body. She sucked in liquid and spit it out. She coughed up mud. She didn't know if they'd been walking for fifteen minutes or for hours. Each step required so much effort. Maybe they'd been walking for days. It was like the pilgrimage to see Pisa, where time stood still, where night and day ran together like a muddy watercolor dream. The water rose past her knees, crept up her thighs. It grabbed at her legs as she walked, pulling her and threatening to knock her down. Was this what Pisa had warned her about? Could Pisa control the weather?

"This is your fault. You should not have driven into the water. You knew that and you did it anyway."

"I did it for you," she said. "I did it to get you back to Chandra. You told me to."

"I didn't tell you to drive into a flood."

"Well, I couldn't drive around it."

They argued back and forth and in circles. It was pointless and exhausting. It took every bit of strength she had just to put one foot in front of the other and keep moving forward. She hoped they were moving in the right direction. Familiar landmarks had disappeared. They had to keep moving. If they kept moving, they would wind up somewhere.

A tree limb about the length of her arm but twice as thick floated past. Then another larger branch went by. The trees are falling down, she thought. It was like a verse in a nursery rhyme, "Down fell the trees, they all fell down." Pisa taught her to have reverence for nature, to respect the earth and not to fight against it. She remembered this as she walked into the floodwaters. Calm and steady. No struggle. No thrashing. Atul was thrashing. He fought the water like an enemy. Pisa had told her if she went to see Atul, it would be bad. This was very bad.

Atul fell. Geneva reached down and yanked him up. His hand was slick and oily with mud. "Be careful."

"I am careful," he said. "I am always careful. This is your fault."

Geneva dropped his hand and walked ahead. "Do you blame me for the rain? Is the rain my fault? Is the flood my fault? The mud and the trees and the sky? All of it? Is that what you believe?"

They came to a downed oak. The oak lay across the road like a dead man, roots a terrible twisted mass of warning: Go back, go back. They could not go back. Geneva hoisted herself up and straddled the massive trunk. Pisa would tell her to respect the water, float don't fight. Atul fought and fell behind, fell down again. The bark scraped her hands and tore her clothes. Her skirt ripped open along a side seam. She pointed. "I can see the steeple from the Sulphur Springs AME Church. The sheriff's office is in the same block. We're almost there."

Atul was still several feet from her, still struggling to reach the tree. His face contorted. She held out her hand. "Here, let me help you." He swatted at her, reached out, and grabbed a jutting branch of the oak, hoisting his body forward and up. The tree shifted, and Geneva grasped its thick trunk tight between her thighs. The water rose impossibly fast. Mother Nature was not fooling around today.

"We should swim from here," she said. Atul didn't

respond. He held on to the branch, struggled forward. "You need to pull yourself up," she said. This time he grabbed her hand. She pulled, but his body was heavier than the hundred-year-old tree between her legs. She repositioned for greater leverage, wedged her hands beneath his armpits. She pulled until her back ached, but Atul didn't budge.

"Why are you so stubborn? I'm trying to help you."

"I don't know," he said. He was crying, though it was hard to tell with so much rain falling.

"Just pull yourself up and over."

"I don't know," he said again.

The water was up to his neck, almost to his chin. It should be easy, Geneva knew, to lift him up. He should float into her arms. Something was wrong.

"I don't know."

"Stop saying that."

The water rose to Atul's mouth. He sobbed and choked on the dirty water.

"You'll be sick," she said. "Don't drink it."

When her arms were limp as taffy, she realized he was stuck. She dived down to see where he was caught. Dark water swirled, muddy and brown. Atul's leg was caught in something, branches from the tree or vines sprouting from the earth. She yanked on his leg, but it didn't budge. Her lungs seemed about to burst. She surfaced, gasped. Atul stared up at the sky, his face lifted to the falling rain. His neck craned to keep his mouth and nose above the rising water. Time was running out. Geneva sucked in a deep breath and dived again. She felt down the length of his leg. His foot, his left foot, was pinned beneath the trunk. She pushed, remembering how it had moved so gracefully just a moment earlier. The oak didn't budge, and Geneva floated away. She swam back, grateful for years spent swimming in rivers and lakes. She was strong enough to swim through these waters, but Atul could not swim. Even once he was free, she'd have to drag him along. How could he live surrounded by rivers and lakes and never learn how to swim? It was like living on top of a mountain and never learning how to walk downhill.

The water rose to Atul's ears. He was stretched as tall as he could stretch. It was not enough.

"Can you get your foot out of your shoe?"

"I don't know."

It seemed these were the only words left in his vocabulary. He choked on a stream of water and coughed, which caused him to swallow more water. His head disappeared beneath the surface, and Geneva pulled him up and tilted his head back.

"I'm going to untie your shoe, make it loose. You pull." She was strong, but also tired. The swirling waters left her muscles soft. She filled her lungs and dived deep, using Atul's body as a guide. His shoe was wedged beneath a large heavy branch, enmeshed in a ropy heap of Spanish moss. She couldn't tell the moss from the shoelaces and kept yanking at the wrong thing. She tugged at his ankle, but the foot was pinned tight. Her body floated to the surface against her will. She had to have air.

Atul's mouth was submerged. He kept his nose above water by holding his head back and craning his neck forward like a rooster crowing. She didn't speak, knowing that he couldn't answer. She dived down and grabbed at the shoe again. The branch pinned his toes and the ball of his foot. If she could lift his heel up, maybe his foot would slide out of the shoe. She worked her fingers around the back of the shoe, pushed his ankle forward, pulled from side to side. She yanked his foot. She yanked the branch. His body shifted. She surfaced and vomited a great mouthful of muddy water. Atul disappeared. Geneva turned round and round, searched for him until she felt the thunk of his body against her leg. She tried to drag him up to the surface, but the water swallowed him whole. Pisa said there would be death. Pisa had warned her.

Plenty of women would have stayed and fought to free the body, dead or alive. Plenty of women would have drowned trying, but not Geneva. In her years, she'd witnessed two unnatural and brutal deaths. Nothing she did now would change the course of tragedy. She left Atul to the beastly water and swam on to save herself.

Chapter Nineteen

Melody told Maurice what the sheriff's deputy had said, about Obi being dangerous.

"It was your friend who nearly got us all killed. You should have seen the way he was driving. He almost hit the little boy. If that man hadn't pulled the kid out of the car, I don't see how he'd have survived." Maurice shook his head. "I've never seen anyone run so fast. I think the only way he'd be dangerous is if someone tried to hurt his son."

Melody didn't think Obi seemed dangerous, either. In fact, he seemed familiar.

"What's going on?" Her father's voice echoed. Without electricity, without the normal hum and buzz of appliances, every word seemed louder. The rain pounding against the roof and windows was such a constant clatter it was almost soothing.

"It's okay, Daddy. Everything's fine."

"Stop saying that. Everything is not fine. Who are all these people in my house?"

"I'm trying to figure that out myself," she snapped at him, and was ashamed. Just minutes ago, she'd thought he was practically dead. "There were some people camping on the land, a man and a young boy. They weren't safe out there."

"They aren't safe in here, either. Get me my gun, boy."

Maurice flinched. "I don't think that's such a good idea."

"What gun?" Melody said.

"I'll get it myself." He dropped his arm down the side of the bed and felt around on the floor.

"Mr. Mahaffey, I don't think it's necessary," Maurice said.

"I'll decide what's necessary. Give me some help, boy."

"I'm not helping you reach that gun. And don't call me boy. We've talked about that."

"I'll call you whatever I want. You're in my house, nigger."

Melody's stomach turned over. She looked at Maurice. The word hung between them, poisoned the air. "Daddy, no," she whispered. "No."

"That's it!" Maurice pointed his finger at Melody. "I already had this out with your mother. I won't put up with that kind of language. I quit. You're on your own."

"Maurice, please." Melody grabbed his arm. She needed his help. The thought of dealing with Obi and Daddy and Bobby and Chris all by herself was too much. "I'm sorry. He knows better. It's the medication. It's the illness."

"It's not, and you know it. He's like every other old white man, thinks he's better than me. Well, I have to draw the line somewhere." Maurice gathered up his bag of syringes and pain medication. "You'll want to get him to a hospital. That oxygen won't last the night." He started toward the kitchen. "I'm going to say good-bye to Bobby."

"What am I supposed to do?" Melody said. "What the hell am I supposed to do now?"

"The hospital will take care of everything," Maurice said.

"Daddy," Melody pleaded with him. "Apologize. You have to apologize to Maurice right now. Say you're sorry."

"It won't make any difference," Maurice said.

"He won't go to a hospital. You know that." Melody followed Maurice into the kitchen. "The phone lines are down. I can't even call the hospital."

"Not my problem."

"You can't just abandon him. He'll die."

"That old man is gonna die soon, no matter what I do."

Melody panicked. She needed Maurice, not just for her father but also for Chris. She needed another adult in the house who wasn't sick or damaged. She didn't know Obi well enough to judge his state of mind. "Please," she said to Maurice. "Please, I'm begging you, don't leave now."

"Leave? Why?" Bobby rushed to Maurice's side. "No! Leave, no. Leave, no. Leave, no."

"I have to." Maurice reached out and touched Bobby's arm. "I'm not leaving you, I'm leaving your father. You know what he's like."

"With you, with you, with you."

"Not now," Maurice said. "Help your sister."

"Me help, me help, me help. Help me." Bobby's mouth contorted. He let out an agonized wail. Melody reached for him as he ran from the kitchen. Maurice followed. She looked around. Chris sat mumbling, hands cradling his injured head. Liam stared up at her. Obi was gone. "Where is your father?"

Chris shifted forward in his chair, rested his elbows on the table. Purple bruises spread across his face, and his swollen nose bent to one side: "I don't feel so great." He sounded like someone with a terrible cold. "Will you pray with me?"

"No," Melody said. "I won't."

"I need help. I keep trying to pray, but it isn't working. I don't feel anything."

Melody knew what it was like to pray and feel nothing. She turned back to Liam. "Where did your father go?"

Liam pointed at the back door. Melody glanced at the windows, but all she saw was the steady gray downpour.

"Our Father," Chris said. "Who art in heaven, hollow is thy name." He stopped, looked up at Melody. "See, that's not right."

"Where is your mother?" Melody asked Liam.

"She left." Liam let out a frustrated sigh.

"Where did she go?"

"I don't remember her." He spoke in a solemn whisper. "Don't tell Daddy, okay?"

Melody pulled Liam into her arms. She didn't know where her own mother was. There was no point interrogating a child. She rocked back and sat on the floor, settling Liam into her lap. "It's okay." She closed her eyes and sniffed his hair. He smelled wild and sweet, like honeysuckle vine.

"Are you going to kick us out?"

"No," Melody said. "Of course not."

"You kicked me out," Chris said.

"I didn't know this would happen, Chris."

"Daddy's nice," Liam said. "You'll see. You don't need to be mad at him."

"Kingdom come, will be done," Chris muttered. "The problem is that it makes no sense."

"I'm not mad." She stroked Liam's hair. It was true; for the first time in a long time, she wasn't angry. Something about the comforting weight of the child on her lap calmed her, even in the middle of this chaos. "Chris, it goes like this: Our Father, who art in heaven, *hallowed* be thy name. Thy kingdom come, thy will be done, on earth as it is in heaven. Amen."

"But what does it mean?"

Melody knew exactly how he felt. The words that once seemed so comforting, so profound, slipped into nothingness.

Melody pushed herself up from the floor. Liam hung around her neck like a monkey. She shifted his weight over to her right hip. He fit perfectly against her, legs wrapped around her waist, arms around her shoulders. "You keep an eye out for Obi," she told Chris. "I'll be right back. Don't go to sleep, okay? Promise me."

"I'm awake," Chris said.

"Keep that ice on your head."

"It's melting." He held up the bag full of slushy water. A stream of it dripped onto the table.

"That's okay," Melody said. "Everything's wet. A little

more water won't hurt anything. I have to check on Bobby. I'll be right back."

She carried Liam with her. "Who is that?" he asked when they passed the bed in the living room.

"That's *my* daddy," Melody said.

"He's very sick," Liam said.

She pushed open the door to Bobby's room and saw Bobby and Maurice mid-clench. They sprang apart when she walked in, but she'd seen enough to know just how close they'd become.

She stepped back and slammed the door on the whole scene. Her face went hot and her legs went weak. She felt winded, like she'd been sprinting. Liam played with her hair, pulled a strand of it between his fingers. He sang a soft, unfamiliar song. He did not seem surprised to find two men kissing. It made sense now, the way Bobby acted around Maurice, the way Maurice touched Bobby with such familiarity and affection. She should have realized. She pulled Liam closer to her, holding him so tightly he began to squirm.

Maurice stepped out into the hallway.

"How could you?" Melody whispered. "He's just a boy."

"He's a grown man."

"He is not. Do you know what happened to him? How it affected his brain? He has the mind of a child!"

Maurice narrowed his eyes. "I know about the baptism. I know all about it."

"He doesn't get it. He doesn't understand."

"He understands plenty. Give him some credit."

"You're going to hurt him."

"You don't know that." Maurice fumbled with his shirt collar. "Look, no one knows about this. We've been very careful."

"Careful? You haven't been careful. You're going to destroy him," Melody said. "Shame on you."

"Hello?" Chris called up the stairs. "Are you up here?"

"We're here," Maurice said.

Chris held his face as he walked. He panted with the effort of climbing the stairs. "I just—" He stopped to rest. "There's water. Downstairs, there's water coming in. It's pretty fast."

"For God's sake, you can't just be wandering around," Melody said. "I told you to stay put."

"No," Maurice said. "It's okay. As long as he feels okay. Probably better to keep the muscles limber."

"I didn't ask for your opinion," Melody snapped.

"I wouldn't say I feel okay." Chris's voice wobbled and broke. "I really wouldn't."

Maurice went to Chris, looked into his eyes. "Your nose is broken," Maurice said. "That's why your face is bruised. Your eyes are dilated."

Liam played with a strand of Melody's hair. Bobby was a boy just like this one. It was not so long ago. "How could you do this to him?" Melody said to Maurice. "You should be ashamed of yourself."

"What bothers you most?" Maurice spat at her in an angry whisper. "Is it that I'm a man or that I'm black?"

"That's not fair," Melody said.

"You're no better than your father," Maurice said. "Bobby told me what happened. He told me all about it.

219

Not that he had to. Everyone knows about that baptism. It's no secret. It changed him, but he isn't ruined and he isn't a child. You can't keep him one by making him stay here."

"I never *made* him do anything," Melody said.

"I'm confused," Chris said.

"So am I," Melody said. "I'm confused as hell." Melody pressed Liam's head into her chest, holding her hand over one ear as if protecting him from the conversation. "You're a pervert. You're a parasite."

"You're a racist bitch who abandoned your brother," Maurice said.

"I am not." Melody's head pounded. It was a horrible accusation. "You're taking advantage of my little brother. You have no right."

"Is there somewhere I could sit down?" Chris said.

"And another thing." Melody's voice rose. "You can't just leave Daddy because you don't like the way he spoke to you. He's not himself, and you know it. He's dying and he's drugged and you can't just walk out on him. Don't you have some sort of code of ethics?"

"I can do whatever I damn well please. You don't own me."

"I'll bet the hospice doesn't allow you to molest brain-damaged boys in the homes where you work. I'll bet they'd love to know all about that."

"He isn't a boy," Maurice said. "He's a full-grown man. Look at him!"

"I'm so tired," Chris said. "Could I just sit down?" Chris leaned against the wall and slid down to the floor like a balloon deflating at the end of a party. His head slumped forward. His eyes closed. A puff of air escaped from his lips.

"You need to keep him awake," Maurice said.

"*I* need to keep him awake? You're the nurse!"

"I'm not his nurse."

Melody was prepared to keep arguing with Maurice, but Bobby stepped into the hallway. His face was red and splotchy. "Sissy, you me left. Left me you. You left me."

"I went to college!"

"And you never came back." Maurice crouched next to Chris, shook him until his eyes opened. "You could have taken Bobby away from here. He thought you would come back for him. He's been waiting for you for years, and you just left him here with that crazy woman and that awful man. How could you do that to him?"

"That crazy woman and that awful man are his parents! They're *my* parents."

"That's no excuse."

"Am I supposed to stay here forever? Is that it? Don't I get a life of my own?" Melody's hand rested on Liam's leg. It was soft as velvet. "We shouldn't be talking about any of this in front of a child. It isn't right."

"I'm not ashamed. We're not doing anything wrong," Maurice said.

"Really?" She let out a scornful laugh. "Then why don't *you* take Bobby out of here? If you're so worried, why don't you two run away together? Take him home to meet your parents, introduce him as your boyfriend. How will that go over?"

"You know I can't do that."

"Why? Because he's white or because he's a boy?"

Maurice looked away.

"What happens when you leave here?" Melody asked. "What's the plan?"

"I don't have a plan," Maurice said.

"Then don't you dare accuse *me* of abandoning him. I'm not the one who was planning to disappear. I'm not the one who was planning to break his heart."

Chris held his head in his hands and rocked back and forth. He muttered the Lord's Prayer. "That's good," Maurice said to him. "Keep talking, keep moving."

"It can't continue. This will kill my father. He can't know anything about this."

"This is not what will kill your father," Maurice said. "You know that."

Bobby trembled. The red splotches on his face darkened and spread. Melody sighed, put Liam down, and pulled Bobby to her. "It's okay," she told him. "You didn't do anything wrong. This isn't your fault."

He pushed her away, yelled at her. "Know I, know I, know I . . . I know I didn't do anything wrong! Stop treating me like a baby. I'm sorry you home came. Came home."

"Our Father," Chris said. "Who art in heaven—"

"Shut up!" Bobby said to Chris. "Shut up. Shut up. Shut up."

Chris looked at Bobby, his mouth still open from the last syllable he'd uttered. He closed his lips with a smack. His eyes were wide. A thin trickle of fresh blood seeped from underneath his bandages. Melody felt trapped in the small hallway. "I'm going to try the phone again," she said. "He doesn't look so good."

A loud crack shook the house. Melody thought it was thunder, but Liam knew better. "Gun," he said in a calm, clear voice.

She sprinted down the stairs. "Daddy?" She missed a step and stumbled wildly. At the bottom, brown, dirty water rose to her ankles. The scent of something sulfurous and ripe hit her as hard as a fist. She gagged.

Obi stood at the foot of her father's bed, pointing a rifle at his chest. Her father gripped a rifle as well, though he seemed worn out by the weight of it. His body was drenched with sweat, and his shoulders hunched around his ears.

"Where is he?" Obi looked at Melody, but kept the gun aimed at her father. "Where is Liam?"

"I'm here, Daddy." Liam came partway down the stairs.

"He's fine," Melody said. "I told you to leave the gun outside."

"He was lying here with a gun when I came in," Obi said. "He shot at me."

Obi seemed either terrified or filled with rage. There was a hole in the wall behind him. The floor was littered with plaster and drywall. Some of it rested in Obi's hair.

"He's dying," Melody said. "You can see how weak he is."

"I'm not so weak I can't protect my house from intruders."

"Daddy," Melody said. "This is Obi. Mama said he could stay on the land."

"You know Genie?"

"My mother knows her," Obi said. "My mother is a friend of your wife."

"Who is your mother?"

"Her name is Pisa."

"I don't know anyone named Pisa." His voice was hollow.

"Put the gun away, Daddy," Melody said. "Put it away before you kill somebody."

The water at Melody's ankles climbed up and reached her calves. The blanket covering her father hung down into the dirty pool. His oxygen tank was partly submerged. "Daddy, I think we need to get you upstairs."

"I'm not going anywhere."

"You need to stop pointing that gun at me, "Obi said.

"Both of you need to put the guns away," Melody said. "Please, I'm begging you, put the guns down."

Chapter Twenty

The old man seemed too weak to move, but he was strong enough to fire his rifle. He was a very bad shot or he was too weak to take aim. Either way, Obi was glad the bullet had whizzed wide past him and into the Sheetrock wall. The last thing Obi wanted to do was shoot this old man, bedridden and pitiful. There was no honor in shooting a creature that couldn't run. Still, he held his own rifle steady and aimed right at the man's heart. His son was nowhere to be seen. Melody and her odd band of men were missing, and this old man seemed out for blood. There was a wild madness in the man's eyes and something else, something ominous. Death. Obi recognized the old dark force in the man's gaze. He was not long for this good earth.

"Who are these people?" The old man's nose dripped snot onto his oxygen tube and upper lip. Death terrified the man. White people never learned how to leave the world with grace. This one was no exception.

Obi stood in the rising water, in the house he never intended to enter, and weighed his options. He heard his mother's voice in the rolling thunder. When he was a boy, his mother told him the story of the Great Flood, the Flood that Destroyed the Whole Earth. She told him about the rising waters, the animals that drowned, the people who panicked, the scent of death in the air. She told him how the sky turned dark and the clouds grew thick and menacing. Some people threw themselves into the rushing water. Some people climbed into the highest trees and cursed the falling rain, but one family stayed calm. One family called on the white beavers for help and built a sturdy wooden raft. They survived, along with one pair of each animal on the earth. It was a very large raft. When the waters receded, the family was alone and afraid until the Great Spirit sent them a message: a raven with an ear of corn in his mouth. The Great Spirit told them to plant the ear of corn, feed themselves, and repopulate the earth. Those people, said Pisa, were their ancestors, and no one born of such brave people should ever be afraid of nature. "Embrace the rain," she told him. "Embrace the wind and the sun and the moon. Be grateful for what nature provides and never raise your fist in anger to the sky." Nature was not the enemy; man was the enemy. Maybe not this man, Obi thought. Maybe this man was just scared and panicked and doing what he thought was best to protect his family. That was something Obi could understand.

Melody was on the stairs now, yelling for him to put the gun away. Liam was with her. The sight of his son calmed him.

"Daddy," Liam said in a quiet, calm voice. "That man is very sick."

"I can see that. I won't hurt him."

"Daddy, I saw two men kissing."

Obi lowered his rifle. He stepped to the side of the man's bed. "Sir," Obi said. "I'm going to take this rifle and put it somewhere safe." Obi reached for the weapon.

"It's safe right here." He hugged it closer.

Obi felt the water lap at his knees. He wondered what would happen if the water kept rising. Could this man walk? Would he drown?

Maurice came down the stairs and stopped where the water started. "I'm leaving."

"I wish you could, but you can't." Melody gestured at the water in the living room. "You can't drive through this. I've already sent one man out into this mess. I won't send another."

Maurice glared at Melody. His upper lip curled. "What's that smell?"

"I'm trying not to think about it."

Obi smelled it, too, a putrid, rotten odor, like a bad egg.

"Do you think the sewage lines have burst?" Melody asked.

Maurice gagged, put his hand over his mouth. He was a weak man, Obi realized. Strong enough physically, but his spirit was weak.

"We need to get upstairs," Melody said. "We need to move Daddy."

Maurice spoke through his hand. "I'm not going down into that."

"You have to help me. I can't lift him by myself."

"I'm not stepping one foot into that nasty water," Maurice said. "Certainly not to help your father. Or you."

"It's your job."

"I quit, remember?"

Maurice was a coward. That was his true nature, and it was on full display right now. Obi slung his rifle across his back, never taking his eyes off the old man.

"I'll carry him," Obi said. "He can't weigh much. Someone will have to get this thing." He pointed to the oxygen tank.

The old man whimpered, released his grip on the rifle, and let his hands fall limp at his sides.

Melody waded across the room to where Obi stood. She picked up the tank as if testing its weight. "I've got it." She was no coward. Her spirit was strong. If Obi had to get mixed up with people, he was glad to be mixed up with her.

Obi put his arms beneath the man's back and knees. He lifted carefully, but the man moaned in pain. He hoped he would never be so fragile. He never wanted Liam to see this kind of weakness in him. The man was limp and Obi was careful not to bump his legs or head as they climbed. It was dry upstairs, and the water let go of him like a great, sucking leech. Melody followed behind, holding the tank close enough to keep the oxygen flowing into the man's nostrils. "Almost there," Obi said, though he wasn't sure where they were taking the man. "I'm Obi, by the way. I don't believe I introduced myself."

"Bruce." The man's voice was a bare croak.

"My mother knows your wife," Obi said. "I'm sorry I scared you. When I came in and my son was gone, I panicked."

Bruce grasped at his shirt and it took Obi a moment to realize he was patting Obi, a gesture of comfort and understanding.

In the hallway upstairs, the injured man slumped in a corner with his head in his hands. Bobby stood over him. He reached down and pinched him as they passed.

Melody pointed them into a bedroom with a handmade quilt on the bed. Obi was glad to see the quilt with its imperfect pattern and the stitching done in mismatched thread. It was good to know this home wasn't filled entirely with things bought from a store. Perhaps if this flood destroyed the earth, this family would be worth saving. He placed Bruce on the bed, gently lowered his head onto the pillow. "Is that okay?"

Bruce blinked at him, his eyes watery and dim. His chin quivered; his hands grasped the quilt. His mouth opened and shut, opened and shut, like he was speaking, but no sound came out. Melody set the tank down next to the bed. She was damp with sweat and soaked below the knees. Her legs were streaked with mud and maybe more. Obi looked at his pants, also covered in the stinking mess. He didn't mind dirt; he lived in dirt and he bathed in river water. He didn't mind animal waste; it was useful for tracking and for masking any scent that was too human, but man's waste disgusted him. It was a portent of illness, of disease and death. He wanted to strip down and discard his filthy pants and boots. He looked behind him at the muddy footprints he'd tracked into the room. "Liam," he said. "Don't touch anything. Don't put your hands in your mouth." The boy nodded and held his hands stiffly away from his body.

"I hate to ask," he said to Melody. "But I think we should all get some fresh clothes, wash some of this filth off. Is there any clean water in the pipes?"

"I don't know." Melody stared down at her father. His breath was ragged and uneven. "You can get some clothes from the closet in the bedroom across the hall. I don't think we have anything that will fit Liam, but I can check and see if my brother has some old stuff."

"Thank you," Obi said. "Can I do anything for you?"

Melody shook her head. Obi lifted Liam and carried him across the hall, passing by the three men without speaking. The injured man slumped in the hallway, but Bobby and Maurice seemed to be arguing. When they saw Obi, they slipped into another room and shut the door. In the room Obi entered, the bed and floor were strewn with newspaper clippings and photographs and dried flowers. Someone had been searching for something here. The closet doors stood open and he pulled out a few clean shirts. They were work shirts, denim and sturdy, though they didn't look as if any work had been done in them. He grabbed a pair of jeans, three sizes too large, and a pair of sneakers that just about fit. There was a bathroom off the hallway and he stepped inside. The faucet sputtered and released a weak brown stream. He undressed Liam, rubbed him as clean as he could with the dry towels and did the same for himself. He slipped on one of the clean shirts from the closet. It wasn't perfect, but it would do for now. He changed into the pair of blue jeans, cinched his belt. The shoes were fine, comfortable even. He wrapped Liam in a towel and car-

ried him, the extra clothing, and a clean towel back into
the room where Melody was standing over her father. "I
found these," he said. "Hope that's okay. Your brother is in
the other room with the door shut. I didn't think I should
bother him."

Melody crossed the room and pulled open a drawer of
the dresser against the wall. "There are T-shirts in here.
They'll be too large for Liam, but at least they're clean."

Obi handed Melody a towel and the extra shirts. "There's
no clean water." He turned away and examined the contents of the drawer she'd opened, and pulled out the smallest shirt he could find, a green cotton tee with white piping
around the arms and neck. It was stamped with the letters
DSU. He scrubbed Liam roughly with the dry towel. Liam
giggled. He slipped the T-shirt over his head. It hung on
him like a dress.

"Your mother is the woman who teaches my mother to
believe in magic, isn't she?" Melody had pulled on one of
the clean denim shirts when his back was turned. She used
one of the towels to scrape the filth from her bare legs.

"You don't believe in magic?"

"I don't, though if you want to prove me wrong and
work a miracle, please go right ahead."

"I'm afraid I don't have my mother's gifts," Obi said. "It
isn't really magic, you know."

"I met her once."

Obi knew why Melody seemed familiar. She was older,
but in her adult features he could discern the face of the
child she had been, the pale skin, the muddy brown eyes,

the nose like a plop of barely risen dough in the center of her face, the lips that disappeared into her mouth when she was anxious. "I was there," he said. "I remember."

Melody's face flushed. "Mama was embarrassed. She never took me back."

"You were a child," Obi said.

"I was ten years old."

"A child. I was only about sixteen or so, myself. I wasn't supposed to be hanging around while my mother worked. She said my maleness was disruptive. It was okay when I was younger, but she said I was becoming so male the clients could smell me, and it made them uneasy." Obi chuckled. He'd been angry with his mother that year, annoyed that she was pushing him away even as he longed to escape. "I was supposed to stay outside and gather the herbs and plants for her."

"But you came in."

"It was so hot that day. I liked being outside. I always have. But that day, there was no shade and no water. I felt like I was baking."

"I remember the heat," Melody said. "The sun was so bright. I got burned. My skin peeled for the next two weeks. I don't know what my mother was thinking, dragging me around like that."

"I kept making excuses to come in. There was a fan in the house and I would stand in front of the fan and drink glass after glass of water. Mother kept telling me to go and I kept saying, 'Just one more glass.'"

"Oh, God, I was so thirsty! They didn't give me anything to drink. I don't know how I had any pee left in me."

Obi laughed. He liked Melody more and more. She was fleshy and soft and pretty in a natural way, not like Eileen, who hid her beauty behind too much makeup and expensive haircuts. "My mother is a seer. She comes from a long line of seers, and her mother taught her how to use herbs and plants to heal. That's not magic."

"Then what is it?" Melody's father moaned and shifted in the bed. She pulled the quilt up over his legs, touched his forehead. "I think his fever is down."

"It's medicine," Obi said. "It's just not medicine cooked up in a lab somewhere."

"We could use some of her medicine right now. I don't know what will happen if the waters keep rising or if Daddy runs out of oxygen. I don't know what to do. I guess your mother would know. That's what a seer is right? Someone who knows what to do?" Her voice sounded thick. She was emotional, but she didn't break down. "I never know the right thing to do."

"Yes, you do," Obi said. "You're doing just fine."

"I've let my brother down."

"You'll make it up to him."

"What if it isn't enough?"

"Then you let it go."

"That's no help at all."

"I'm not my mother. I'm no seer."

Melody walked across the room to the window. "I think the levees have failed. It's the only reason the water would be so high. It'll get worse before it gets better."

"We were camping on the river." Obi decided to trust Melody. If anything happened to him during this storm or in the future, he knew he could trust her with Liam. "There was a misunderstanding with some boys."

"Is that what happened to your face? A misunderstanding?"

Obi touched the wound beneath his eye. "This? This was just an accident."

"What happened on the river?"

Obi told her most of it. "Those boys were on something. They were crazed." He told her about how the boy came at him with a knife and how he fought back, how anyone would fight back under the circumstances. He told her his knife slipped, that he hadn't meant to hurt the boy. He did not tell her he thought he'd killed the boy. He did not want this woman to think of him as a killer. That would not serve any of them.

"Accidents, misunderstandings, a failure to read the weather. You really aren't a seer. You'd think you might get some of your mother's gifts."

"Not me," Obi said. "I think Liam shows promise, though."

Liam stood at the foot of the bed, looking at the old man.

"I'll do anything to protect my son," Obi said. "You can understand that. I can't afford trouble with the law, with anyone. That's why I went for my rifle. I don't want to use it, but I will."

"You'll be safe here," Melody assured him. "At least as safe as the rest of us."

Before Obi could thank her, the old man sat straight up in bed. He looked filled with strength. His hair stood out around his head, and color rushed into his face. Obi saw what he must have looked like in better times: a robust man, a strong man.

"Daddy." Melody leaned in and Obi saw that she loved her father. Her eyes locked on his and she reached for his hands. "Daddy, what is it?"

"Genie," the dying man said.

"No, Daddy, it's me. It's Melody." Her voice was gentle, soft. Obi wished he could help her, but he knew he could not.

"Genie." The man's voice was strong and clear, not a hint of weakness. "Genie, I'm dying."

Obi watched the man's spirit leave his body and he knew the man's life had been filled with sorrow and darkness and terrible pain. Death was a relief, if only a temporary one. Obi whispered the words his mother had taught him to say in the presence of death. "Mother Earth, Father of Ancestors, He Who Lives Beyond the Heavens, make a new world for this man. No death, only a new world."

Chapter Twenty-one

Geneva became a wild animal. Somewhere between the tree that took Atul and the sheriff's office, she gave up on being civilized and threw her full lot in with Mother Nature. Bruised and tossed around mercilessly by the rising waters, her skin was scraped raw, her clothes torn and useless. By the time she clawed her way up the concrete steps of the county building, she considered each new pain a triumph. Pain was just proof of life. That was true for as long as Geneva could remember.

She stumbled, barefoot and half-dressed, into the sheriff's office, where Boggs and Chandra sat. Her teeth clacked together violently. She couldn't stop shivering.

Boggs stood. "Dear God. Are you okay?"

"No." She heaved up a vile stream of mustard-colored water. "I'm not okay." She kept retching even when her body was empty. A faint bit of cinnamon stuck in the back of her throat, and that was worse than the bitter bile that filled her mouth.

"No, I reckon you are not." Boggs brought her a dry wool blanket and wrapped it around her shoulders, handed her a stack of brown paper towels. She took the towels and scraped the wad across her tongue. She was shivering so hard she bit her own hand.

"Where's my father?" Chandra said. "Where is he?"

Geneva sat in a hard plastic chair, put her head between her knees. "I lost him."

"What do you mean, you lost him? How could you lose him?" Chandra spat at Geneva, angry and full of contempt. Soon enough she'd figure out that grief was a more appropriate emotion.

Geneva lifted her head. The room spun. "The water was too high. He couldn't swim."

"Now, just a minute." Boggs brought her a paper cup filled with lukewarm water. "What are you saying?"

"I tried to save him, but the tree wouldn't let him go. He couldn't swim." She kept saying he couldn't swim, though she knew damn well that swimming wouldn't have saved him. There was nothing logical about what she said. There was no reason left in the world.

"Where is my father?" Chandra lunged and slapped Geneva again and again across the face.

"Settle down." Boggs pulled Chandra away. "You wanna tell me what happened?"

"He couldn't swim." Geneva didn't know why they were having such a hard time understanding. "We wrecked the car and tried to walk. The water kept rising. He got stuck. There was a tree, a beautiful tree. The tree wanted Atul and it took him. If you want to blame someone, blame the tree. Blame the rain." She couldn't say it any plainer.

"You are the rain." Chandra said. "You are a flood of misery."

"We have rescue boats out now," Boggs said. "Where did you lose track of him? I'll radio for help."

"I didn't lose track of him. He's gone." She peered into the rain. "There are no boats out there."

"There are," Bogg said. "The Red Cross radioed in; they're evacuating the low-lying areas. They're evacuating damn near everything. Shelter's at the middle school. It's on a ridge. Trustees are out with sandbags."

"It's too late for Atul." She looked at Chandra. "Do you understand?" Chandra glared, her face tight and red. She would kill Geneva if given the chance. Geneva could see that. "Do you understand what I'm telling you, Chandra? Your father is gone."

She pulled the blanket tight around her chest. "Please," she said to Boggs. "You need to send someone to my house. It takes on water even in small storms. My husband is dying. He won't make it upstairs. He won't escape if the water rises."

"We're covering the whole county," Boggs said. "It's a big county."

"We're on the far edge. About a quarter mile off County Road 240."

"I spoke with your daughter," Boggs said. "They're fine."

"But our house floods," Geneva said. "If the levees give way, our house will flood quickly. You have to do something."

"The levees gave way some time ago," Boggs said. "We're doing what we can. We're doing everything we can."

"We have to find my father." Chandra's voice was tight and small. She turned to Boggs, balled her fists, and slammed against his chest. "Do something! Send someone!"

"Look," Boggs said. "The boats are out. We'll find him."

They might find him, Geneva knew, but they wouldn't save him. It was too late for that. Chandra sat, slack-jawed and ugly in her ill-fitting clothes and her deliberately un-flattering haircut. Geneva should never have brought her here. Geneva should have listened to Pisa.

"My family needs help," Geneva said. "I have a bad feeling. Can I get on one of those boats?"

"Ma'am, I can't call a rescue boat off the job because you have a bad feeling." Boggs walked to his desk, scooped the wad of wet tobacco from a sheet of paper, and tucked it into his jaw.

"My husband is dying. They need me."

"You only care about yourself," Chandra said. "What about my father? How could you leave him?"

"If it weren't for you, your father wouldn't be out in this storm." Geneva turned her anger on Chandra. "He was worried sick about you. He wanted to get back here to you. That's why we were stuck in the flood. That's why we had the wreck. That's why your father is not here."

"I hate you." Chandra wiped her nose on the back of her bare arm. A thin, viscous strand of snot hung down in front of her lip.

Boggs spit into a Styrofoam cup, passed Chandra a box of tissues. "Sheriff has a fishing boat out back. Wife won't let him keep it at the house."

"I can drive." Geneva shrugged off the blanket.

"Your daughter mentioned that a man and a little boy were camping out on your land. You know anything about that?" Boggs spit a wet brown stream into his cup. "Matches the description of the man Chandra says attacked her friend. Could be dangerous."

"I can handle a boat," Geneva said. "You can stay here with Chandra."

"We're all sticking together," Boggs said. "I'll radio for one of the rescue boats to meet us. By the time we get there, they should be sweeping the edge of the county anyhow, and you should all get to the shelter." He pulled on a pair of thigh-high waders as he spoke, dropped a pair in front of Chandra, and handed a pair to Geneva. "They'll be too big, but better than nothing. Put 'em on."

Boggs steered the boat through the thick, dirty water. Geneva thought she would never be dry again. Water poured into the boat. They should be prepared to bail, Boggs told them. His cheek bulged and he spit great brown streams of tobacco overboard at regular intervals. Geneva pointed out the way she thought they should go, but the familiar landmarks had disappeared. Without a sun in the sky, without black roads and green signs and yellow houses and brown fields, she was lost in a world of sodden gray. The churches were her only guideposts. Monuments to God and man rose up through the colorless anonymity. If she kept them to her left, they would be heading in the right direction. They passed the tall white cross of Crossroads Baptist, the bright blue cross of Friendship AME, the steeple of First

Baptist, the bell tower of Holy Mary. Geneva directed Deputy Boggs through the Bible Belt one notch at a time. For the first time since the baptism of her son, she was grateful for man's enormous ego in building houses of worship.

"Hoo boy, this is a mess!" Boggs had to shout to be heard. "Sheriff's daughter isn't going to be happy. Bet they'll cancel the wedding."

"Who cares about some stupid wedding?" Chandra screamed, but her voice was thin against the storm.

"Right," Boggs said. "Not so important in the scheme of things."

Chandra bared her teeth and tucked her chin. She folded her arms up tight. She might have been trying to protect herself from the rain, but Geneva knew better. The girl was wound tight, literally and figuratively. She was in a rage and, like the river in a storm, she would not be contained for long.

Geneva wished she had the package Pisa had given her, the one with the herbs and the chants. She tried to remember the blessings she'd said over Bobby and Melody through the years, but they all ran together like gibberish. She wondered if that was all Pisa had ever given her, just a bunch of gibberish. But, of course, it was Pisa who'd warned her that there would be great violence if she went to see Atul. There was no gibberish in that warning, and Geneva should have heeded it. She directed Boggs east through a forest of trees, a path dense and dark on a sunny day turned gothic nightmare by the storm. Chandra huddled herself tighter. She seemed to be shrinking.

241

Finally Geneva's home appeared. It was squat, a mere half the house she remembered, much of it hidden beneath the water. "That's it."

Boggs approached slowly. "Don't want to alarm anyone. Keep your eyes on the house. If you see anyone moving around, let me know."

Geneva squinted into the rain. She wished there were some way to signal to them.

"The first floor is flooded." She hoped Melody had managed to get Bruce upstairs. "I need to go in. I can't see anything from here."

"You're not going anywhere." Boggs spit for emphasis.

"It's my family," Geneva said. "I have to go. Let me go inside."

"Can't do it," Boggs said. "Might be dangerous, and I can't send you in there. I'll go in and send them out."

He spoke to Chandra. "I'll bring everyone out. If the man is in there, you can identify him. You don't need to be afraid. I'll apprehend him."

"What if he isn't in there?" Chandra said. "What if he's out here somewhere, watching us? What if he's just waiting for you to leave so he can come over here and shut me up? He'll kill me. I know he will."

"I don't think that's particularly likely in this storm." Boggs reached under his seat in the boat and pulled out a box. He fumbled with the latch until the box sprang open.

"Is that a gun?" Chandra leaned forward, hand out.

"A flare gun." Boggs released a stream of brown spit. "If you need me, just shoot this into the air." He showed her how to use the gun.

"You won't see it if you're inside."

"This is ridiculous," Geneva said. "She'll kill us with that thing. She'll blow a hole in the boat."

"I will not!"

As they argued, Boggs stepped from the boat to the submerged front porch. Water rose as high as his hips. He tethered a rope around a porch railing and let the boat float away from the house. The rope was long and left them bobbing in the rain a good twenty feet away.

"Hey!" Geneva shouted, but Boggs was gone.

Chandra turned the flare gun over and over in her hands, like a child with a new toy.

"Be careful with that!" Geneva said. "It's dangerous."

"Don't tell me what to do." Chandra cradled the flare gun against her chest and glared at Geneva. "You just sit there and shut up."

Chapter Twenty-two

Melody's father collapsed onto the pillow, onto the quilt his mother had sewn in her dying days when her eyesight grew weak, a quilt with mismatched threads, orange turning to red and red to black. Melody had always loved the quilt in spite of its ugly flaws. She loved her father the same way. The fabric of the quilt was thin, so soft that lumps of cotton batting shown through. The blue veins in her father's arms were stark, his rib cage a ladder. His chest convulsed as the last rattling breath left his body. His face transformed from a mask of agitation and pain to a calm and peaceful expression. His eyes remained open. He smiled.

Melody felt like she'd been punched. His death shocked her. Shocked her despite its inevitability. She'd had only a couple of days to get used to the idea that her father was dying, and while those two days were pretty damned convincing, she wasn't ready for this.

"I'm sorry," Obi said.

"Oh, God." Melody fell back into an old rocking chair. "He was so sick. But still, I . . ."

Liam climbed on the bed before Melody could stop him.

He pulled a woven strand from around his neck and laid it on her father's chest. "Don't be sad," he told her. "He feels better now."

Melody touched the woven strand. "What is this?"

"It's for safe travels," he explained. "Protection."

"Did your grandma give you this?"

Liam nodded. "He needs it more than I do."

Melody doubted that was true, but she appreciated the thought. Liam climbed onto her lap, rested his head against her chest. Maybe he did have his grandmother's gifts. She rocked him and stroked his silky hair. She could sit there forever, not caring if the waters rose, not worrying about what her brother was doing with some strange man, not knowing whether Chris was okay, not fretting about her mother. None of it seemed to matter more than this boy on her lap. Melody was worn out and sick of trying. She was sick of being angry, sick of feeling useless. And it wasn't just the past two days that left her feeling that way. She'd been pissed off for the past three years. Hell, she'd been furious since Bobby's baptism. All that anger was a waste of time. It didn't change a thing, and it left her feeling wrung out. A man's voice cut through her reverie. He called for her, called her by name. Melody thought God was coming for her, coming to prove his existence in the midst of disaster. It was the first sign of God she'd witnessed in years. It seemed appropriate that he'd show up now. But, of course, it wasn't God at all.

Obi stood, put his hands on his rifle. Melody jumped up, holding Liam in her arms. "I'll handle it," she said. "No need to pull out the artillery."

She hugged Liam closer and stepped into the hallway. Chris was still hunched in a corner, mumbling meaningless prayers. Maurice and Bobby appeared from Bobby's room. A man wearing a uniform draped in a plastic poncho emerged at the top of the stairs.

"Melody? I'm Deputy Buster Boggs."

Melody stared at him.

"We talked on the phone."

"You're that man from the sheriff's office?"

"Deputy Boggs."

Melody sighed. "Daddy's dead." She didn't know why she said it. This man didn't know her father.

Boggs held his gun pointed out in front of him, angled toward the ground.

"Dead?"

"He was sick," Melody said. "Very sick."

"I am sorry about that." Boggs glanced at Maurice, Bobby, and Chris. His mouth contorted as he ran his tongue along his bottom teeth. Melody thought he looked like a frog.

"Who is this boy's father?" Boggs looked at Melody as if she might be hiding Obi in her pocket.

Liam's hand squeezed and released the back of her neck like a kitten's paws kneading. "You don't need to worry about him. Can you put that gun down, please? There's no need for guns here."

Boggs lowered his gun to his side. "You said he was dangerous."

Melody shook her head. "No, *you* said he was dangerous."

"He may well be."

"He isn't. He's a good man." Melody believed that was true. "Did you find my mother?"

"She's safe. We've got a boat outside. More on the way."

"Mama!" Bobby sprinted toward the stairs.

Boggs lifted his gun. "Stay right where you are."

Melody stepped in front of Bobby. "No! Put that gun down. Put the gun down now!" Things were getting out of hand. She wrapped one arm tighter around Liam and slipped the other one behind her back, taking Bobby's hand in her own.

"Do what I say. Just stay put," Boggs said. "No need to panic."

"I am panicking," Chris said. "I think there is every need."

"What happened here?" Boggs stepped closer to Chris and stared at his bruised face, his bandaged head.

"There was a car accident. I tried to call an ambulance, but the phone lines are down."

"He has a concussion," Maurice said. "He's got a pretty good cut on his head, and his nose is broken."

"Who are you?" Boggs said.

"I used to work here. I'm a nurse."

"Look here," Boggs said. "Your sewage lines are busted and the water is rising. We need to get everyone out of here."

"The situation is dangerous," Melody said. "But we are not." She pointed to the men in the hallway, identified them to Boggs. "And this is Liam. I think you can see that he's no threat. Now, take us away from here."

"Where is the boy's father?"

Melody kept quiet. If Obi wanted to reveal himself, he would. If not, she would protect him as far as she could. She worried about what the sight of this man in a uniform would do to him. She was afraid one of them would shoot without thinking.

"Take us out of here," Melody said. "Please, just get us out of this god-awful house."

Boggs dipped his tongue between his bottom teeth and his lips. He looked from Maurice to Bobby to Chris and back to Melody. She could see he was considering his next move. He gave her a quick nod and gestured with his gun to the staircase. "Women and children first."

Melody was relieved. "Come on, Bobby. Let's go see Mama."

Bobby kept his grip on Melody's hand. Maurice and Chris followed them down the stairs. Melody could hear Chris muttering his prayer behind her. She still held Liam in her arms, and she knew Obi wouldn't like her taking his son so far away from him. What choice did she have? What would George Walter say about her choices now? She hoped Obi knew she would protect Liam. She would keep Liam safe until Obi was ready to care for him again. He would have to trust her. She hoped he could.

The water downstairs rose to her hips; the smell was un-believable. "Let's get out of here," Melody said.

"Out," Bobby said.

"Out," Liam said.

They stepped out into the raging storm. Melody could barely make out a boat floating in the murky gray distance. The boat looked like a papier-mâché project gone wrong, nothing more than gluey wet newspaper floating in a bucket of paint.

The buzz of a motor cut through the rain. A man wearing a bright yellow poncho piloted another boat, sidled it right next to them, and shouted, "Let's go. Let's load up."

Melody looked back and forth between the smaller boat, where she assumed her mother waited, and the larger boat being steered by this yellow-clad stranger. She stepped toward the yellow. "Thank God you're here."

The man reached out an arm and hoisted Melody and Liam into the boat. "We have a shelter set up at the middle school. Blankets, dry clothes, food."

Melody shivered. The denim shirt she wore, her father's shirt, grew waterlogged and heavy. She wrapped her arms tighter around Liam, knew he must be freezing in her old thin T-shirt.

The man's voice whipped around in the fierce wind. "Let's go." He gestured to Bobby.

"Mama," Bobby said. "I want to go with Mama."

"We need to keep moving," the man said. "There are other people who need help."

"Bobby, get in the boat!" Melody yelled.

Chris staggered past Bobby and Maurice and climbed into the boat, banging down hard on his knees. He didn't seem fazed. He continued with his meaningless prayer. "Our Father, who art in heaven . . ." He prayed as he pulled himself onto one of the bench seats.

"He's been in an accident!" Melody said. "He needs a doctor."

"There are doctors at the shelter. They'll have a look at him. He's walking, which makes him better off than some others I've seen."

"I'm worried about his head."

"Let's get moving, then. How many are in there?"

"Just the deputy," she said. "And these men here."

"And Daddy!" Liam pleaded. "Don't forget Daddy."

Melody patted Liam on the back. She put her lips against the man's ear and said as quietly as she could while still making herself heard over the storm, "This boy's father is in there. There's some trouble. I don't know if he'll come."

"We won't come back," the man said.

Melody nodded. Boggs stepped out the front door and lifted his hand to the man in the boat.

"I got 'em!" the man shouted.

Boggs pushed Maurice and Bobby forward until they had no choice but to climb into the boat. "Take these two and get the two women from the sheriff's boat," Boggs said. "I'm going back in after a man. We'll take the small boat."

"I'll drop them at the shelter and head back out for another sweep."

Boggs disappeared into the house. Melody hoped Obi would either escape or surrender peacefully, but she couldn't imagine him doing either. Bobby and Maurice settled into the boat, and everyone donned an orange life vest. The vests were familiar to Melody, the same kind Old Grandaddy kept in his fishing boat, four puffy sections with a hole in the center and a web of adjustable canvas straps. "I don't have a child size," the man said. Melody loosened the straps on her jacket and slipped the vest over both Liam's head and her own. She pulled the straps tight enough to hold the child close. "Is that okay?"

"Don't let go," Liam said.

The man in yellow fired up the motor and steered toward the smaller boat. It was a matter of traveling a few yards, but the rain was so heavy and the sky so dark they were right next to the boat before Melody saw the girl curled up in the bottom like a gasping fish.

"I'll be damned," the man said.

"Mama!" Bobby yelled. "Where's my mama?"

The girl looked up at them. "Please help me."

"Mama, Mama, Mama!"

The man lifted the girl into their boat. "I thought there were two of you."

The girl didn't respond. He slipped a life vest over her shoulders and pushed her down onto the bench seat next to Melody and Liam. She was tiny, fragile, her skin the color of caramel, her short hair so black that it seemed blue.

Melody realized she desperately wanted to see her mother, not because she was angry, but because she was scared and sad and lost. She couldn't remember ever wanting her mother so much. "Where is Mama?"

The girl shivered and looked away.

"We have to move," the man said. "We have to get to shelter."

"But where could she be? There's nowhere to go."

The man looked out over the roiling waters and steered the boat away as Bobby howled like a wounded animal. "No, no, no, no. Nononononononononono!" Rain slashed against Melody's skin, sharp as razor blades and cold. She hugged Liam tighter. The rain turned from stinging sheets to pounding drops as they made their way across the water. Storm sirens wailed, a mournful keening sound. The tornadoes would come next. Melody had been through storms like this before, though none quite so fast-moving and destructive. The tornadoes always came at some point. The man steered the boat with care. Melody saw other boats in the distance, other families being rescued, other people who were scared and wet and suddenly homeless.

Liam's heart pounded against her chest. His soaked hair tickled her cheek. The man in yellow steered through the mess. Trees that had survived for more than a hundred years lay in their path, causing the man to backtrack several times and find a new route. A multitude of water moccasins slithered across a downed tree branch. Electrical lines danced across the water, throwing sparks like fireworks. A sulfurous odor hung in the air, the smell of an Easter egg discovered on a hot May afternoon.

The girl next to Melody stared, mute and gaping. Chris grasped at the Lord's Prayer, mangled the words. Church spires and steeples rose up all around them as they traveled to higher ground. All the rescue boats were full of God-fearing, churchgoing, income-tithing people, and where was their reward? Where was their prosperity? The heavy hand of God settled over them, blocking out the light and destroying the crops. Pastors began preparing their sermons. They would reference Noah, of course, and talk about the importance of faith during times of hardship. People would find a way to rebuild their homes and plant new crops, but it wouldn't matter. God or Satan or Mother Nature would destroy it all again. Maybe next time there would be a drought or fire or hail. No amount of prayer would do anything to stop it, but neither would logic nor reason nor science.

Bobby leaned forward and touched her shoulder. He put his face next to hers and shouted above the roar of the boat motor. "Are you going to again leave me, again leave me, again leave me? Leave me again?"

She reached up and put her hand on top of his. "Don't worry. I'm right here." Maybe Maurice was right about Bobby. Maybe he wasn't so damaged. Maybe his biggest problem was just that he lived in a place where he could never be himself.

"We'll start over." She wasn't sure he heard her, but she said it again. It comforted her to say the words. "We'll all start over."

"Start over, start over," Liam sang.

Melody laughed. She thought about George Walter and his strange advice. George Walter was right. She had choices to make. She could change things for Bobby and for herself, but she couldn't do it by running away from home, from Mama, from her past.

She nuzzled Liam's neck with her nose, smelled his green scent and pointed ahead to show him where they were going. She hoped the deputy wouldn't hurt Obi. Liam needed his father, and Melody wanted to see Obi again.

The sturdy middle school sat high on a ridge, atop a man-made rise. It was a strong, ugly building, made of brick and concrete, a gray squatting beacon of safety. A line of sodden people trudged through the front doors. A helicopter hovered in the distance. The rain slowed perceptibly. The boat moved forward. Melody tightened her grip around Liam's waist and sang a soft song against his ear.

Chapter Twenty-three

Obi hid behind the bedroom door. The dead man was stretched out on the bed, but Obi could still feel his presence in the room. It wasn't a good feeling, but Obi didn't fear the dead. He was far more afraid of the man in the hallway, the man with the gun. Behind the door, his heart pounded so fiercely, it felt like his chest would blow open. He held his rifle steady, one hand on the barrel, one finger on the trigger. He would fire if it came to that.

His mind raced through all the events that led him to this moment. Bad decisions, bad choices, a long string of them stretched out for years and years. He never should have married Eileen, though without her, he would not have Liam. He could not regret the time he'd spent with Liam on the river. He surely did not regret taking Liam away from the fat, lazy life Eileen provided for him. When he thought it through, he only had one real, lasting regret: He regretted the incident with the boy in the woods. He regretted the hell out of that. If he could go back and just walk away, he would. Even now he felt the cold knife in his palm as it slipped into the boy's neck. It was like slicing through soft cheese.

The voices in the hallway rose and fell. He heard Melody tell the man to put away his weapon. He heard Bobby crying for his mother. Then the voices faded, and Obi knew he was alone in the house with the deputy. There were only two ways out of the room—the door, which led to the hallway and the man with the gun, and the window, through which he could see the sturdy branches of an oak tree, the same tree he'd considered climbing to get a better look into the house. The oak's branches looked strong, comfortable even. If he could hang on and resist the pull of the wind, he might make it. It wasn't a terrible plan. He could ride out the storm in the arms of the oak and then disappear into the land. Melody would care for Liam until he found them. He would find them.

The storm crashed against the house. The floor shifted beneath his feet. Footsteps approached. He raised the rifle to his shoulder and steadied it. He breathed in. He breathed out. Ten steps to the window. Ten steps. Ten steps. Ten steps. Oh, God. His feet felt rooted to the floor. The body on the bed released a noisy, gassy expulsion. The room filled with a putrid stench. Obi stepped forward on rubbery legs. His heart hammered in his chest. His palms were slick with sweat. Footsteps echoed through the hallway beyond the door. There was no time. The man with the gun would find him soon. He sprinted forward, toward the window and the strong oak tree beyond. He slung his rifle strap around his body to free his hands. The window was stuck tight. It didn't budge, no matter how hard he yanked it. He lifted the butt of his rifle to break the glass, but then realized all he had to do was turn the latch. The window slid open, and Obi hooked one leg over the windowsill. A gust of wind nearly knocked him back inside.

The man with the gun raced into the room, ordered him to stop. Obi was perched on the window like a crow. He would fly or drown, but he would not surrender. Rain poured past him into the house. He leaned toward the arms of the tree, cradling his rifle against his chest.

"I'll shoot!"

Obi wavered. He wasn't ready to die.

"Show me your hands."

The man moved closer. Obi rocked on the window ledge—one-two-three—pushed off hard with the soles of his boots against the good solid brick of the house. He stretched his arms wide and reached for the largest branch. His left shoulder pitched forward with a painful sting, but he grabbed hold of the tree with his right arm. He shimmied forward on a thick, rough branch until he found the spot where the branch touched the trunk, and he settled down in the crook. He was below the window now, out of sight of the man with the gun. He touched his left shoulder. A wash of pink seeped through his shirt, diluted by the pouring rain.

"Are you crazy?"

Obi looked up. The man with the gun was leaning out the window, yelling down at him.

"You didn't kill me," Obi said.

"I wasn't trying to!" the man shouted. "I just want to talk to you. I have a few questions."

"I've got nothing to say," Obi said. "Let me be."

"I can't do that."

Obi shifted, and the pain in his left shoulder grew diffuse. The bullet had lodged in a wedge of bone and would stay there until the day he died, a day that was still more than fifty years away, though Obi couldn't know that. The limb where he sat was nearly as wide as an overstuffed chair, and he had no fear of falling. He pulled his rifle up and aimed it through a smattering of branches. The man yanked his head back into the house. Obi waited. He would wait for the flood to end, for the waters to recede, and then he'd fetch Liam and do whatever he had to do to keep them both safe and free. They would take new names, dye their hair, move somewhere far away. As long as they were together, they would be at home.

"Come on back inside. You'll die out there."

The man's face was barely visible behind the shaft of his rifle. Rain poured down and blurred Obi's vision. It was a disadvantage to be the one below, the one outside.

"I don't intend to hurt you," the man said.

"You shot me!"

"I was trying to get you to stop. I wasn't aiming to kill."

Obi pointed his rifle toward the sound of the man's voice. The longer he held the barrel up into the falling rain, the greater the chance it would let him down when he needed it. His back and neck ached. His shoulder throbbed. The man kept talking, trying to convince him to come back inside.

"We've got doctors at the shelter. Why don't you come with me? That wound is superficial at best."

"You don't know that." Obi lowered his rifle. The man leaned farther out the window into the pouring rain.

"I don't intend to hurt you. I just have some questions."

"I don't have any answers for you. Just leave me here."

They were at an impasse. The man was dogged in his desire to bring Obi in, and Obi was just as determined to stay free. He looked down. Water swirled beneath him, gray and menacing, but just water after all. His mother always told him to embrace nature, never fight it. This water was the same water he'd bathed in and cooked with while they lived along the river. Maybe it was tainted now, but it was still his water, the water he sought out whenever they set up camp, the water that gave him life over these past years with his son.

Obi bit his tongue hard, tasted blood in his mouth. He pressed his back against the sturdy trunk and said a quick thanks to the tree. He looked skyward again. The man in the window stared down, waiting for Obi to climb up to him. The man was just doing his job, but Obi couldn't risk prison. Instead of cold, spring rain he would be surrounded by cold, steel bars. There would be no private moments, no stars to count at night, no searching for the man in the moon with Liam, no storytelling by the fire after dinner, no fish wiggling beneath his palms nor dirt beneath his feet. His son would grow up soft and resentful. His mother would be ashamed. It was not a life he could live.

Obi dropped into the swirling waters. He let go of his rifle and plunged deep beneath the surface. The water was strong. He struggled at first and the current pulled him deeper. He remembered to trust the water, to let it carry him. His head bobbed above the surface and he relaxed. There was no way to tell which direction the water flowed. All the familiar landmarks were gone. There was no sun in the sky to point the way or tell the time. He became part of something vast, infinite. A woman waved to him from her second-story balcony. He waved back and smiled. In the distance, he heard the roar of motorboats and sirens, but it had nothing to do with him. He was no longer a mere man. He was transformed, a creature of the water and the earth and the sky. His instincts would take him home.

Chapter Twenty-four

The water sucked and pulled at Geneva. It turned her end over end, until she wasn't sure which direction was up. Foul water entered her nose and mouth. She thrashed against the current, gasped greedy gulps of wet air when her head broke the surface. She swam. For the second time that day, she gave herself over to Mother Nature and swam as hard as she could. When she was in the boat arguing with Chandra, the house had seemed close enough. Now it seemed miles away. As soon as Boggs left them bobbing on the end of that long rope, Chandra went mad. She pointed the flare gun at Geneva and made all sorts of nasty accusations. Geneva was a whore, a witch, an evil shrew. The girl ranted on and on. Geneva tried to calm her, and when that didn't work, she struck back. She called Chandra a liar, a coward, a stupid girl. It was ugly and childish, and Geneva wasn't proud of herself, but the day hadn't led to many proud moments and she didn't intend to dwell on it. If she'd stayed in the boat, Chandra would have set off that flare gun. Geneva didn't figure a shot from a flare would kill her, but it would burn hot enough. Jumping into the flood seemed a safer option. It also seemed the quickest way to reach her family. Boggs had no right to keep her away. She struggled to stay afloat, her arms and legs numb with exhaustion. She couldn't see a foot in front of her. Was the house that way? Or this way? Geneva knew the violence Pisa had warned her about wasn't Atul turning on her, wasn't Atul's death, wasn't her argument with Chandra; it was this moment when the wide world turned against her and took her to task for all the damage she'd done. It was too late to be sorry, but she was sorry. She was sorry for leaving Bruce when he needed her most, sorry for pushing her daughter away to set her free, sorry for everything that had led to Bobby being less than he should be, sorry for the whole mess with her mother and, most of all, she was sorry she hadn't listened to Pisa. She was mighty sorry about that.

The water tossed her under and around, up and down, side to side until Geneva stopped struggling and gave herself over to the currents. Time stopped. There was no way to tell how long she'd been in the water. She didn't know where she was, or if she was anywhere at all. It occurred to her that she might be dead and this might be hell. This endless waterlogged nightmare seemed far worse than any fiery afterlife she could imagine. It was right about the point she'd consigned herself to an everlasting watery grave that she felt something solid. She reached out and realized that she was being tossed against her own porch, her own beloved house now half-submerged in the hellish flood. She grabbed hold and pulled herself forward, pulled her battered body onto the porch. It was the longest journey she'd ever taken, but she'd made it. She'd made it home.

She coughed up dark streams of toxic water and dragged herself into the house, past the submerged stairs, everything slick with mud and filth. "Hello?" Geneva didn't want to surprise anyone. She climbed to the second floor; her bare feet slipped beneath her and she came down hard on one knee. Hot pain shot through her leg, but it didn't slow her down. She crawled forward. The small hallway between the bedrooms was streaked with footprints and blood. Geneva pulled herself up, leaned against the wall to take the pressure off her throbbing knee. Her skirt wrapped itself around her waist and legs like shackles. She tugged at the stubborn zipper, and the fabric tore away from her body like paper. She peeled off her blouse and stood panting, wearing nothing but a bra and a pair of silk panties. She hopped forward. "Bruce? Are you here?"

In her bedroom, the contents of her memory box were strewn across the bed, old newspaper clippings and photo albums and dried corsages from dances she'd long forgotten. The dried bouquet from her wedding lay on the floor, its daisy petals long gone and only the prickly stems of baby's breath still discernible in the faded, rotting, lilac-colored ribbon. She bent to pick up the bouquet and had to steady herself against the antique cedar dresser, the one her great-granddaddy made. The drawers of her dresser were open, everything spilled out onto the floor. It was a mess, and there was no sign of her husband. She clutched the bouquet to her chest and limped slowly across the hall to Bobby's room, where nothing had changed.

She thought she heard her husband call her name, but maybe it was just the howling wind. She clutched the bouquet against her bare stomach and moved painfully toward Melody's bedroom, where she found Bruce. Her husband stared at the ceiling, his mouth wide open like he was about to speak. He wore a faded pair of filthy cotton pajamas. Rain poured through an open window. Geneva lurched toward the bed. "Let me help you." Geneva shivered. "Let me keep you warm." With one hand, she shimmied her torn and dirty underwear down around her ankles. She unhooked her bra and let it fall onto the floor. The bouquet in her hand fell apart, but she held tight to the coil of ribbon. A bit of rusted wire poked through and scratched her palm. She wiped the blood on the quilt, lay the bouquet beside her husband. She undressed him, moving aside a strand of something that looked like one of Pisa's creations. She removed his humiliating diaper last, tossing it as hard as she could toward the open window, but she was too weak. The filthy diaper hit the wall and slid onto the floor. Geneva picked up her wedding bouquet and laid the strand of herbs across her husband's chest. She curled up next to him and closed her eyes. She was so very tired.

Snippets of her life floated past and she snatched at memories. She was ten years old. Her mother called her into the dark room. "Sing to me," she said. Her mother closed her eyes and hummed along. Genie thought it was a good sign. Her mother would get well. She would bake cookies and take Genie to school. She would sew Genie a new dress for church. Genie sang louder. Her mother's eyes flew open. "Who is this?"

"It's me, Mama."

"You are filthy. Everything is filthy and disgusting."

It was true. Her mother wouldn't allow her to open the windows when she was feeling dark. The sheets hadn't been changed in weeks. There was a sticky bit of liquid spilled across her mother's bedside table. Bourbon, most likely. Pill bottles were piled on the table. The doctor kept prescribing the pills to help her mother sleep. She slept too much. It didn't matter.

"Bring me your father's razor."

Genie refused. Her father was in the fields, bossing around a hundred men. He was making cotton for the whole world. It would be late before he got home, and Genie was afraid of what her mother would do with the razor.

"Now!" Her mother yelled. She picked up a glass from the bedside table and hurled it.

Genie ducked. Shards of glass skittered across the wood floor. Genie got the razor. It was long and straight and very sharp. She loved to watch her father shave, loved the scraping sound of blade against skin. Her father took good care of things like razors and farm equipment. He did not have time to care for his wife.

Her mother's hair was glorious, black and shiny and thick with natural waves. Genie watched as she chopped through it. Ragged hunks gathered in the bed. She was a bird in a nest. She cut the hair shorter and closer to her head. She scraped the blade along her scalp. Blood appeared, bubbling up and dripping down her nearly bald head. It pooled and coagulated in the bits of scraggly hair she left behind. Genie kept her voice gentle, soothing. "Mama, don't hurt yourself."

She brought a damp washcloth from the bathroom and crawled into bed with her mother. She stroked the cloth across her mother's bloody scalp, tenderly blotting the nicks and scrapes. That's all it was, nicks and scrapes. Her mother reached up with her left hand and grabbed a hunk of Genie's hair. She sliced through it with the blade, and Genie stared, horrified, at the mass of her own hair floating down to mingle with her mother's hair on the bed. Genie leapt away. She fled, running down the stairs so fast that she pitched forward and fell hard. She felt her right wrist twist beneath the weight of her body, and a sharp pain shot up her arm to her shoulder. She ran out the back door, where miles of cotton stretched out like strands of pearls in the searing late afternoon sunshine. She ran across the backyard to her father's shed. She pulled and pulled on the door, but it was locked tight. She touched the mangled edge of her freshly chopped hair and sobbed. Her wrist throbbed. She looked toward the house and saw her mother in the window, staring at her. Genie realized that her mother's illness was confined to that room and that she would never leave as long as she was in the dark place. Genie's heartbeat slowed and she stared back at her mother, a bird trapped in a cage, trapped in a nest made from her own feathers. Not me, Genie thought.

She was sixteen. Her mother took her to see Pisa. Genie saw that Pisa was powerful, and she could be powerful, too.

She tried to explain it to her mother, but her mother was weak. She went along for as long as she could, but she kept slipping back into the darkness.

She was twenty, beautiful and strong and surrounded by girls who wanted to look like her, boys who wanted to be with her. Powerful, she was powerful. She was the queen of Delta State and everyone thought she had a shot at Miss Mississippi. Her fingers were long and graceful and practically melted into the ivory of the piano as she played classical music, pop tunes, ragtime, gospel. She loved the cool feel of the keys and the way they gently warmed at her touch.

Her father was proud of her, but also impatient. "Come home," he said. "Your mother needs you."

"No," she told him. "I want to stay."

"You'll go back. When your mother is well."

She went. What choice did she have? Her mother was in bed, in the dark room. She stared at Genie with her stone-dead eyes, though Genie thought she saw a glint of satisfaction beneath her mother's cold glare. She was jealous. Jealous of her daughter's beauty, her daughter's life. She'd once been the beautiful one, but her beauty faded with each bout of darkness. She was nothing but a husk.

She was twenty-three. It was the longest dark period yet. College was like a dream from some other life. Some girl from Clinton, a tap dancer of all things, was crowned Miss Mississippi. Genie cooked dinner for her father. She cleaned the house and shopped for groceries. She tried to convince her father to hire some help. It was 1963, and her father ran one of the most prosperous farms in three states. He employed an army of black men to care for his fields, but he refused to hire even one of their wives or daughters to help Genie in his house. "I won't have every nigger in White Forest gossiping about your mother," he said. "We take care of our own."

Genie brought her mother tall glasses of bourbon. She read to her from the local paper. There were race riots in Alabama. Myrlie Evers wanted her husband's killer brought to justice, but it wasn't going to happen for another thirty years. Three men were lynched in Neshoba County, two of them white. "That'll teach those Yankees to mess around down here," her mother said.

"They just want to vote, Mama. Black people want to vote."

"This place is too dangerous for ordinary people," her mother said. "It's crawling with things that will eat them alive. It's eating me alive. It will eat you, too." Her mother looked like something devoured and spit up. She was so thin Genie could see the bones underneath her paper skin. Her mother was never going to get better. Every day, she slipped further into the darkness. "Why am I still here?" she asked Genie. "I thought I'd be gone by now." Genie tried to make her feel better, offered to brush her hair, to bathe her, to dress her in nice clothes, but her mother wouldn't have it. "Why?" She asked the question again and again. "What's the point?" Genie couldn't provide an answer. "You'll be better off when I'm gone," her mother said, but then she cackled and turned wild-eyed. "Or maybe not. Maybe you'll just take my place."

Never, Genie thought.

Every day, Genie woke up and put on a dress, applied some makeup, brushed her hair. She did it to remind herself she was worth the attention, even if the only admirer she had was the one in the mirror. She did it to keep from sinking into filth and sadness like her mother. Her college classmates had moved on. They got married, got pregnant, not always in that order. Some were working in town. A handful headed off to California, searching for something they didn't even know they needed. Genie was locked in place. She couldn't move forward and she couldn't move away. She met Bruce that summer. He drove a truck for Grantham Feed & Supply, and he delivered pesticides, herbicides, and fertilizer to her father's farm. He showed up every two weeks in the summer months, rolled barrels of poison from the back of his truck into her father's shed. She brought him sweet tea and he lingered longer than necessary. Her father did not approve, but Genie cared less and less about her father's approval. As long as her mother was sick, her father would not let Genie go.

Genie's father was leaving for two days. The members of the Delta Council called an emergency meeting to discuss the uprisings taking place across the region. Workers were demanding breaks and asking for better wages. He had to go. He gave Genie the keys to the shed and told her Bruce would be by with supplies. "Just lock everything up," he told her. "Don't stand around talking to that redneck.

Just lock it up and get back inside. Take care of your mother."

Genie took the key. She put on her best sundress, crisp cotton printed with golden sunflowers. She brushed mascara on her lashes until her eyelids felt heavy, painted her lips bright red. She brushed her hair until her scalp felt charged with electricity. Then she went into the dark room. Sometimes her mother was more alert in the mornings, but today she was drowsy and despondent, glancing up at Genie with hooded eyes. "Why are you all whored up?" That voice, muffled and sharp at once, eliminated any doubt she might have.

"Here's your drink." Genie pressed a glass of watered-down bourbon to her mother's lips.

Her mother slurped and some of the liquid dribbled down her chin. "Weak," she said.

"Well, it's early. We'll save the strong stuff for later."

She waited. Bruce pulled up at ten o'clock in the morning and Genie greeted him with a smile. She jingled the keys at him and explained that her father was attending a meeting in Cleveland. She hopped into the passenger seat of the truck and rode with Bruce to the shed around back, watched him unload the barrels from the bed of the truck, and asked him questions about each one. He explained which powder killed which weed and what to use for rodents. He asked her to stand back and he donned a pair of gloves, snapped a paper mask over his nose and mouth, and rolled out the last barrel. It was marked with a skull and crossbones on all sides and stamped with warnings about inhalation, ingestion, and dermal exposure. Genie locked the door to the shed and took Bruce inside. He was nervous, and when he was nervous, he stuttered. She served him a piece of lemon meringue pie and a cup of coffee. She let her hand rest on his forearm and told him someday the farm would be hers. "All of it," she said. "All of this land will belong to me and to my husband." She looked him right in the eye when she said the word "husband." His face flushed red and she smiled.

She let him kiss her, tasted the sweet tangy lemon and bitter coffee on his tongue. He pressed himself against her, and his desire chased away any darkness that threatened her. She needed to be needed. He groped at her, grabbing at various parts of her as if clutching for a life preserver. She reached down and unbuckled his belt, unzipped his blue jeans. He sprang from them as if freed from prison. She lifted her skirt, pushed her panties down around her knees, and gasped as he thrust into her. It was over before it began. He convulsed and pulled away, leaving behind a sticky trail on her thigh. She knew nothing of sex and assumed that was it. They lay side by side on the cold tile floor of her parents' kitchen. Genie felt restless, dissatisfied. Bruce looked at her. "You're the prettiest girl I've ever seen."

Genie shrugged. She knew she was pretty.

"I'm not rich," Bruce said.

"I don't care."

"I'm not handsome."

"I'm sick of handsome people."

He rolled on top of her, supporting most of his weight on his elbows. "I'm not good."

"Neither am I." She guided him into her and pressed

herself hard against him until she felt something like pleasure.

She sent him off with another piece of pie and a thermos full of coffee. He promised to return in better clothes and with a good shave to talk to her father.

Genie waited until the dust from his truck settled before heading back out to the shed. She put on a pair of yellow kitchen gloves, pleased with the way they matched her dress. She tied one of her father's bandannas around her nose and mouth, and used a crowbar to pry open the barrel, the one with the skull and crossbones. She dipped a tablespoonful of the white powder into a clean glass. It looked like laundry detergent, nothing more. She closed the barrel, tamped the lid down all around with a hammer. Inside the house, she crushed a dozen of her mother's sleeping pills into a fine powder with a wooden rolling pin, the same pin she'd used to roll out the piecrust early that morning. She filled the glass half-full with bourbon and stirred until most of the cloudiness disappeared, packed in some ice and fresh mint leaves, and topped it off with sweet tea. She carried it upstairs right away, afraid that if she hesitated, she would lose her nerve.

"What have you been doing?" Her mother's voice croaked like a bullfrog.

"I made you a special drink."

She held the glass to her mother's lips. Should she be wearing gloves even now? Her mother sipped and then took a larger gulp. "It's sweet," she said.

"You like it sweet."

Her mother nodded. Genie pulled the glass away; maybe

it wasn't too late to stop this. Her mother grabbed for the drink.

"Is it too weak?" Genie asked. "I can fix a fresh one."

Her mother pulled the glass to her lips, took long greedy gulps. "It'll do."

Too late to stop anything, Genie realized, and better that way. Her mother was miserable, pathetic. Genie would do what her father couldn't; she would set her mother free. She would free herself. She stroked her mother's filthy hair, a film of grease against her palm. "Finish it up before the ice melts."

Her mother did as she was told. Geneva, for she was Geneva now and not a frivolous Genie, waited. "It'll be better this way," she told her mother. "You'll see. You'll be happier now." Her mother's face turned gray and she clutched at her stomach. She gasped. She clawed at her throat, retched and convulsed. Her bowels released and the stench that filled the room sent Geneva to the window. She flung it open and allowed fresh air into the room for the first time in years. When she turned around, her mother was dead.

Geneva couldn't let anyone see her mother in such a state. Her mother deserved better than that. She bathed her with lavender-scented bath soap and a bucket of warm water. The breeze from the open window mingled with the clean scent of soap, and the stench of despair retreated. Geneva washed her mother's greasy hair, dried it with the softest towel she could find, and brushed it until it shone. She pulled her mother's finest nightgown from the closet, an ivory satin gown with lace around the hemline. It looked like a wedding dress. The soft fabric slid across her mother's limp body. Geneva pulled clean sheets over her mother and made the bed around her. Then she set to work on her mother's face. Moisturizer, a hint of cream rouge, a wash of pale pink lipstick, the barest brush of eye shadow; it was subtle but perfect. Geneva stepped back. Her mother was beautiful. For the first time in years, she seemed content, peaceful. Geneva draped a quilt across her mother's legs, folded the soft fabric prettily. In life, her mother was a terror. In death, she looked like the subject of a dreamy painting. Geneva kissed her mother's forehead and then, impulsively, pressed her lips against her mother's cold lips. "I'm sorry," she whispered. "I didn't know what else to do."

Geneva hauled the gloves, the old bandanna, and the soiled sheets out back, where she buried them among the graves of the family pets. Only then did she call the doctor and report that her mother had asked for her pills.

"How many did she take?"

"I don't know," Geneva said. "How many did you give her?"

Geneva's father put a notice in the paper that said his wife had died after a long illness. He buried her in the Baptist cemetery and he got back to work. Geneva was too old to return to college. She'd seen too much to go back to the life where she was nothing more than a pretty girl. Sometimes, in the middle of the night, she woke in a panic, certain that she could hear her mother's voice calling for her. She married Bruce against her father's wishes. She was pregnant when her father walked her down the aisle, her stomach filled with a secret weight. On her honeymoon in

Florida, she miscarried. She stared down at the bloody mess in the toilet while her new husband begged her to hurry up. They had dinner reservations at a restaurant on the beach in Fort Walton. She flushed and fixed her makeup in the cloudy hotel mirror.

When they returned home, her father tried to teach Bruce how to run the farm. Geneva went to see Pisa. She told her about her mother's death, about the baby, about Bruce. Pisa laid hands on her stomach. "There are plenty more babies to be conceived. That one was not meant to live, just as your mother was not meant to live."

"I didn't know what else to do," Geneva said. "I thought it was the best thing. Now I don't know. Maybe I'm being punished. Maybe no baby will want me."

"You should look to the future," Pisa told her. "You cannot live your life if you are always looking back."

She was twenty-six and heavy with a baby due any day. She waddled through the house, preparing meals for her father and husband. They teased her about being fat, but when she looked in the mirror, she knew she was more beautiful than she'd ever been. She rubbed her stomach with oils that Pisa gave her. The baby inside her turned over as if swimming with pleasure. "It's a daughter," Pisa said. Geneva worried about raising a daughter. A boy, it seemed, would be easier. Geneva promised herself that she would never hold her daughter too close.

She was twenty-nine and her daughter was bouncing up and down on her bed. "Fatty fatty, two by four, can't get through the bathroom door." The smell of Bruce's cigarettes made her nauseated. Geneva hoisted herself from bed and waddled into the bathroom. "Mine," Geneva said, rubbing her hands against her swollen belly. A boy would be easier.

She was forty-one and her son was reborn as an angel. She loved him twice as much. Her daughter was someone she barely recognized.

She was fifty-one, and her life was slipping away. She opened her eyes and saw her daughter. "Mama." Her daughter's voice came to her as through a canyon. She clutched at Bruce. Bruce would save her. She reached for his hand, but his bones crumbled to dust beneath her grip.

Her body was lifted up and set down again. God was trying to decide whether to keep her. She heard voices, and when she opened her eyes, she saw lights so bright they made her head throb. Angels or demons surrounded her; she could not distinguish. A cold pinch on her arm sent a wave of warmth through her body. It was the darkness that her mother embraced, the darkness she'd fought for so long. It was a comfort, and Geneva understood why her mother succumbed to it.

Chapter Twenty-five

AFTER THE FLOOD

The floodwaters receded, leaving behind piles of soggy debris and the threat of sinkholes along paved roads. A series of downed power lines sparked alongside the blacktop of Highway 49. The air filled with dangerous smells: sulfur, gasoline, ammonia, mold. Search and rescue teams abandoned their boats and moved across the land on foot or in recreational vehicles normally used for hunting game. Now they hunted bodies, dead or alive.

A child was found inside an antique armoire, his body curled like a comma around a stack of hand-embroidered dish towels. The child was unmarred by the water, and the firefighter who found him thought he was sleeping until he lifted the boy's stiff body. The firefighter, best known for his temper and his time as the star quarterback of the local high school a decade before, broke down and called out for his mommy.

An old lady, maybe the oldest lady in the whole county, rode out the storm on the roof of her house, shielding herself and her three basset hounds with a roll of gardening tarp meant to keep frost off tomatoes. She had to carry each of the hounds up to the roof, hoisting their saggy, heavy flesh through an open window onto a second-story balcony, and then pulling them up one at a time. Everyone laughed, imagining the ninety-pound, ninety-nine-year-old lady lifting the dogs with their long ears and short legs and woeful howling up onto the roof. And how did they get back down? Someone always asked this, chuckling at the very idea.

A man who'd been a drinker his whole life, who was well known as nothing but a sorry drunk, fell suddenly sober for the first time in two decades and saw the face of God in the storm clouds. He was cured of his craving for whiskey. "Just don't want it no more," he said with a look on his face that told you that this lack of wanting was a miracle too big to explain.

Another woman, said to be eccentric by polite people and downright loony by folks who were less genteel, was discovered naked and filthy in bed with her dead husband. Her leg was broken and she was so dehydrated that her lips had turned white. Her hair—her thick, black, shiny curtain of beauty—had gone completely silver. Some people said she looked like a witch, something they'd always kind of suspected. Other people said she looked like an angel, like someone who'd seen God and then been returned to earth.

These were the stories people told in the days after the flood. Redemption, miracles, supernatural visions, close brushes with God. Not since Noah and Moses and Abraham had there been so many people receiving messages from on high. Everyone, it seemed, knew someone who knew someone who swore each tall tale was the gospel truth.

Melody was inclined to believe none of it, except of course the part about the woman with her dead husband, the woman whose hair turned suddenly silver, though Melody suspected the transformation had more to do with the corrosive floodwaters stripping away Miss Clairol than with any sort of divine intervention.

She stroked Mama's hair, wiry and coarse between her fingers. At the shelter, everyone said her mother was dead. Sheriff Randall was the one who told her that her mother was alive and had been airlifted to a hospital in Memphis. Melody's first thought on seeing Mama was that death might have been a blessing. Her body was broken, her face marked with lines Melody hadn't seen before and, of course, there was the loss of that beautiful black hair. When Melody found herself alone in the hospital room with Mama for a few brief moments, she was struck with the dark thought that she could spare Mama the pain of recovery, the pain of seeing herself suddenly aged. A pillow across her face or a bit of poison inserted into the tube delivering medicine, either would do the trick. As soon as she thought it, she went cold. When had she become capable of such thoughts?

"Melody?" Mama opened her eyes.

"I'm here, Mama."

"Don't hurt me."

It was like her mother had read her dark thoughts. Melody

flushed with shame. She called for the nurse, who adjusted the drip attached to Mama's arm. Mama slipped back into unconsciousness.

"She seems scared."

The nurse made a note on a chart. "Who knows what she's thinking. She's been through a terrible trauma." The nurse looked at Melody. "So have you. You should get some sleep."

"I know," Melody said. "I will." She knew she wouldn't, not anytime soon. She didn't mind. Since the storm, she'd been busy and useful. It felt good to be useful.

"The painkillers sometimes cause strange dreams," the woman told her. "We'll start weaning her off as soon as we can."

The woman in the bed across the room called out, "Praise Jesus!" in a high-pitched voice.

"See what I mean?" The nurse disappeared behind the curtain to tend to the woman, another flood victim.

Melody had asked about a private room, but the hospital was crowded. Since they rolled the woman in, she'd been telling the same story. This woman swore she'd seen a man in the water, a man unfazed by the rushing currents and the swirling depths. The man, she said, floated past her as gently as if he were out for a leisurely swim. The man had dark hair and skin the color of cedar. "He didn't walk on water," the woman told Melody. "It was more like he was part of the water." The woman thought she'd seen Jesus and that he had saved her. She was rescued moments later and had been close to drowning. "Thank you, Jesus!" she shouted. "Praise Jesus!"

Bobby pushed open the heavy door and entered the room with Liam. The child's mouth was covered in something. Chocolate? "Come here." She pulled Liam onto her lap and used a tissue to wipe his face. He grinned at her. It was blackberry jam smeared across his lips. Slightly better than chocolate, Melody figured. Obi would not approve of too much junk food. Her stomach ached when she thought of Obi. There was no word of him, and Melody wanted to believe that no news meant he was alive somewhere, hiding and waiting. Pisa seemed to believe that was true. How had she put it? She said she could feel her son's "essence in the physical world and not yet in the spiritual realm." It had not been difficult to track down Pisa. Many women knew her, knew where her house stood three counties away. The sheriff managed to find a phone number and get the woman on the line once the phones were restored. Melody filled her in, told her that her grandson was safe and her son was missing. Melody explained they were heading to Memphis with an emergency crew to see her mother. "I'd like to bring Liam along," she said. "The roads to get him back to you won't open for a few more days at least, maybe a week. I'll bring him to you as soon as I'm able. I promise."

She handed the phone to Liam and let him talk to his grandmother until the volunteer in charge of the phone started shooting her dirty looks. The phone lines were only sporadically in use, and people were waiting for a turn.

Today, just three days later, when the man on the news announced the roads were open, Melody prepared to make the drive. It would be even better to wait a few more days, she knew. There would be traffic and still some detours, but she had promised. She would get Liam to his grandmother by nightfall.

Her mother's eyes fluttered opened again. The fear was gone, but she didn't seem to recognize Melody.

"Mama," Melody said. "This is Liam, do you remember Liam?"

Geneva stared at the boy, a blank expression on her face.

"This is Obi's son, Pisa's grandson."

At the mention of Pisa, Mama's eyes flickered. Somewhere, beneath the drugs and the trauma, Mama remembered. The nurses told Melody to talk to her, to be conversational, normal. Melody read to her. She bought a newspaper and read from different sections. Mostly, she read news from the style section, beauty tips and Hollywood gossip and fashion advice. She avoided news of the flood, which filled the front section. Occasionally she read a dry article from the business section or something about national politics. Mama drifted in and out of sleep. She seemed to be dreaming even when awake.

"We're taking him home," Melody said. "We're going back today."

"You're leaving me?"

"Just for a day. Bobby will stay with you."

"We're a family," she said. "You can't keep secrets from me."

Melody didn't know what kind of secrets her mother thought she was keeping, but she played along. "I wouldn't dream of keeping secrets from you, Mama."

"I'm going to tell you all about the shed. We can't have secrets."

"I can't wait to hear all about it. It sounds like one hell of a story." Melody wondered if she meant Old Grand-daddy's toolshed or some other shed long gone. Her mother seemed haunted by memories and kept mixing up the past with the present.

Bobby stood beside Melody. "Mama, Mama, Mama."

"Angel boy." Mama reached out and took Bobby's hand. She squeezed her eyes shut. Fat tears rolled across her temples and into her hair.

"You'll be okay here today?" Melody asked Bobby. "I'll be back tonight. It'll be late."

"My boy," Mama said. "My beautiful boy."

"Come back," Bobby said.

"I promise." She touched his arm, was grateful he didn't pull away. "I'll drive like the wind."

At the shelter, after sitting for hours with Bobby and Liam on the hard bleachers, she'd stood to stretch her legs. Bobby grabbed her arm and begged, "Don't!" People turned to stare at them as Melody shushed Bobby and tried to pull away. He was scared of being left alone. Melody stayed by his side. She and Bobby and Liam walked the floors of the shelter together and made a game of it. "Jump-ing jacks," Bobby would call out, and the three of them would stop where they were and perform a set of ten. "Somersault!" Liam called, and they rolled across the dirty floor. Melody tried to enlist the girl from the boat to join them, but the girl sat hunched in a corner like a rodent, feasting on handfuls of sugary breakfast cereal. Maurice had disappeared. The crowds in the gym were segregated, not by any formal agreement but just because that's the way things were done. Bobby understood that Maurice could not sit with him and that he could not join the large, dark knot of people on the far side of the gym.

Liam told them stories about white dogs and hawks and coyotes. He spoke of his father as if he would see him soon. Melody hoped that was true. She knew Boggs had neither arrested Obi nor brought him in for questioning. The sheriff told her Obi had disappeared into the storm. Could he survive? Melody hoped he could.

The sheriff asked her about the girl who'd been rescued with them. "Deputy Boggs thinks she knows more than she's saying. Deputy Boggs thinks she's hiding something."

"I don't know anything about her," Melody said.

"I'm sorry about your father."

He turned to leave. Melody called after him. "If you do find Obi, what will happen to him?"

The sheriff shrugged. "All we have is the story from the girl, and she seems confused. No one else has reported a thing. No missing persons report, nothing. Boggs only wanted to question him. He may have been overzealous in his efforts. He feels terrible about scaring the man. Unless we find some evidence to support the girl's story, I don't know what we'd charge him with." Sheriff Randall dropped his head and scuffed his foot against the floor. He wrapped her in a big bear hug that left her gasping. "Tell your mama that I said hello. You take good care of Genie, you hear?"

★ ★ ★

Now Melody handed Liam over to Bobby, asked her brother to wash the child's face. "We'll be leaving soon." She turned to her mother. Seeing her laid out in a hospital bed took Melody back to the day of Bobby's baptism. Back then, she was filled with terror and fury, and she realized she'd carried those feelings around for a solid decade. But no more. Somewhere in the midst of the storm, her terror and fury were washed away. Back then, her mother said she'd saved Bobby and she didn't have the strength to save Melody, too. Now Melody knew she didn't need saving, not by her mother and not by religion. "I'm going to see Pisa," she said. "Is there anything you want me to tell her?"

"I'm sorry," Geneva said.

"I'll let her know."

"Not her."

Melody's mother had never apologized to her for anything, and she wasn't apologizing now. She was in her head, hallucinating from the drugs. "I killed her. I didn't know what else to do. I was so young, just like you are now. I couldn't see any other way. She wanted to go. You'd have done the same."

"What are you talking about, Mama?"

"We were trapped," she said. "I set her free. I saved myself. You don't know what it's like to be stuck. I did the best I could, you know. I always did the best I could."

When her mother was better and no longer on heavy painkillers, Melody planned to tell her that she knew exactly what it felt like to be stuck. There was no point trying to get through to her now, though. "I'll be back soon," she said.

"I did the only thing I knew to do," her mother said. "I did the best I could."

Melody made one more stop before leaving the hospital. Chris's face was swathed in bandages. The doctors broke his nose again to reset it, but it would always be crooked. The bruising around his eyes had softened, and the black was fading into spectacular shades of mottled green and yellow. His head, where the doctors had drilled in and removed fluid from his brain, was shaved and stark on the white pillow.

"They said I can go home tomorrow," Chris said. "I don't really have a home." She knew what he meant. He didn't have anywhere that felt like home.

"Your parents will be glad to see you. I'm sure they're worried sick."

"My mother organized a prayer chain with the women at church. Someone is praying for me around the clock. They all took half-hour increments. Dad said she posted a schedule on the refrigerator."

Melody laughed. "She wants to do something. It's what she knows."

Chris grimaced. "I can't feel God anymore. I used to pray and know that he was there, listening. Now, it's just empty."

"Maybe that's what God is," she said. "Just emptiness that we fill up with whatever we need."

"That's depressing."

"Well, I haven't really got it figured out. I could be wrong."

"I feel like a fraud," Chris said. "I don't know what I'm supposed to do now."

"No one has to do anything in this world," Melody said, parroting George Walter. The strange man who had picked her up on the side of the road had been right about so many things. "Everything in life is a choice."

"If that's true, you should choose to keep singing. There's nothing phony about your voice."

"I'll see you tomorrow," Melody said. "I'll stop by and say good-bye before they release you."

Melody drove for more than five hours, navigating the cheap rental car through numerous detours. She bounced across old, rutted roads marked only by numbers or not marked at all. Mud caked the tires, and dust settled over the car until it became a clay-colored insect crawling across the land. She taught Liam songs to pass the time, taught him how to sing in rounds, how to do simple harmonies. He had a clear, sweet alto. By the time she pulled into the gravel drive in front of Pisa's small wooden house, she knew she would miss Liam terribly.

There was not much storm damage here, just scattered tree limbs and shingles blown off the roof. Pisa stepped onto the front porch, and Liam sprinted to her. Melody recognized her from the childhood visit. She hadn't changed.

"You are Geneva's lost songbird," Pisa said.

"Not lost," Melody said. "Found."

"I see that." Pisa gestured for her to come inside the house, but Melody stayed put.

287

"Let me fix you something to eat."

"I have a long drive back to Memphis. The roads are still tricky, and I'd like to get the worst of it behind me while I have some light."

"Wait a moment. I have something for you." Pisa ducked into the house. Liam followed, and Melody wondered if she'd get a chance to say good-bye. Pisa emerged with a small wooden box. "There are some things in here for you and some for your mother." She pried open the lid, and Melody smelled the strong scent of cedar. Pisa pulled out a transparent fabric pouch that smelled of camphor and over-ripe plums. "Give this to your mother. Tell her to hold it against her chest and say these words." She plucked out a folded piece of paper. "It will speed her healing." She handed Melody a bit of whitewashed fossil or bone suspended on a frayed bit of red thread. "This is for you."

Melody took the trinket from Pisa, turned it over in her hands. It was about the size of a silver dollar, ovoid with jagged edges and the imprint of something organic pressed into its surface, an insect or the veins of a plant. The thread left red streaks across her palm where she touched it.

"I can't take this."

"It's yours," Pisa said. "I've been saving it for you."

Melody tried to press the trinket back on Pisa, but the woman refused to take hold of it. "I don't believe in this stuff. I'm not my mother."

"You certainly are not," Pisa said. "You certainly are not your mother. Your mother was not her mother. Your mother is not you."

Melody wondered what Pisa would make of George

Walter and what George Walter would think of Pisa. They seemed so sure of themselves, but they couldn't both be correct.

"You are not your mother, but you are not so different from her as you believe," Pisa said. "When you have your own daughter, you'll understand how much you share with your mother."

"I'm not even sure I'll have children." Melody pressed the object toward Pisa.

"Keep it," Pisa insisted. "You don't have to believe in something for it to be true."

Melody closed her hand around the object. She liked the way it felt in her palm, cool and substantial and sturdy.

"It's a piece of bone from the sternum of a white dog. The imprint is from the feather of a hawk. It will guide you and bring clarity."

Melody slipped the bone into her pocket.

"Your mother is a strong woman. She makes her own way. She doesn't always listen as closely as she should. Not to me and not to herself."

And certainly not to me, Melody thought. "I should get back to her," she told Pisa. "And to Bobby."

"Your grandmother was weak. Not like you. Not like your mother."

Melody rubbed her thumb across the cool bone in her pocket. The sun dipped toward the horizon. She should get back on the road before nightfall, but she didn't move. "I never knew my grandmother. Mama never talked about her much. I know she died young."

"Your mother was afraid to turn out like her mother. She

took matters into her own hands. It was reckless, but it wasn't wrong."

"What are you saying?"

"Ask your mother. I think she'll tell you now. The point is, she didn't become her mother. Neither will you."

The conversation raised more questions than it answered, and Melody wanted to probe deeper, but Liam ran onto the porch and threw himself against Melody's legs. She stumbled as the force of his body wrapped around her knees. "Come back," Liam said. "When Daddy gets here, you come back."

"I will," she promised. She stroked his silky red hair. "I will come right back here and see you. We'll sing some more songs together."

"I know we will," Liam said. "That's why I'm not sad."

"I really should go," she said to Pisa.

Pisa gripped Melody's shoulders and peered into her eyes. "You don't have to believe in me," she said. "But you should believe in something."

"I'll try," Melody said. "But the stuff most people believe in seems like a bunch of voodoo to me. No offense."

Pisa smiled like a woman who'd never been offended. "Take care of your mother. Be kind to her. You are stronger than she is. You will do better than she did. Your daughter will do better than you. That is the way the world works." Pisa gave Melody's shoulders one last, hard squeeze before letting go. "Come back to see me. Bring your mother."

Melody made no promises. She climbed back into the

dirt-crusted car and drove. The journey was lonely and quiet without Liam. She focused on the world outside the car, took in the wreckage of the storm. A group of men in an old Chevy turned off the road ahead of her and parked in front of a small house. Melody slowed to watch. The house seemed not worth saving, a shack even in better times, but the men unloaded lumber and tools and a case of beer. The roof had been lifted right off the house, and the front porch was mostly gone. The frame listed to the east. The men consulted, retrieved tools, and set to work. One of them glanced up at Melody. She'd stopped the car in the middle of the road. She waved and drove on. All across the Delta, people were beginning the hard work of rebuilding. What else could they do?

She pulled Pisa's gift from her pocket and looped the string around her neck. The bone fell heavy and grew warm against her chest. It seemed to pulse with life. Light faded from the sky. Something streaked across the road in front of her, something wild and large and gray. A coyote. The beast turned its head and locked eyes with Melody as it bounded and disappeared into a grove of pine trees. She recognized Obi's gaze. He would be home soon, and she would return, just as she'd promised Liam.

The sun dipped; the sky turned gray and pink. The ravaged fields on either side of the road began to twinkle and blink with light. She put her hand on the bone at her chest, took comfort in its warmth and weight. The fireflies led her north toward Mama and Bobby and her future, whatever that might be. Pisa had said she was stronger than her mother. Melody felt strong. She felt strong and calm and fearless. There was no telling what would happen next. She had so many choices to make.

She sang as she drove into the night. Her voice filled the car, floated out into the darkness, and joined the chorus of crickets, bullfrogs, old dogs, and the howl of a wild coyote.